LIGHTS OVER
CLOUD LAKE

NATHAN HYSTAD

Cover art: Tom Edwards Design

Typography by: Beaulistic Book Services

Edited by: Scarlett R Algee

Proofed and Formatted by: BZ Hercules

ISBN-13: 9781081856076

Also By Nathan Hystad

Acknowledgements

This is the first time I've written an acknowledgement, and it's past due. Writing a book seems like a solitary process from the outside, but I find it to be quite the opposite. *Lights Over Cloud Lake* is the eighteenth novel I've written, and each book gives me something different.

First of all, I want to thank my wife Christen, who has supported my dream from the start. She's put up with my obsession with reading, writing, and everything in between, and it means a lot to me to have a partner in all of this. She's become my sounding board and my first line of defense, reading my books before anyone else sees them. Thank you, Christen. For everything.

I have a great group of author friends to lean on, to talk with, and discuss the small things, and sometimes the big life things with. To the Collective, and beyond, I thank you for being there throughout this journey. I wish each and every one of you the success you deserve.

Thank you to Scarlett Algee, my editor. She's been with me from the start, and she's become invaluable to my process. I count myself lucky she still makes time to red-mark my manuscripts, and I'm thrilled we've been able to work together for this long. Her advice and suggestions make each book that much better. Here's to many more.

Thank you to BZ Hercules for formatting and being my last line of defense on my books. You are a wonderful person, and a pleasure to work with.

Tom Edwards, you've been a dream to work alongside for all of my covers. From back in the *Explorations* days, you've created your artistic magic, and have made my visions of covers come to life each and every time.

Huge thanks to Steve Beaulieu for doing the typography on this book, and for being an overall awesome dude.

And last but not least, I dedicate this book to my mom. She's been gone for almost eight years, and I miss her every day. She taught me to read. She taught me to love words. She showed me the magic behind a book, and for that I will be eternally grateful. This one's for you, Mom.

August 2ⁿᵈ – 2001

"Very good, Jessica. Yes, let go of your surroundings." Dr. Hendricks' voice was soothing, lulling me into deep breaths. I didn't think it would work, but my eyelids became heavy, my chest rising and falling in perfect rhythm.

"How old are you, Jessica?" the doctor asked.

"Fourteen," I said.

"Good. What is your name?" I heard scribbling on a notepad as he jotted my answers down with a pencil.

"Jessica Bailey Carver."

"Very good." More scratching. "Where did you go on July thirteenth?"

My eye twitched. "To Cloud Lake's Summer Kick-Off," I told him, fully aware he wanted a different answer.

He slowed the pace of his words. "When you left, you walked home, is that correct?"

"Yes. No. I ran." I didn't tell him why, but I could picture my bleeding legs, the red welts from the tree branches.

"Why were you running?"

"I was trying to get home, but…"

"What is it, Jessica? What happened when you got out

1

of the trees?" Dr. Hendricks asked, unable to hide the impatience from his voice.

"I was in Mr. Martin's yard. It was bright, so bright." I lifted a hand and placed it over my eyes, recalling with such clarity how white-hot it had burned.

"Was Mr. Martin there?" he asked.

"I saw him that night, but not there," I said truthfully. Dad had been grilling me on it for the last week, but I couldn't tell him what he wanted to hear.

"Where were you taken?" Dr. Hendricks asked, and I sensed him shifting in his seat.

My eye twitched again. I saw images in my mind—a bed, tubes, shadows—but never a face. I told him this, and he kept probing with deeper questions, ones I was unable to give firm answers to. Dad was in the room, and he made a whimpering sound in his throat as I deflected. I didn't know where I was in my memories. Everything was a jumbled mess.

"Could it have been inside a room? Dirt floor? A wooden staircase?" he asked.

I scanned through the memories and shook my head. "I don't think so."

"*Could* it have been?" he asked, emphasizing the first word.

"I guess. It could have been," I finally relented. I didn't want to be here any longer; I wanted to push the painful images from my mind and go home.

"Thank you." He snapped his fingers, though I didn't know if that was supposed to do anything. My eyes slowly opened, and I glanced over at my dad, who exhibited a sad smile. A "chin up, sport" kind of gaze.

"Are we done?" I asked.

Dr. Hendricks nodded. "I need to speak with your father. Do you mind waiting out there with your sister?"

I shook my head and walked away on shaky legs. Zoe sat in the cramped waiting room, flipping through a magazine with some overdressed model on the cover.

"You okay?" she asked, peering over at me from behind the magazine.

I raised a finger to my lips and crept to the door, which I'd left open a crack.

"It isn't uncommon for someone who's been through this kind of traumatic event, Brian. She's scared. She's seeing things in clips, almost like random photos from her internal camera. They don't make sense to her, but they might in time." Dr. Hendricks' voice was clear as he spoke to my dad.

"What about the lights? She's making it sound as if…" my dad started.

"It could be a flashlight. Maybe there were floodlights inside the room. There are too many factors," the doctor said.

"What's the next step?" Dad asked him.

"I suggest she be medicated for something this intense. She needs to be calmed down, to handle the anxiety and stress of what happened to her," Dr. Hendricks advised.

"For how long?"

"As long as she needs it," he answered.

Dad let out a sigh, and I could picture his cheeks deflating like a balloon on the other side of the wall. "Do I make another appointment with you?"

"No, Brian. I don't often deal with this level of trauma, but I can recommend a few professionals who'll really be able to make inroads with your daughter," the doctor said.

"Thank you."

"Hold her tight. It's not often you hear about the victim making it home in a case like this." I shivered at his words.

3

"I will. Thanks for the help, doc," Dad said, and I ran across the room, sitting beside Zoe. She passed me a magazine, and I opened it, pretending to read an article.

"Ready to go?" Dad asked us.

I nodded, unable to forget the pictures that had flashed over my mind in Dr. Hendricks' office. Part of me wished I knew what had really happened to me; the other part wanted to go home and forget any of it ever occurred.

July 7th – 2020

My feet were aching as I strolled through the gallery. It wasn't the ideal time to wear a new pair of shoes, especially after a long day on the streets of Manhattan. I'd roamed from street vendor to street vendor, talking to the proprietors about their food: where they came from, how long they'd been in the city. Most of them had been affable, and almost all had offered me free food.

A woman carrying a silver tray of hors d'oeuvres passed by, stopping near me, holding the crab puffs out. I shook my head, unable to stomach the thought of eating another bite today. Or this week. Or ever.

The gallery was one I'd been to a few times before; each showcased an amazingly talented New York artist's works. This one was for a woman who called herself "Persephone," and I understood the reference as I scanned through the wonderful paintings surrounding the gallery. The Greek goddess of the same name had been abducted, brought to the underworld to become the queen and wife of Hades.

I stopped in front of a giant canopy and instantly recognized the farmer's field—the corn crops, the trees in the distance, the night sky—as a classic alien scene. I'd read enough books and watched all the documentaries to know this was the ideal setting for such a sighting. I looked up at the seven-foot-tall painting and saw the flying saucer above. It wasn't cartoony; not quite round, but jagged instead, as if molded by a child who'd been told to make a UFO.

Goosebumps rose on my arms as I stared at it.

"What do you think?" a woman asked. Her scent drifted towards me before I saw her, a mix of roses and sandalwood. She wasn't what I normally expected from an artist at this gallery. I thought I'd look down to see bare feet and wild curly hair. But she was slight, short, with midnight pumps and a sleek gray dress. Her hair was pulled into a ponytail, and her lips matched the color of her shoes.

"It's brilliant," I told her, actually meaning it. Too often I went to these shows having to try to decipher the artist's meaning behind some elusively obscure statue or painting. She was clear with her intentions.

Her gaze drifted to the badge around my neck. "The *Brownstone Beat*. Can't say I've heard of you," she said.

"We're online. Kind of a niche following, but strong supporters. I've worked there for a while. I can only assume you're Persephone?" I asked, and her eyes lit up.

"Why, yes, I am." She looked at my name again. "Eva. Eva Heart."

I peered to the side, seeing another alien-centered painting. This one was crop circles: large rings connected by long lines. It reminded me of a chemical compound image. Two parts hydrogen, one part oxygen.

"Do you believe?" I asked, feeling foolish for even asking.

Persephone nodded. "I do. If we think we're alone out there, we're even more egocentric than I thought," she laughed.

"I agree," I said quietly.

"You do? How intriguing. I don't know many people

in the city that believe in aliens, UFOs, or abductions. It's a little too… country for them," Persephone said.

"I haven't always lived here," I said with a smile.

A man waved at Persephone, and she touched me lightly on the arm. "Give me your card, and I'd be happy to meet up to do an interview for your magazine," she said.

I fished one from my small clutch and slipped it to her. "I will. Thank you."

"Pleasure is mine," she said, walking away, heels clicking on the tile floor.

Barns would be thrilled I'd landed such a high-profile artist. I'd hesitated about coming tonight and had really only done so because no one else at the office had been able to use the press pass. Harry had a date, and I knew the others had likely made up excuses.

I walked around the gallery for a few more minutes before heading outside. It was muggy during the day, but as the moon rose high in the sky, the city air cooled, and I took the opportunity to walk home. My feet were sore, but it was only ten blocks.

The city was my safe place, as crazy as it sounded, but I suddenly felt trapped by it. I needed a vacation, or at least a few days in a bed and breakfast out in the Hamptons. I had a friend with a place out there. Maybe it was time I took her up on the offer to use it. Seeing those paintings had broken through one of my many barriers, and I could feel the dread seeping into the walls now.

I was alone on the street, and where I'd felt safe a minute ago, I was worried now. The alleys were dark, too dark, the streetlights casting uneasy shadows on the road. A taxi whizzed by, and I tried to flag it down, but it kept driving, the light off.

My legs moved faster, and I was halfway home when my heel snapped. I stumbled forward, dropping my clutch on the sidewalk. "Great timing, Eva," I scolded myself, picking up both heel and bag. I limped along, and after another block, I kicked both shoes off, tossing them into a trash can. A man sat leaned against a closed bookstore, his hat between his legs, a cardboard sign held up even though his chin pressed against his chest.

I moved around him, almost running now. My pills were at home, and the desire to pop one overwhelmed me as I jogged the last excruciating block. My keys were stuck on the bottom of my bag when I opened it, and the streetlight went out. I turned to see it flicker back on, then off again, until it was strobing brightly. Finally, I was inside the building, and I ran up the stairs, arriving at my suite. I locked the door behind me, sliding my back against the slab, breathing heavily.

My pills were on the countertop where I'd left them with my full-sized purse, and I went to the bottle, swallowing one with a sip of water. I hadn't had an attack like this for a long time, and I sat in my living room, turning on the lamp beside me.

"It'll pass. They always pass," I told myself. And I was right.

July 9th – 2020

"Close the door," my boss Chris Barns said as his gaze remained glued to his laptop. "Take a seat, Eva."

I perched on one of the two chairs in his corner office overlooking Fifth Avenue. Our website wasn't quite established enough to be on one of the higher floors, but even from here, I could see a piece of the Empire State Building, and I actually preferred to hear the traffic from the busy street below. The constant hum of the city in motion calmed me. If there was one thing I feared, it was the dead silence I rarely had living in Manhattan.

I stayed motionless, waiting for Barns to speak, but he just mumbled as he tapped away on his keyboard. I waited two minutes and cleared my throat.

"Sorry. You know how it is…" He closed the laptop and removed his glasses, setting them on the desktop. His office was immaculate. Bookshelves filled the one wall, with first edition classics behind locked glass sliding doors, and he even had a few plants thriving near the window. I had it on good authority that Barns knew nothing about the care of his ficus and jades, because his assistant frequently complained about having to water them.

His desk was a direct contrast to the rest of the office. It was filled with stacks of dog-eared books, folders, and strewn-out paperwork. Half of the sheets had old dried coffee rings on them, and I smiled at his erratic demeanor. He was unpredictable, but it was part of the reason I enjoyed working for the man.

"What did you want to see me about?" I asked. I was in the middle of an article about the cleanliness of Manhattan's street-food vendor business and was itching to get back to it so I could finish up. Barns had a penchant for grabbing shawarma from the one outside our office, and I suspected he'd stop as soon as he skimmed my work.

"I have something for you. Something… big." Barns relaxed his posture and stared me in the eyes. He wasn't much of an eye-contact boss, and his gaze was unsettling. His voice lowered as he spoke again. "You know Cloud Lake in Maine, right?"

My eyes sprang open. Why was he asking about it? My heart raced inside my chest, and whiteness threatened to creep over my vision. I saw Barns' mouth move but didn't hear the words as my pulse pounded in my eardrums.

"Eva? Are you okay?" His expression was full of worry.

I settled and breathed slowly. "I'm fine. Not feeling

well," I lied. "Why did you ask about Cloud Lake?" I tried to make the query sound innocent, but the crack in my voice gave me away. I'd been on edge ever since the other night, and this wasn't helping things.

Barns furrowed his brow and ran a hand through his thinning gray hair. "There's a story waiting to be told. Could be a big one. I wanted to send you, since you grew up around there," he said.

"I didn't grow up there. We spent a few summers at the Lake when I was a kid. My grandmother owned it," I corrected him, not wanting to be attached to the place any more than I already was. His eyes widened at my snappy comment.

"Either way, you know the lay of the land, maybe some of the locals. You can do some digging the others might not be able to," he said.

I was almost afraid to ask, but I had to. "What's the angle?"

He leaned forward, elbows on his desk. "There've been a few sightings. Strange things in the sky."

"Are you telling me you think there are UFOs in Cloud Lake?" I asked, trying to add a pleasant air to the question, as if I found the entire idea preposterous.

He shrugged, clicking a pen repetitively. "All I'm saying is the sightings have been noted all around the region."

"Any video proof?" I asked.

"Not that I've seen yet," he said.

"In this day and age?"

"Do you want the job or not?" Barns was annoyed at my attitude, and I needed to do something different than the usual. Plus, a deep-seated part of me was salivating at the idea of a UFO piece. The more rational part was dreading the idea. It had been so long since I'd let myself think about Cloud Lake and that summer. Maybe it was time.

Time to open up long-sealed boxes inside me.

"I do, but isn't this a little 'trashy magazine' for us? We like to do exposés on the environment, city pieces, and the odd political piece to gain visibility. Why Cloud Lake?" I asked.

"Because we need something to stand out. We're dying here, Eva." Barns appeared five years older as he said this. His chest caved in as his posture slackened, and I saw the bags under his eyes, dark and heavy.

"I… I didn't know. Is there anything I can do?" It was a dumb question. I was one of ten regular writers at the online magazine. I had no ability to save it.

"You can go to Cloud Lake and write a damned good story. Get a real take on it. Talk to the people. Find anyone who claims to have seen the UFO. I heard there may even be one or two of them who believe they were abducted. Work out the details. Do what you do so well and have done for the last five years. Only do it better than ever, because we need something to make the difference." Barns seemed to notice he was melting into the desk, and he sat up straighter, putting his glasses on. He flipped open his laptop, and the old editor-in-chief came to the surface. He started typing, and I knew it was time to go.

"When do I go?" I asked.

"Saturday. Get your current piece finished and send it to me by tomorrow." He didn't look up, and I left him there, clacking away at his keys. Before I shut the glass door, he hollered at me. "Eva!" I peeked my head back inside, and he gave me a feeble grin. "I smell a book deal on this one. It could be just what you need."

A book deal? He was pressing his excitement a little too far. "I guess we'll find out," I said, and closed the door. Readers did like pieces like this. I should know. I'd devoured almost every article and book on the subject over the last two decades. There was no way Barns had obtained that information, though. He must have remembered me talking about Cloud Lake, but I couldn't recall an instance when I would have brought the subject up with my boss. I was almost sure of that.

Our magazine held half the office space on the fifth floor, and the center of the area was made up of cubicles. Barns had tried to give them a fancy edge, slate-topped desks over a classy hardwood floor, but they were still tiny boxes within the office, where you could hear every bit of your neighbor's business whether you wanted to or not.

I glanced to the edge of the space where the top two contributors' private offices stood, and tried to push the jealousy away. I worked hard or harder than those two, but one was Barns' nephew, and the other wore short skirts and tight tops, something I wasn't willing to do to have an office. Harry noticed me staring through his glass palace, and he gave me a wave. Instead of acknowledging him, I pretended I hadn't been looking his way, and flipped open my laptop.

Karen was gossiping to someone on her phone about her bust of a date last night, and I grabbed my noise-canceling headphones, cranking some Chopin to drown the annoying woman's conversation out. Maybe a few days out of town would do me some good.

Hearing the words *Cloud Lake* had been enough to send jolts of fear into the soles of my feet, but now, only a few minutes later, a deep-down part of me was excited. I hadn't been there since I was an optimistic fourteen-year-old girl, and after that last summer, I'd never managed to be that person again. Maybe it was my chance to reclaim what I'd lost. Isn't that what we all strive for? If there was one thing all the therapy had taught me, it was that I needed to let the past go. Mine in particular was so bizarre, I'd had to go through three professionals before I found one who took me seriously.

I closed my eyes as the song reached its crescendo and tried to focus on finishing my article. The second my fingers touched the keyboard, I felt a tap on my shoulder. I spun to see Harry there, smiling widely. He mouthed something I couldn't hear, and I tugged the headphones from my ears.

"Sorry, what's that?" I asked.

"I'm asking if you wanted to grab lunch." Harry asked me to lunch once a week, and I always gave him the same answer. Today, I noticed a pleading in his eyes I hadn't seen before, and the truth was, I knew he'd have confidential news on the magazine's future. After seeing the concern from Barns, my curiosity was piqued.

"Sure," I answered, getting a surprised eyebrow lift in return.

"Great. Let me grab my jacket," he said.

It was the middle of summer, and Harry was collecting his blazer. The guy never left home without one, and I had to admit it was a good look for him. I watched him walk away, and I wondered why it was I hadn't accepted his advances before. It wasn't as though I had a line-up at my apartment door, pleading for dates.

One of the biggest cities in the world, and it felt like the dating pool was closed for a filter replacement all year round.

Ten minutes later, Harry and I were dining on a cramped patio, while hundreds of businesspeople and tourists alike passed us on the sidewalk, many with bewildered expressions as they pointed to the Empire State Building.

"Do you ever tire of this?" Harry asked.

"What?"

"This." He motioned to the people and the street. "The city. I don't know. Maybe it won't be such a bad thing." He stopped and glanced at me, seemingly aware he'd said something he shouldn't have.

"So we *are* closing." I reached for my water, feeling the urge to have something a little stronger today.

He nodded. "Maybe. Either way, I'm out. Barns can't afford to keep me, even if we find a way to survive. Ad revenue's way down. We can't keep making a living at these stories about... what are you doing now?" he asked.

"Food vendors." I pointed at one across the street, the smell of roasting meat emanating from the small trailer. The man inside was sweating profusely, and a few people were lined up, waiting for their chance to order.

"Right. If we lose our jobs, what are you going to do?" Harry asked me.

I hadn't thought about it. "I only found out a few minutes ago. I haven't had a chance to ruminate quite yet." I waved our young waitress down. "Scotch on the rocks, with a twist."

Harry grinned. "Make it two." He held up peace fingers. "I saw you in there with my uncle. What was that all about?" he asked.

It was hard for anything to happen at the magazine without the entire office knowing instantly. I thought I'd just answered my own question of why I'd never dated Harry. "I'm going to Maine for a story."

"Maine? That's in the budget?" Harry tilted his head, and when our drinks came, he sipped generously and set the glass down. "Sorry. The whole thing has me a little flustered. Maine. What's the scoop?"

"UFO sightings." I said it while staring at my glass.

"UFOs. Now why is old Uncle Barns interested in that?" Harry asked.

"He thinks it'll be a good human piece. You know how these supernatural and abduction shows are all the rage these days? He probably reasons we can sign a book or documentary deal with one of the big streaming channels," I said. The truth was, it didn't seem like Barns to choose this story. It felt far too coincidental for me to be sent to Cloud Lake.

I hadn't thought of the place for at least five years. Well, that wasn't quite true, but I'd done my best to avoid thinking about it. It would only send me into a deep spiral of despair when I did, even though I knew none of my memories were real. I'd constructed them to hide the real truth, but even that escaped me.

"I hope you have a good time. You wouldn't be interested in having some company while you're up there, would you?" Harry asked, a fire glowing in his eyes now.

I shook my head. The last thing I needed was Harry seeing the real me, especially in that setting. I had no idea how I was going to respond to returning there, but I felt strong enough. I had a barrier around my mind so powerful, I could handle anything. That, and a purse full of pills.

"I shouldn't be gone long. Only a couple of days, I'm hoping. In and out," I said, without having any sort of a plan yet. Saturday was two days away; just enough time to pack and prepare.

"I can't say I'm not disappointed. I'll be honest with you, mostly because this lunchtime Scotch is hitting me and I might not be here next week. I always thought you and I were going to become a thing." Harry ordered another drink and glanced at my full glass.

I didn't know what to say, so I changed the subject and we chatted idly about the magazine and where our lives might take us when it all ended.

July 10th – 2020

"You can't be serious." My sister Zoe leaned toward the camera, shock spread plainly over her face.

"Why not?" I asked.

"Cloud Lake. I mean, come on, Jess. You're seriously going to go there after all these years? After what happened?" Zoe loved being dramatic, and this was no exception.

"Don't call me that," I told her quietly.

"I'm sorry, but I'll never get used to your new name. But I'll try to call you Eva. Does it really matter anymore?" Zoe asked.

It might not to her, but Zoe hadn't gone through what I had. No one had to deal with the aftermath of that summer in the same twisted way that had been forced upon me. "No one will know who I am. They won't remember me, Zoe." I was hoping that much was true. I was no longer the skinny fourteen-year-old girl waiting to fill out my halter tops and have guys interested in me. I was in my thirties and an almost-successful writer.

"Not that bad? We left that cabin and never returned. Don't you remember Grandma…"

I cut her off. "I don't want to talk about that. It's fine, Zoe. I'm going to ask about the sightings."

"*The sightings*. You make it sound like it's no big deal. Is this really even for work?" she pressed me. It was well past dinner time, and my stomach growled as we talked. We tried to have face to face discussions online as often as we could, which these days meant once every three or four months, as if our lives were so busy we couldn't carve out ten minutes every two weeks.

"It's for work. Remember Clark?" I asked, and she finally smiled.

"How could I forget? I wonder what he looks like

now," Zoe pondered.

"Well, it seems like the kind of place where people are born and never leave, so how about I look him up for you?" I said with a laugh.

"If you do, tell him his kisses need a little work." Zoe faked a sloppy kiss at the camera, and I heard someone shouting for her in the distance. "Uhhhhh, I have to go, Jes… Eva. Never have kids, okay?"

I was so far from that part of my life, I didn't even reply. "Say hi to everyone for me. Maybe I can come visit soon." When Zoe had first moved to Texas, she swore we'd visit each other, but I hadn't been there in three years. Her kids were growing up fast, and I hadn't been involved in their lives at all.

"Sounds good," Zoe said, and it was clear from her tone she didn't believe me.

"Talk soon." I closed the program and sat at my small kitchen island's stool, looking at the clock. "One more day."

I kept the laptop open and typed a search in the browser bar. *Cloud Lake UFO.* A few recent articles showed up, each nothing more than a couple sentences about a local seeing bright lights in the sky. Nothing definitive. I bit my lower lip and changed the search. *Cloud Lake Abductions.* More results showed up, and I clicked on the most current. I got an image of a middle-aged man in a plaid jacket, his wild auburn hair tucked under a classic green farmer's cap.

Chester Brown was on his porch on July sixth when he spotted a light over his crops. Chester has been a long-time resident of Cloud Lake and claims this isn't the first time he's seen the same brilliant flashes in the night sky.

"I was out back, like most nights, rockin' in my chair, when they showed up. It was like the Fourth of July come a couple days late."

When asked about what the alleged Unidentified Flying Object looked like, Brown had this to say. "Couldn't see much other than the light. My eyes are old, but I think I saw it between flashes. Flat, round, not of this Earth."

Brown says this is the third time he's seen something like this in fifty years on his land, and doubts it will be his last.

"Cloud Lake is something of a hot spot. We've had all them missing persons, a cousin of mine included."

Cloud Lake's history of strange sightings continues, but is there more to it than an elderly farmer's poor eyesight? Only time will tell.

I rolled my eyes at the badly-written local Cloud Lake article. This was the epitome of a desperate fluff piece, but behind every story was a glimmer of truth, and I needed to find it. I cringed at the thought of having to go over the lacking details with Chester Brown, but I knew I'd have to. I'd put ten on it that he had a barrel of homemade moonshine in his barn somewhere.

I scrolled through the page, and one link stood out. The headline was more than familiar to me. This wasn't about alien abductions, but about a young girl taken from outside a cabin in 2001. Tears formed in my eyes, and I closed the laptop, all of my composure threatening to explode into a million pieces.

I wasn't going to go there. I couldn't. I breathed, putting my walls up again. I stood, took a sip of my now tepid coffee, and pulled the drawer open on the far side of my kitchen island. Inside, half a dozen pill bottles met my gaze, and I searched for the right one, popping the top and swallowing the contents with a dry gulp.

As I waited for the effects to calm me, I scanned over my apartment. It was far nicer than anything I should've been able to afford on my midrange salary, but I was grateful each day that I'd been gifted the inheritance from my grandmother. I missed her so much, and blamed myself for her eventual passing. Dad and Zoe would have talked sense into me if they knew I'd ever thought that, but I couldn't help it.

I wondered what her cabin looked like now. I knew there was no way I'd be able to return to it while in Cloud Lake. For all I knew, it had been torn down and redeveloped as high-cost lake property, like most of those old lots were these days.

My wallet sat on the countertop, and I unfolded it, looking at my driver's license. My hair was darker in the image, a different version of myself. For some reason, I liked to change my look every two years, as if on a strict calendar. I glanced in the window over my sink, finding the reflection of a blonde woman, one with more wear lines than in the license photo, but also with a little more serenity. The card had my address and showed my court-changed name: Eva Heart. It had been so long ago, I almost didn't know who Jess Carver was anymore.

I scoured my fridge for some leftover pad Thai and finished my coffee before deciding I was too strung out to go to bed quite yet. I drew a bath in my clawfoot tub. It sat over the unit's original hardwood, refinished before I'd moved in five years ago. As I slipped into the steaming water, I tried not to think about diving off the dock at Grandma's cabin into Cloud Lake.

July 11ᵗʰ – 2020

I woke to my sunrise-simulation alarm clock, the light cascading over my fair-sized bedroom, waking me calmly, instead of the incessant beeping of a regular alarm. These days, I did anything to help mitigate my anxiety. This was something I could control, and I liked this alarm setting my day off on the right foot.

Everything was packed and waiting by my door; all I had to do was shower and have a bite before initiating the long drive up the coast to Maine. The truth was, I hadn't been in that state since 2001 and hadn't expected to ever go back. I sat on the bed, rubbing my eyes, and I had a momentary lapse in my calm demeanor. What the hell was I doing? How could I go there after everything that had happened?

The almost twenty-years-older version of myself pushed the fears away, and I resolved to be strong. If I could do this report and return home in one piece, I'd have beaten the one thing that held so much power over my entire life. I wondered if everyone had that definitive moment in their lives, where they stood at a crossroads like this. There was always one moment that would set you up for the rest of your days, or take you down. I was determined to make sure this was my defining instant.

Forty minutes later, I shut off the coffee maker after filling my to-go cup, and I checked to make sure everything was turned off inside my apartment. I was only planning on being gone for three or four days, tops, so I didn't bother tossing the cream in my fridge and hoped the spinach would stay fresh.

My apartment was one located in the heart of Chelsea, and I loved the neighborhood. I was also lucky enough to have underground parking, which came at a premium, like everything in Manhattan. The elevator took me and my suitcase to the bottom level, and I walked into the parkade. It was always a little darker than I liked, and I fought hard to not picture things lurking in the shadows or around the corners.

I glanced at the video cameras set up around the space, their lights blinking red, telling me they were activated. The building super told me the parkade was as safe as they came, but I still held my breath as I crossed to my car, the alarm beeping off as I pressed my fob. Once I was behind the security of my car's locked doors, I calmed myself.

My audiobook began to play as my car connected to my cell phone via Bluetooth.

I pulled out of the parking lot, entering the quiet Chelsea side street. It was seven in the morning, and the roads were nearly silent as a few taxis drove by, several early risers taking their leashed four-legged friends to do their morning business. The guy who owned the corner market down the street from me waved as he washed the sidewalks in front of his store. He was always smiling, and I tried to emulate his mood as I cruised by toward Twelfth.

Already, I could see a half dozen runners on the High Line as I drove underneath it, heading for the Hudson. I merged right and found myself on the road I'd taken so many times over the last few years as I went to visit my dad in his small house outside Hartford. He'd always had this dream of moving to Connecticut and had finally done so six years earlier. Now he seemed bored out there.

I settled in for the drive, trying to not project anything that was about to happen. I'd trained my mind for this kind of thing. *Forget the past, don't stress the future. You are here.* I repeated the mantra and turned up the audiobook volume. It was a non-fiction piece about abductions in New Mexico, and it was my second time listening through.

"For every one of the abductions, the victims noted lights. Sometimes the lights are flashing, and others say they're focused beams from high above; but nearly every single case file on record recalls the lights. I took it upon myself to interview Dr. Morty Hershfeld about this phenomenon, and he had some interesting theories on the topic."

The narrator was a doctor himself, but not one who was much respected in the medical field. Mostly because he claimed to have been taken as a child and had made it his lifelong mission to prove that abductions weren't solely made up by drug abusers and the mentally ill. I'd read a few books by Dr. Donald Teller but still didn't know how much of his writing was pandering to the masses.

Another voice carried through my car speakers. "*Alien abductions weren't recognized, at least in modern culture, until the early nineteen sixties. This has led to a lot of speculation, blaming television shows and pulp science fiction as having influence on our minds. Why hadn't we seen UFOs before we knew what a flying light might be? It does beg a few questions, but I believe there were sightings, many of which remain unrecorded.*

"*There are examples of light in the skies in ancient texts in China and India, as well as Egypt. The ancient Mayans had drawings that could represent otherworldly beings. But others would argue they were only drawing the sun with a beam of light emerging from it. There's no way to know for sure, but as I've stated, I believe that not only have we been visited by beings from other planets, we also are living among them.*"

My flesh crawled as I heard Hershfeld's statement. He'd received a lot of flack, but I appreciated his willingness to document the abductees and experiencers he'd worked with.

Donald Teller took over once again. "*Straight from the leading doctor in the field: aliens are real, and they might well be among us as we speak. You all know I'm a believer, but if they're among us now, we better watch out. I don't think that's going to end well.*

"*Chapter Three: Abductions in the night.*" I pressed the off button and sank into the driver's seat. I couldn't listen to the rest right now. I had to prepare my questions for the residents of Cloud Lake, and I flipped my phone over to the dictating app and started listing off queries. Some were meant to support their claims, to make the interviewee comfortable; then I'd follow with something to push them to give all their truth away.

An hour or so later, I turned off the dictating and

thought about the circumstances of the writing job. How had Barns known about my connection to Cloud Lake? Everything that had happened to me there was done to Jessica Carver, not to Eva Heart. There was no chance I'd ever brought the name of my old family summer spot up at work, and definitely not with Barns. Had I mentioned it to Harry? It was the only logical answer.

I was also one hundred percent certain no one knew about my obsession with aliens. Abductions, Roswell, crop circles; I was a regular freak in a normal woman's body. I tried to think if I'd ever cared about it before that summer in 2001, but couldn't recall. It felt like there was so much I didn't know about myself before that time, as if I was re-born when my dad found me, wrapping me in his strong arms, his tears of joy splashing against my face. I'd never felt safer than in that moment, and as I drove through Connecticut, I almost made the exit to stop and see him.

"Don't be stupid, Eva," I said. Even talking to myself, I used my new name, another thing I'd trained myself to do. I figured in another two years, I wouldn't even have to remember to say Eva. It would be as natural as breathing.

Plus, if I stopped to see Dad, he'd only freak out and try to stop me from going to Cloud Lake. He couldn't haul out of there soon enough, and I could still hear his muttering about how he'd never return to that hellhole. Once the police had let us leave, it was like a switch had flipped inside of him, and he'd rushed Zoe and me out of there in our old Bronco. I could still feel the sweltering heat of the red nylon seats sticking to the back of my legs.

Someone honked, alerting me I was veering into oncoming traffic. I swerved to the right and received another honk from the lane beside me for my efforts. My heart was racing, and I blinked quickly, feeling the adrenaline coursing through my body. I had to pull it together. All the thoughts about my past were flooding through my barriers, the walls I'd spent thousands of dollars of therapy on to learn to build. Maybe this wasn't a good idea. Zoe's look should have been enough to warn me off.

She was two years older than me. She remembered more about it and had been there for the week I hadn't.

As if on cue, the phone rang, and my sister's name appeared on the console screen. I was too worked up to answer it. I couldn't let her know I was starting to worry myself, or the call would end with me turning around. I needed the story, and I needed the closure.

The rest of the drive was quiet, and I managed to hold my composure as I sped through Connecticut, then into Massachusetts, which I still was sure I said wrong every time I tried to pronounce it. It was almost noon by the time I was halfway through New Hampshire, and I still had several hours before arriving at Cloud Lake. My stomach was tight, but it definitely grumbled as I saw weather-worn signs for New Hampshire's best burger.

I decided this spot would be as good as any, and I pulled off at the next exit. The diner was paired with a gas station, and it was full service: something I didn't find very often any longer. I rolled the window down, and a fifty-year-old man in a blue jumpsuit walked over, wiping his hands on a dirty rag. "Fill 'er?" he asked with a gap-toothed smile.

His gaze lingered on me, moving to my chest, and I crossed my arms instinctively. I had the urge to leave, to drive away, but the cap was already popped, and my tank was almost empty. I rolled the window up halfway and nodded. "Fill it."

I'd forgotten what it was like out here in the real world. New York had its own share of interesting characters, but here in the country, it was a different entity. This man's eyes were wild, and I couldn't help but be reminded of Peter Martin. When he was done with the gas, he asked if I needed anything else, and the implication behind his words was enough to make me shove the money in his hands and take off, forgetting I was ever hungry.

I fumbled with my purse as I merged onto the interstate and pulled out a pill bottle. I popped one in my mouth and took a swig of cold coffee from my cup.

I was going to get this over with and move on. It was time for me to stop living like this. I had to. I glanced at myself in the rearview mirror, seeing sparkling blue eyes staring back at me. I had to do it for her, the girl I used to be, and I vowed at that moment to be better than I was yesterday. I didn't need to have a breakdown every time someone like Martin watched me. I could fight that, and would.

With new determination, I drove into Maine, heading north for another hour or so, until my GPS told me to exit off the main road. I followed the secondary, the divided highway turning to a single lane in each direction. Even for a Saturday afternoon, the traffic was light here, and I saw the destination of Cloud Lake on the car's navigation screen.

I soaked it all in and let the breeze from the open window cool me, cutting the air conditioning off. It was bright out, and I wore sunglasses to counter the glare. The trees were tall and healthy, the heat combined with the greenery collaborating to send a glorious scent into the car. I peered down the road and saw the lake in the distance, faintly beyond the quaint main street I was nearing.

The *Welcome to Cloud Lake* sign greeted me, and I slowed to a stop, pulling over on the side of the road to look at it. It was so familiar, the blue sky painted on the wooden sign flaking now, unlike when I was a kid. I closed my eyes, and for the first time in nearly twenty years, I re-membered something about that summer.

July 3rd – 2001

"Dad, do we really have to come here again? It's soooooo boring," I said as I gazed out the window. I was going to be stuck staring at a swamp all summer, fending off mosquitos while Katie and Britt got to swim at the pool. Luke was working there as a lifeguard, and I could already picture them lying out, watching him from behind their cheap plastic heart-shaped sunglasses as he sat in the lifeguard chair, blowing his whistle.

Even Zoe thought Luke was cute, though she wouldn't admit it.

"You say that every year." Zoe glanced over at me from the front passenger seat, blowing a bubble with her gum. It popped, falling flat against her chin.

"So?" It was my only retort. She was right. I always complained, at least since I'd passed the line from little girl to teenager. I did usually end up having fun, though.

"Listen. You girls don't know how lucky we are to spend our summers here. How many parents do you know who are given this much time off?" Dad asked, and I

26

glanced up to see him waggling his eyebrows at me in the rearview mirror.

Dad was the gym teacher at the high school, the same school that Zoe went to and that I'd be starting at next year. I was mortified at the idea of being in a class with my dad. Zoe had told me all the horror stories already, and I knew it was going to be worse for me. Dad didn't seem to get it. He thought having his daughters in his gym class was the best thing in the world.

"Sounds terrible, Dad. A whole summer with you working, and us being able to do whatever we want to with minimal supervision," Zoe said, flipping her hand between the seats of the Bronco. I slapped her some skin, and she blew another bubble.

"And now you know why we're coming to stay at Grandma's cabin again." Dad laughed, a hearty, boisterous sound that I still found comforting. I always pictured him as I did when I was a little girl, his big voice pushing through his thick moustache. Even now, with a full beard and much less hair, he was the same strong pillar of a man.

"I hope Grandma doesn't try making us sew stuff again," I said. "I swear she's using us as child labor. You should call someone about that, Dad."

He laughed again. "I don't know where you kids come up with this stuff. My mother only wants to spend time with you. She's in her seventies. Do you expect her to drive you to the mall to scope out hotties?"

Zoe slapped a hand over her mouth. "Dad, can you never say that again?" She looked over at me, a sparkle in her wide eyes. God, Zoe was so pretty. I only wished I had half the natural beauty of my sister. I managed to make a few heads turn from the boys in my class when I tried hard enough, but my sister…she had all the attention, all the time.

She'd turned sixteen a few weeks ago, and she was still fighting with Dad, trying to persuade him to let her get her license. That would be great for me, since I was two years from having that kind of freedom. He'd promised Zoe she could practice over the summer, and if he thought she was good enough, he'd take her to the exam himself.

I rolled the window down and stuck an arm out, feeling the hot breeze against my skin. I loved the summer. The sun, the wispy white clouds, the soft lapping of Cloud Lake as we lay on the end of the dock, trying to decide what movie to watch that night. It was a magical time, and even trapped in a fourteen-year-old's body, I somehow appreciated it.

"Maybe this won't be so bad," I heard Zoe say, and I followed the direction of her head. A boy was cutting the grass near the town entrance, a bright blue sign welcoming us to Cloud Lake. The boy was in a muscle shirt, long basketball shorts drifted past his knees, and his hair flopped over the side of his face.

Dad slowed as we entered town, and Zoe unabashedly waved to the kid. He nodded and kept cutting the grass, sending the staple smell of summer into the car windows. Zoe was right. Maybe it wouldn't be so bad.

July 11th – 2020

A car honked behind me, and I realized I was taking up half the road; the shoulder here was only a couple feet wide. I waved them by as I soaked in the town sign, and when the car had passed me, I let out a deep breath. I'd pictured the drive to Cloud Lake so vividly, it had me reeling in my driver's seat. I could clearly smell the grass.

The sound of a mower lingered in the air, and I glanced to where Clark had been mowing so many years ago. The same patch was long now, full of weeds, and I wondered when they took park maintenance out of the budget.

I literally hadn't thought about that summer in so long. It had been wiped from my mind, along with so many other things during that time, but now it was as if the key to that memory's locked box had been located. I wondered what else was going to come rushing back now that I'd returned.

I flicked the blinker on and pulled onto the quiet road, heading into town. The power lines hung low over the first few buildings, and I noticed very little had changed. If you'd asked me ten minutes ago what the first business was on Main, I wouldn't have been able to answer. Now I saw Buddy's Diner and instinctively pulled my car over, parking at an angle in front of the restaurant. I hadn't eaten since this morning, other than the protein bar I always kept in my purse for just such emergencies.

I checked the email from Barns to see where he'd put me up. I didn't remember if the town had much in the way of hotels, but I was happily surprised to see he'd found me a private cabin at the Lake. It was much preferable to a seedy motel, where cheap tourists filed in with their five kids and inflatable noodles, screaming in the pool until midnight.

I pushed the door open to Buddy's, the sound of the chimes comforting. I inhaled, smelling exactly what one would expect from a place like that: fry grease and old coffee. It was endearing. I'd spent so long in New York eating at bistros and writing in fancy coffee shops, I'd almost forgotten what it was like to be on the road. When I'd first started in journalism, I worked for one of the big guys and spent a year traveling across the eastern seaboard, covering stories from "The Secrets of Cape Cod" to "Hurricane Sally: The Aftermath." I'd learned a lot, but after burning through an engine in eleven months, I'd decided something a little more stable was necessary.

I waited for someone to seat me, and when no one came, I walked to the counter, pulling out a stool. A woman with darkly-dyed curly red hair turned to notice me, and she smiled like she didn't have a care in the world.

"What can I get you, dear?" she asked sweetly. She had an edge to her voice, like she'd been married twice and smoked two packs of menthols a day. I instantly warmed to her. I glanced at her nametag, wondering if she'd worked here before. Isabelle. It sounded familiar. No, there was no way someone would be at the same diner for twenty years.

"Coffee," I said, "and a menu, please."

She nodded and poured some dark brew into a chipped white cup, passing a plate with cream and sugar on it. "Where you from?"

"New York," I said, picking up the extra-large laminated menu. I searched over it, knowing if I didn't order something like a burger and fries or a sandwich, I was risking my stomach's health.

"Quite a ways for a pretty girl like you to come. What's it like living in the big city?" Isabelle asked.

"Not much different than anywhere, I guess. You wake up, go to work for someone, and go home at night. Hopefully find a few minutes of peace and solitude in between." I smiled, matching her mood.

"Amen, sister. Spoken like a woman awake to the world. What'll you have?" she asked, eyeing my menu. I glanced around, finally noticing the few other tables in the place with people at them. Kids drew on a placemat behind me, as I could see them in the mirror behind Isabelle. Their mom was staring out the window, looking for a happiness she'd likely lost some years ago. I did that. Whenever I met someone new, I'd always make up stories about them in my mind. It was a quirk of mine.

Four seats down the counter, a farmer sat reading the

newspaper. In the day of digital newspapers and maga-
zines, I'd returned to the place time forgot, and my first
minute inside Cloud Lake, I was a witness to someone still
reading a paper. He licked a finger and flipped the page,
glancing up as he caught me staring.

"Miss? Did you want some food?" Isabelle asked again.

"Sorry. It was a long drive. I'll take a cheeseburger and
fries. Hold the onion." I slid the menu over to her, and she
gave me another patented grin as she eyed me up and down
casually. I was in good shape, or at least mediocre shape. I
liked to go to yoga twice a week, and I walked everywhere
I could, so in my opinion, that allowed me to eat something
bad for me once in a while. This was one of those times.

The chimes rang out again as I took a sip of the strong
coffee. I added in a little more cream as a man came up to
the counter. He didn't look at me, but I caught his eyes in
the mirror. They were dark, sad eyes. I imagined he'd recently had a loss in his family. A brother, maybe a child.
He was tormented by it. I broke my stare at the mirror and
chided myself for being so foolish. I was here to do a job,
not play childish games.

"Hey, Izzy. Here for my dinner," he said as the waitress
appeared from the kitchen.

"Like clockwork." She passed him a brown bag, grease
already seeping through the edges. He slipped a ten-dollar
bill onto the counter before pulling out two singles and
adding them to the note.

Isabelle beamed at him, and he finally looked at me,
nodding slightly before heading out the door.

It was later than I'd thought. I glanced at my watch to
see it was almost six. I didn't know what time the cabin
office would be open until, but I suspected it wasn't very
late in this sleepy community. "Isabelle, would you mind
making mine to go too?" I asked her.

Minutes later, I was in my car, the bag of food on the passenger floorboard of my car, and a hot coffee filling my steel cup. I drove leisurely past a grocery store, post office, gas station, and laundromat. It was all coming back to me, dripping familiarity as I headed toward the lake and the cabins. I had their address plugged into my nav system, but I found I didn't even need it as I wound my way through the tiny village and onto the gravel road leading to the lake.

The cabins were on the right, and I pulled up to them, seeing a few other cars parked in front of the various stand-alone units. They were dark wood log cabins with peaked metal roofs. I found myself looking forward to the stay as I got out of the car. It had been so long since I'd been in an idyllic setting like this. The closest I got to nature was strolling the Great Lawn in Central Park once a month, and only if it was warm enough.

Tall birch trees mixed with some aspens, and their leaves rustled in the wind as I glanced up at them, using my hand as a visor. The sun was already beginning its descent into the west, and I glanced to the lake, seeing the murky water reflecting the bright rays. My gaze settled across the water to the shore, where I saw a few cabins. I knew that was where my grandma's cabin had been, and the hair on the back of my neck rose.

"Hello, can I help you?" a voice asked from behind me.

I turned to see a young man standing on the porch of one of the units, this one marked OFFICE. The closed sign was flipped, and I grimaced.

"Sorry, I'm running late. I'm Eva Heart. I should have a reservation," I said.

The dirty-blond-haired man nodded, and he ran to the office, his flip-flops slapping the soles of his feet with each step. He returned a moment later with a key; the placard attached to it had the number ten etched into the wood.

"Just down the path, right by the lake at the end. It's my favorite one," the guy said. He had an easygoing tone, and I assumed he'd grown up in the area. There was a casual local vibe surrounding him.

"Thank you…" I scanned for a nametag that wasn't there, and he clued in.

"Trevor. Call the number on the back of the key if you need help with anything. The office is closed, but I live in here for the summer." He jerked a thumb at the cabin labeled *Office*.

"That must be an interesting job." I started for the car when I thought of something. "Hey, Trevor."

He glanced at me with shaggy blond hair in his eyes. He reminded me of a puppy. "Yes, Miss Heart?"

"You can call me Eva. I've heard some rumors about UFOs around here. What do you think about that?" I asked it softly, as if I didn't have a care in the world one way or another.

His head tilted to the sky as he stepped closer to me, the gravel crunching under his sandals. "You know, I never used to believe in that kind of thing. My uncle swears he's witnessed lights a few times, unexplainable movements, and he always told us about them when we were kids. I always listened with interest, but as I got older, I laughed his ramblings off.

"He'd sit us around a firepit out back of our house and tell us about the Grays. You know… long fingers, skinny bodies, big black eyes on oversized heads?"

I nodded as sweat dripped down my sides. I was leaning forward, listening to every word closely.

"And by the end of the tale, he'd break out a flashlight and start flickering it, mimicking the patterns he could recall. His breath would smell like cheap beer and cigarettes, and his eyes would turn crazy," he said.

"Are you implying you believe now?" I asked Trevor.

He nodded, ran a hand through his thick hair, and sighed. "I don't know why I'm telling you this."

"Go on," I urged him.

"My uncle disappeared when I was twelve. Vanished. One day there, next day gone. Poof." His fingers stretched out like he was doing a magic trick.

"And you think these Grays had something to do with it?" I asked, wishing I had some water. My tongue was threatening to stick to the roof of my mouth.

"I don't know… when you say it like that, it sounds so stupid," he said.

"Trevor, I work for a magazine out of Manhattan. Would you mind coming over to the cabin tomorrow for coffee? I'd love to talk to you about your uncle," I said, hoping I wasn't coming on too strong. The second person in town I'd spoken to, and he had a connection to the lights. Was this a coincidence? Hell, I bet if I went back to Buddy's Diner, Isabelle probably had her own tale about the UFOs.

I might have hit the jackpot here in Cloud Lake. Maybe I'd get to write the book I'd always wanted to after all, and about my childhood summer home, nonetheless.

"I don't think so, Miss Heart."

"Eva," I corrected him, and he stared at me with intensity.

"Eva. There are a lot of people around that will be happy to talk to you, though."

"Can you give me some leads?" I asked hopefully. He was probably ten years younger than me, but I batted my eyelashes a little, instantly feeling foolish for it.

He gave me a goofy smile and nodded. "I'll point you in the right direction. Have a good night, Miss… Eva." And with that, he was off.

I slid into my car and drove onto the gravel road between the cabins. A young family sat around a firepit, roasting wieners, the smell of charred flesh suddenly making me queasy. I glanced at the bag with a burger and fries and considered tossing it.

No, I needed to eat something; that much was clear. I waved at the family, receiving a dubious stare from the mother in return. The kids were oblivious as they prodded their hot dogs deep into the coals, likely covering them in charcoal in the process.

An elderly couple sat on their porch, the woman with her face in a paperback. The man rocked in a chair, sipping a can of Coors Light. The silver bullet. I imagined their lives. They've been married for forty years, and even though they don't say much to each other these days, their bond is strong. They bicker occasionally, but for the most part, they smile at one another as they go for long walks at dawn.

They come to Cloud Lake every year, and have for thirty years, ever since their kids were young. Now they're all grown up, with kids of their own, their lives too busy to sneak away to the cabins for the summers, so here the old couple is, alone but at peace with it.

I snapped out of it as I saw cabin number ten, right at the end of the keyhole-shaped driveway. I took the roundabout and parked in front of the unit before rolling up the window.

Minutes later, all my stuff was inside, and I surveyed my home for the next few nights. There was a bedroom tucked in the left corner, and a bathroom to the right. Inside the living room was a wood-burning fireplace, but it was too hot to use that now. Behind me sat the compact kitchen, the kind with curtains under the sink instead of cabinets. It was dated, a little run down, but extremely cozy. I didn't mind it one bit.

Everything was made of cedar and still held the faded patented scent so many years later. I soaked it all in.

I settled my bag into the bedroom and freshened up in the bathroom before forcing myself to eat. I took it outside, behind my cabin, and sat at the picnic table overlooking the lake. It was becoming dark, and I could hear the crackle of nearby cabin dwellers' outdoor fires, the smell transporting me to that summer. I remembered more of that first day as I stared at the water, juices of the now-cold burger running down my chin.

July 3rd – 2001

"Don't leave them in there too long, girls," Grandma said.

She was right. I pulled the metal stick from the firepit and touched the hot dog, checking to see if it was cooked on the inside.

Zoe leaned in close and whispered, "Remind you of something?"

I smacked her arm away. "Gross. You're disgusting."

"You wish you weren't thinking the same thing," she said, giggling. Grandma didn't seem to notice, or she was good at pretending not to hear our secret discussions.

I looked over at her, amazed at how much older she seemed this summer. We'd visited her at Christmas, and again at Easter, but now I could really see the illness spreading. I loved that woman with an excessive amount of my heart. She was the only female role model I had as a kid, and even though her ideas were a little dated at times, she was my rock.

I couldn't begin to guess how many times I'd picked up the phone over the last four years to talk to her about nothing and everything. As I stared at her through the flickering flames of our fire, guilt racked me. She was in treatment, and I'd stopped calling every week because I'd become too busy with school, drama club, and friends.

I made a vow to spend as much time with her that summer as I could. From the looks of things, I wasn't going to get many more chances. "Grandma, I love you." I said this without thought, and she tore her gaze from her crossword puzzle, eyes rheumy but aware.

"I love you too, Jessica Carver. You too, Zoe," she said.

"What'd I miss?" Dad asked as he walked from the pier. He was holding two small fish. He'd spend twenty-three hours a day out there if we'd let him.

"We're about to eat, Brian. Pull up a stump," Grandma said. She always called the chairs "stumps" if they were around the firepit. I used to think it was silly; now it was endearing.

"Sounds good to me. Let me put these on ice, and we'll fry them up tomorrow," Dad said.

"I can't wait." Zoe rolled her eyes back in her head and stuck her tongue out, making me laugh. We hated fish, especially the little ones caught in the murky Cloud Lake water, but we didn't complain. Dad loved it so much, and there were certain things we let him get away with. Socks and sandals wasn't one of them.

I made my hot dog bun while Grandma broke the news. "I've signed you girls up for some activities this summer."

My stomach sank. "Grandma, we're too old for that stuff," I pleaded.

"Maybe Jess can go, but I'm sixteen. I don't plan on playing skip rope with the girls at camp this year," Zoe said, without a hint of give in her voice.

"I know that, girls. That's why I volunteered you two to help out at the Cloud Lake Summer Kick-Off next week," Grandma said.

I loved the party more than I'd admit. It was so idyllic. Bonfires, motorboats, parasailing, and barbecues. Last year was so much fun, and Zoe even sneaked off with some boy. I caught them holding hands by the docks, but she told me nothing else happened, even though I saw the hickey. She must have thought I was a real rube to believe her lies.

"What are we going to be doing?" Zoe asked, and I noticed my dad watching Grandma as he jammed his hot dog into the flames.

"I don't know. Volunteer stuff. There's the kids…"

"You want us to babysit a bunch of snot-nosed kids while the adults all drink too much and get high when they don't think we're looking?" Zoe spouted. My mouth formed a small O in surprise. Dad only grinned.

"She's not wrong, Mom," he said.

"It'll be good for you girls, if only for a few hours. Anyway, it's better than being stuck at home, isn't it?" Grandma asked.

"Not if I was at the pool with Luke saving me from drowning," I muttered, but no one seemed to hear me.

The cabin beside Grandma's was always empty when we came for the summer, but I saw the light flicker on as I ate my dinner.

"Someone next door?" Dad asked.

"Yeah. That's Peter. He's finally retired, so he's going to be out here most of the year now. Or as long as he can sneak out to fish at dawn, he says," Grandma said.

"I guess I better make friends with him, then," Dad said.

Something about Grandma's expression set off warning bells. "You might want to keep your distance, Brian."

"Why?" Dad asked, a half grin on his face.

Grandma's serious tone broke, and she laughed. "Because then we'll never see you. Now come on, who's up for a game of Scrabble?"

July 11th – 2020

The lights to the cabin beside me flicked on, and I couldn't help but think of Peter's cabin next to Grandma's. I hadn't realized how repressed my memories of that summer were, but being here was surreal at the moment.

A figure emerged from my neighbor's cabin, and she waved. "Hi. Guess you just checked in?" the woman asked. She came over to me, and I noticed how much of a freak I must have appeared. I was in the dark, no lantern, no flashlight, resolved to sit at a table with empty food trays in the late evening dimness.

"I arrived here an hour or so ago." I peeked at my phone and saw I'd been reminiscing internally for nearly two hours. "Maybe longer."

The girl had an LED lantern with her, and she turned it on, setting it on the table. "Want some company?"

She was around my age, with dark-brown shoulder-length hair, and she looked tired, or nervous. She was right at home in a pair of jeans and a dark sleeveless blouse. I motioned for her to have a seat across from me. "I'm Eva," I said, without thinking twice about my own name.

"Clare." She extended her hand, and I shook it, wishing we could have bypassed the formality.

I went into friendly reporter mode. "What brings you here to Cloud Lake, Clare?"

She glanced over at the lake. It was beautiful right now. Calm, unmoving, like a sheet of pristine ice. It reflected hundreds of stars, the crescent moon hanging on the near side of the water.

I cleared my throat, and she snapped out of her reverie.

"I'm here with my husband. He's a developer, and his company's looking at building a resort here."

"Here? At Cloud Lake?" I was shocked at the notion of choosing this place to build any sort of resort. Sure, it was quiet and peaceful, but not a great location for mass tourism.

"We're hitting another three lakes in Maine this summer. Dan is in charge of researching all the costs and sites. He gets a feel for the people, the town council, the local law enforcement. He really does his homework." Clare smiled, but it felt forced.

"And you hang out for the ride?" I asked.

She nodded. "It can be a little boring. We were trying to…" I saw her hand roam to her belly subconsciously, before she noticed it. Her palm slapped the top of the table and stayed there. "Anyway, it's nice to have a neighbor here. You staying long, Eva?"

"Don't think so. I'm here for a story."

Her eyes lit up. "You're a writer?"

"Journalist, but yeah, I'm a writer too," I said. It always surprised me how interesting people's reactions were when they learned I was a writer. Anyone could do it if they put their minds to it, so I never really understood why it was so fascinating.

"That's great. I used to think I had a book in me," Clare said.

I'd also heard this response nearly every time someone asked me what I did for a living.

"What would you write about?" I prodded.

"I don't know. Maybe a romance. Girl gets swept off her feet. Happily ever after." Her words had a hint of sadness behind them. "Do you want a glass of wine?" she asked, and I found that I did. "I have a fire prepped. Why don't you come next door, and we'll sit outside there for a while?"

"Where's Dan?" I asked after her husband.

"He's out. Probably at the local bar getting a feeling for the locals' take on a resort. He says he likes to pump the idea of a boost to the town's commerce by talking to the workers and small business owners. And if they're anywhere in Cloud Lake on a Saturday night, it's the Sticky Pig Pub. Or so he claims," Clare said, and I saw something there: deep-seated regret, or pain. I didn't have to guess at her story; she was telling it to me with her eyes.

I wanted to remind her she could leave. Go home without him and find someone who would bring her out on a Saturday night. Find someone who loved and appreciated her, and gave her the chance to thrive at life, but I kept my trap zipped and nodded. "I'd love a glass of wine, Clare."

She brightened at this, and I made a quick stop inside my cabin to throw away the remnants of dinner and grab my cell phone. I'd missed a call from my dad, and I didn't have the energy to hear the voicemail. I had a suspicion that Zoe had broken the news to him, and the last thing I needed at that moment was to hear my dad's accusing voice. It hurt more than ever now, as I started to remember that summer again.

My dad was so different, so carefree and loving, but not in a claustrophobic way. That all changed for the next five years, until I finally broke free and went to college. Even then, it had been constant texts, phone calls, and impromptu visits.

I left my phone on the table and headed over to Clare's, where the fire in the pit was starting to roar. This woman knew how to make a good fire. If there was one skill Zoe and I had learned from our time at Cloud Lake, it was how to make a good fire. Two, if you counted how to pee in a lake with poise.

She already had two glasses of red wine poured, and liberal ones at that. I didn't even ask what kind it was. I didn't drink often, and one was close enough to the other for my tastes.

"I was so rude, taking over the conversation. What are you here for? What kind of story?" Clare asked with interest.

I didn't know how much to say; definitely not anything about my own fascination with the topic. "Have you heard the rumors about UFOs and aliens in the area?"

Clare shook her head. "No. Are you kidding me?" Her gaze darted around the darkness beyond the flickering flames.

"I'm not saying it's real, but there have been enough sightings that my boss sent me here to do a piece on it. 'Cloud Lake: Hot Spot or Hoax?' That's only a working title." I laughed, and she lifted her glass to clink to mine.

"Well, I like it. I wonder if Dan's heard about these sightings. What have you found out so far?" she asked.

"Nothing. I only arrived a few hours ago, but I did a little digging, and there have been visuals on strange lights in the sky, and other occurrences over the last forty years," I said, taking a sip.

"I didn't think anyone still believed in that kind of thing. Haven't they all been explained away, like weather balloons or stealth bombers, that kind of thing?" Clare asked, surprising me that she even knew that much about it.

"There are still a lot of sightings, but most of it ends up being fake. Doctored images, and with every kid having the ability to make CG videos, they pop up online all the time. I do still think there are a large group of people out there that do see something, or at least believe they see something," I said.

"Are they crazy?" she asked. A chorus of frogs erupted into the night, creating an eerie soundtrack to our discussion.

"There have been a lot of doctors working over these kinds of cases, but for the most part, there are no signs of abuse or mental illness. They're truly unexplained," I said.

"You seem to know a lot about this. No wonder your boss sent you for the story." Clare's glass was empty, and I glanced at mine, which was basically untouched.

"What is there to do around town?" I asked her, as if I hadn't spent most of my childhood summers here. A lot could have changed in that time, but judging by Main Street when I drove into town, nothing had.

"Not a lot. I've mostly been going for walks and taking the canoe out onto the lake. If you do either, bring bugspray, because it's been nasty around here," she advised.

We talked for a while longer, and I finished my glass of wine, feeling the effects. I was a lightweight, and it didn't mix well with my medication. We said our goodbyes, and ten minutes later, I was in bed, wearing a t-shirt instead of pajamas in the hot summer night. It was muggy inside, and I slid the window open wide, instantly relieved as the breeze carried in fresh cool air. An owl hooted, perhaps claiming a prize catch in the night.

By the time I began to doze off, I'd started to remember something else about that summer. It wasn't clear like the other scenes; more imagery than anything. Before I drifted away to sleep, lights blasted through my open window, against the wood paneling. The wall by the bed began to shake, vibrating as if by a terrible force outside my cabin. My breath caught in my chest, and my eyes sprang wide open, the rest of my body unable to move.

I told myself I had to move. I couldn't stay in bed, not with this happening. I jolted upright, ready to run, when I

43

saw the lights move away. It was a big diesel truck, and someone got out of the passenger side before the engine rumbled again, taking the vehicle around the keyhole toward the gravel road.

"You need to relax, Jess," I told myself. Jess! Why had I used my old name? I was getting rattled being here. The lights, the shaking walls. It was all too familiar.

I stayed awake for another hour before finally falling asleep.

July 12th – 2020

"I'm here to see Sheriff McCrae," I told the robust woman behind the receptionist's desk.

"Do you have an appointment?" she asked, using her middle finger to push her glasses up the bridge of her nose.

I shook my head. "No, but I can make one if you like."

A door opened and a man stepped out of his office. He had crumbs on his shirt, and a piece of a donut stuck to the side of his mouth. Time hadn't been on Sheriff McCrae's side. My brief recollection of him was a strong and macho man with a full head of hair. I think he might have been wearing a cape in my memory.

There was no recognition in his eyes as his stare met mine. Why would there be? "Who's this, Patty?"

"Eva Heart from New York. I'm interested in talking to you about the recent event," I said, sticking my hand out like an old pro. He took it, and I shook with purpose, like my dad had taught me. He grimaced.

"About the missing persons?" he asked, wiping the crumb from his lips.

This piqued my interest, so I went with it. "Yes,

exactly."

"Why don't you come inside?" McCrae glanced at Patty, who was glaring at me. "Hold my calls, okay?"

She nodded, and I followed the sheriff into his office. It was like stepping through a time machine. He had a singing fish mounted on his wall, dusty antlers behind his desk, and an old six-disc changer, along with a stack of CDs with names of bands from the seventies, stuff my dad used to listen to when we were young.

"Pop a squat," he said, pointing at one of the orange chairs across from his desk.

I obliged. "What can you tell me about the missing persons?" I pressed, grabbing my recording device.

He glanced at it, looking like he might request I discard it, but spoke anyway. "There isn't a lot to tell. Mark Fisher was known to be into some bad stuff. We've booked him twice on minor drug-related charges, so the fact that he up and disappeared wasn't too surprising. Even his brother isn't overly concerned."

I made a mental note to track down Mark Fisher's brother. "What else?"

"Then there's Tucker. He's been spouting nonsense about aliens for years now, and I think he finally had a few too many bottles of vodka. We spent some time combing the lake but haven't managed to find him yet. I suspect he'll turn up soon, but hopefully not until after the Cloud Lake Summer Kick-Off," McCrae said.

"You haven't done the Kick-Off yet?" I asked, realizing my mistake. I had to be more cautious.

"What do you know about that?" he asked, leaning forward.

I stammered, "I've read about it. I thought you did it closer to the beginning of the month."

"No, we changed it to the third week of the month. We

found the last two weeks of July and the first week of August were our busiest, so we wanted to overlap it. We've been doing that for over ten years, so your intel must be dated," he told me. "You sticking around for it? It's quite the festivity."

"I'm only here for a few days," I said.

"Well, it's this Thursday if you're interested. Where were we?" McCrae asked. I noticed his computer was one of those old clunky towers that you never saw anymore, and his monitor was thick, at least ten or so years old. I guessed the Cloud Lake sheriff's budget wasn't too flush.

"What do you think about the possibility of a resort coming to Cloud Lake?" I asked. I wanted to know more about the vanished people, but the timing on the question was too perfect.

His eyes grew wide at my query. "How did you hear about that? You must be a good reporter, because I only had the call from Mr. Newton an hour ago, wanting to meet to discuss it. I also received calls from a few of the local business owners, excited at the prospect."

I smiled innocently. "I have my sources."

"Well, hold on to them, because they're ahead of the curve," he said.

"I take it all this talk about aliens visiting Cloud Lake wouldn't be too good for business, then?" I asked.

McCrae picked up a pen and flipped it between his fingers. "You'd be surprised how many people around here think the town should roll with it. It's been attracting press, and there's even a tour coming to town this week to see the lay of the land and watch for a UFO. Insanity, if you ask me."

I was glad to have made this meeting. This was the exact kind of thing I needed for my article. "Can you give me any details about this tour?"

"Go see Henry at the feed store. He's the one crazy enough to let them on his property. He's even got some of them camping out for the night in tents. He's done it for a few years now." I could tell the sheriff didn't believe in the sightings, and that he didn't think the missing citizens of Cloud Lake were related to all the UFO talk. I couldn't blame him. He wasn't a believer; most people weren't. Hell, I wasn't even sure if I was.

"I will. Was there anyone else missing?" I asked, seeing McCrae's interest in me beginning to wane.

His gaze lowered to his desk, and he nodded. "Carly. The Miller girl. It was only a few days ago, and she was having a sleepover at a friend's house about a block from her own house. The kids claim she left in the middle of the night, but no one saw her do it. She never made it home."

I swallowed hard. "How old is this girl?"

"Thirteen. Real shame. We didn't find a damned sign of her anywhere," he said. "This town hasn't been so devastated in years. We searched for three days straight, and the volunteers are still going, though not as strong as usual. No sign of her anywhere. No suspects. It has us in a real pickle." His gaze drifted to the wall, where an old faded newspaper article stuck to a cork board. The date was only too familiar for me, printed on July 16th, 2001. I closed my eyes and took a deep breath, wanting to fish a pill from my purse. I couldn't do that in front of him, so I excused myself.

"Thank you for seeing me on such short notice." I was suddenly sure he'd recognize me. That he'd take my hand, his eyes going wide, and ask me how I was doing after all these years, but he didn't.

"You're welcome, Mrs. Heart," he said.

"Miss Heart. Not married," I said.

"Don't let the men of Cloud Lake know that. They'll

be lining up," he said innocently enough.

"I'll keep that in mind." I left him to his work and raced past Patty at the receptionist's desk, heading outside and instantly feeling the morning heat. I used to love the warm summers and had become used to them again in New York City. It didn't get much hotter waiting for the number three, two platforms beneath Broadway after a day in the park. Still, this was abnormally hot for Cloud Lake. I didn't recall these kinds of temperatures when we used to stay here, but I could have been wrong.

I slid into my car and turned it on, feeling the cool press of air conditioning against my skin. I had on a sleeveless green blouse and gray capris, finishing off with leather sandals. It looked professional, but was airy enough to not overheat in. Even after my moment of near-panic, I found I didn't feel like drowning it out with a pill, so I left my purse where it was. Something about being here was changing me, and I wanted to accept my reality for now.

I found my tablet and opened the file on the home page labeled *Cloud Lake Agenda*. I added a note to talk to Henry at the feed store, find out who Mark Fisher's brother was, and speak to the Millers about their missing daughter. The wound would be fresh, and I considered broaching the subject with someone that Carly was friends with, someone close but not in the family, who might be willing to talk.

Add that to the bullet points about locating Chester Brown, the farmer from the article I'd found in the local county's online paper, and I had quite the task list ahead of me. I used a stylus to cross off one of my lines and scanned through the rest, wondering which to take first.

- ~~Talk to the local Sheriff's department~~
- Locate Chester Brown's address and interview him
- Locate Mark Fisher's brother

- Talk to Summer Kick-Off committee council member
- Locate Carly Miller family, friends, and/or parents
- Go to the feed store and talk to Henry about the Tourist UFO watch group
- I added one more item that might have been more personal than story-related, but I typed it anyway.
- Find out if Clark still lives in Cloud Lake

Satisfied I had a good jumping-off point for the story, I decided to go to the feed store first. I popped up an online map of the town and searched for anything remotely close to that description. Nothing came up. I decided to drive around Main to find it. Cloud Lake was a lot of things, but widespread it was not.

I found the place within ten minutes. The main drag was quiet on a Sunday morning; the only people that seemed to be out and about were heading to church. I drove past the store with a hay bale on the logo and followed two older cars with dressed-up families inside. They pulled over and entered the church's gravel parking lot, kicking up dust at me.

I parked beside an elderly man, who exited his car, staring at me with judging eyes. He was in a suit that had to be twenty years old, dark brown with an awful pastel-blue tie. I smiled at him and stepped out, unsure why I was bothering coming here. I glanced at the sign along the street, seeing the letters that spelled out this week's sermon topic.

The only light in the sky you should worship is the Lord, our savior.

I snapped a picture of it with my cell phone. Now that would make a great image for the article. I sneaked around it, crossing the street to take another with the church in the backdrop, making sure there were no prying eyes as I did this.

I guess I missed one.

"Miss, what are you doing?" a man asked from beside the church entrance. He wasn't dressed up like the others, but he had a nice polo on, and he wore a smile that could melt a stick of butter in seconds.

I shoved my phone inside my pocket and walked over to him. "I'm visiting here for a few days, and I wanted some pictures of the trip. Are you heading in?" I asked the stranger.

He didn't make a move. "Visiting, hey? I guess you could say I am too." He stuck his hand out. "John Oliver."

"Eva. Eva Heart." I shook his hand, getting a firm grip in return. His eyes were intense, and I had a hard time placing his age. He had the eyes of someone who'd seen a lot, but the smooth cheeks and disposition of someone younger, maybe my age.

"Well, Eva, pleasure to meet you. Would you mind if we sat together? I don't really know many people around town," he said.

I was usually more cautious than this, but he was handsome, and we were going inside a church. How much danger could it put me in? "Sounds good."

The place wasn't large, and I recalled there being a handful of other denominations in town. This one was Baptist, and I was instantly transported into another lifetime, hearing the hymns being sung to the rhythm of an organ. For a while after my ordeal, Dad used to force Zoe and me to attend church. We hated it, and I honestly didn't believe my dad benefitted much from it either. He was searching for something and hoped it would help me. It hadn't.

"How about here?" John asked, motioning to the rear pew, which was empty save one older woman wearing a thick sweater. The church didn't appear to be air-conditioned, and I wondered how she wasn't sweating in droves.

The music stopped, and a hefty man clothed in a robe emerged onto the stage, his presence instantly filling the room. The entire congregation seemed to lean toward him, and I found it all unsettling.

"Good morning, family. We've been over the recent news already, and we've prayed for the recovery of Carly Miller." I watched as his gaze lingered on a couple with a small boy near the front of the church. The woman was crying, and I marked her outfit. That was clearly Mrs. Miller. A woman from beside her reached over the small boy and clutched her hand. I marked her too. She was the one I needed to talk to.

"There's been a lot of talk in town lately about visitors from other planets, seeking our people, our family to take, and do ungodly things to their bodies and minds. We need to squash these blasphemous ideas from the world around us." He raised his big hands, thick fingers clenched together, and I thought he might be able to choke a tree with those puppies.

"There are no unexplained lights over Cloud Lake. There are only clouded minds and souls."

A chorus of amens rang through the crowd, but John and I remained silent. We sat there for the next hour while the pastor spoke of God's absolute power, and how we were his only children in the vast universe. I fought to concentrate as I scanned the crowd, making up stories in my head about most of them. I wondered if anyone in this room had sighted the lights above the town over the last couple weeks, and bet that at least some of them had.

By the time it was over, the rest of the congregation was standing, talking and laughing, shaking hands and hugging, and I made for the exit, John following me. "That was… interesting," he said, holding the door to outside open for me. I stepped out into the scorching late-morning sun and covered my eyes with a flat palm.

"What do you believe, John?" I asked, and he shrugged.

"I believe in a god, but I also believe there could be beings on other worlds. Whether they've deemed us worthy enough to visit is another story entirely," he said, passing me another infectious smile.

I glanced at my phone, seeing it was almost noon.

"Do you have somewhere to be?" he asked, and I shook my head, even though I kind of did. "Then how about lunch? We can go to the lake. I'm staying right on the water."

I hesitated, and he seemed to understand. "You meet me at the picnic table in thirty minutes. Here's the address." He scribbled it on the back of a business card and passed it to me.

My breath caught at the street name. "You okay?" he asked.

"Sure. I'm fine. Just hot. Can I bring anything?" I asked.

"I'd love your conversation. It'll be nice to have a meal with someone again. See you soon?" he asked, heading for a two-door Ford truck.

"See you soon," I replied, wondering what I was getting myself into.

Once inside my car, I keyed the address into my tablet, and my suspicions were right on. The Beach Boys played on the local radio station as I stared at the screen. The cabin was next to my Grandma's. The one Peter Martin used to own. The man who was now in prison.

July 5th – 2001

The water was chilly as I jumped in off the dock, pulling my knees into my chest as I plunged deep into the lake. I emerged, spitting a mouthful of water at Zoe, who was floating on a yellow inflatable pool bed. It had a cup holder, and her can of Coke almost fell over as she splashed me. One of the Beach Boys' songs played on the radio sitting on the end of the dock, rabbit ears high in the sky. They crooned about surfing, sun, and girls, as if there was nothing else in the world.

"Stop messing around. You're going to make me fall in," Zoe said. She was in one of her moods today.

I smoothed my long wet hair and waded over to her. Seaweed licked the bottoms of my feet, and I pictured a monster underneath trying to grab at my ankles. I headed over toward the beach, where the weeds had been trimmed, and planted my feet on the sand.

"Ew, Jess, are you peeing again?" Zoe asked, finally breaking into a smile. The sun was high in the distance, and I made a face at her and grabbed another floating lounger off the dock, climbing onto it after pulling a soda can from the cooler.

"You wish," I said, making no sense.

"God, sometimes I wish you were older," Zoe said, and I believed her. We were always close, but I could feel us starting to drift apart. Soon she'd be driving, going to college... having sex with boys. I almost blushed as I thought about the last one, and pushed it away. I knew we'd always be sisters, but I didn't want to lose my best friend too.

"I'm sorry, Zoe. I'll stop being such a baby," I promised, and she smiled again.

"Good. Now... Dad's gone fishing, and Grandma's at the doctor's with that neighbor lady. What do you say we take the car and head into town?" Zoe's eyes were full of mischief, and I instantly wanted to tell her what a horrible idea that was. But that was what a little girl would say, not a woman's best friend.

"Deal," I said, partly aware of the huge mistake we'd be making.

We floated for a while longer, talking about where we'd go when we got to town. We could ride our bikes—it was only like fifteen minutes from here—but Zoe had it in her to take Dad's car. She said it would be cooler, and maybe we'd run into that grass-cutting boy. That sold me on the whole adventure. I closed my eyes as we floated, the intense sun pressing against my water-resistant sunscreen, and imagined his strong arms wrapping around me.

He kissed me softly, awkwardly, because I didn't know what a kiss was supposed to feel like. It was all a little too PG for even my own mind, but I went with it.

"What are you doing?" Zoe asked me, breaking me from the spell I was under.

"Nothing," I lied, and wiped my lips with a damp arm.

"Come on, let's get dry and changed," Zoe said, and that was when I saw him.

The old neighbor guy was on his deck, facing us. Zoe didn't seem to notice, and she stood on the dock, water dripping from her small two-piece bikini. I saw the man's eyes linger on my sister's body, and I cleared my throat, trying to warn Zoe.

She didn't get the hint. "Are you getting out?" she asked, and I shook my head, walking to the beach instead of climbing onto the dock. Sand clung to my feet as I ran to the cabin, glancing back to see the man still staring at Zoe, not even attempting to hide his leering gaze. My skin was flush with goosebumps, and all sorts of alarm bells were ringing.

Zoe arrived a minute later, a towel wrapped around her midsection. "What was that all about?"

"Didn't you notice the neighbor? He was creeping all over you," I said, my voice cracking.

Zoe looked over her shoulder. She was smiling. "Hope he got a good show," she said, and I was disturbed at the comment.

"You shouldn't let him stare at you," I said firmly.

"What am I supposed to do? He was standing on his dock. You don't know he was even watching us. You always make such a big deal out of everything," Zoe said, and I bristled at the accusation.

She hadn't seen his eyes squinting, or the way his lip quivered as he stood frozen in time. I wondered if I should tell Dad later, and decided I would.

"Just drop it, Jess. Let's go into town," she said.

"Do you mind if we take the bikes?" I asked, feeling like enough bad things had already happened today.

Zoe appraised me as only a big sister could; she lifted her white sunglasses from her eyes and stared hard at me. "Fine. But if we see that cute boy, you have to tell him what a good driver I am," she said, and I stuck out my pinky finger.

"Deal." I was thrilled she actually listened to me, and we wound our way to the cabin and inside, away from the glances of the man next door.

July 12th – 2020

I had a half hour, and that was enough time to make a pit stop at the feed store to talk to this Henry character. A few minutes later, I was entering the shop, finding it nearly empty. Truth be told, I was amazed the place was even open on a Sunday. Most of these small towns closed down on Sundays, and nothing was open past eight during the week.

A grumpy woman stood behind a cashier's desk, and I walked by her, heading further inside. Skids of fertilizer sat on the floor, as if that were an impulse item here in Cloud Lake. I turned to the woman, about to ask for Henry, when I saw a man disappearing into a tiny office. I followed him, knocking on the door. When no one answered, I tried the door handle, depressing it.

"Hello? Henry?" I called, sticking my head into the staff kitchen.

He returned to the room, a bewildered look on his face. He was older than I expected, shock-white hair combed to the side. He was clean-shaven and wore a crisp red button-up short-sleeved shirt.

"Can I help you?" he asked.

"Henry?" I asked.

"That's what my nametag says." He smiled, tapping his chest, before realizing he wasn't wearing one.

"I was talking to the sheriff this morning, and he told me I should speak to you about the campout on your land this week," I said, leaving out who I was.

"So you want to pitch a tent and wait for ET to swing by for a visit, do you?" he asked, his eyes dancing around.

"I guess I do," I said.

"Show up Tuesday night, and bring a tent and sleeping bag. I'm told there'll be a grill out there too, if you fancy a steak." He looked like he thought he might have offended me. "Unless you're one of them vegans or whatever."

I laughed and shook my head. "No. Sounds good. Where's your place?"

He gave me directions, drawn on the white space of a flyer for his store.

"Have you seen the lights?" I asked him.

He glanced to the door and then behind him, making

sure no one was looking. It all felt a little set up for my liking. "I have. More than once. They seem to favor my land for some reason. Close to the lake, fertile soil, lots of lowing cows. Had some of my cows taken from me too."

"Just who are *they?*" I asked him.

"You know. Aliens from another planet. The Grays."

I leaned in, my voice quiet. "Have you seen them?"

He advanced as well, so our faces were only inches apart. "Nope," he said too loudly. "But I know they're there."

"Why, then? Do you expect to them to drop by?" I asked, wondering if this was all a big scam. I expected we'd see lights, but they'd be from a remote-controlled drone or something even more obvious. Maybe old Henry here was going to don a rubber suit, complete with glowing fingers, and chase us around.

"Who knows? They come when they feel like it. They don't send me a calendar invite, or whatever you kids call it," Henry said.

I chuckled and shook his hand again. "Good to meet you, Henry." I lifted the paper with his crude map on it. "I'll see you on Tuesday."

I walked through the store and picked out a small one-person tent, and settled on the cheapest sleeping bag. I didn't expect to need one with the heat, and as I stood at the register, I grabbed some sunscreen and a can of insect repellent. I had almost forgotten about my lunch date and checked the time, seeing I was already five minutes late. I swiped my card and told the grumpy woman to have a nice day. She didn't reply.

I left, and my car led me around the lake; my first time on this particular road in many years. I had mixed feelings about heading near my grandma's cabin. Before I came to Cloud Lake, I promised myself I wouldn't set foot near it, but now that I was here, it felt childish and foolish to stay away. It was only a cabin, and Peter Martin was long gone. So was my grandma.

As I drove down the side road heading toward the water, I passed a few familiar homes. How many of them still had the original occupants in them? Likely they'd been sold or passed down to the next generation by now. I neared Grandma's cabin and slowed. It was unkempt, tall grass around it, looking like it hadn't been manicured in quite some time. Who owned it? From the looks of the property, they'd deserted it ages ago. The cabin itself was in dire condition, the old cedar shingles were curled and sporadically placed on the roof, and the windows were boarded up tight.

I spotted the place where Peter Martin used to live, and thought about that first time Zoe and I had been swimming in the lake and he had watched my sister with an unapologetic stare. I should have said something to my dad that day, but Zoe told me I was crazy. She'd reasoned that men had been checking her out for a year already, and Mr. Martin was no different.

I had only been fourteen, and my big sister's word was gold. I could have saved myself some serious trouble if I'd spoken up.

I heard a knock on my window. John was standing there with a serving tray of food and a smile.

"Sorry, I wasn't sure I had the right place," I lied as I stepped out of the car.

I saw him glance into the back seat, where the tent sat in a bag with the tags on it. "Going camping?"

"Something like that," I said, not explaining any further. I wanted to visit Chester Brown's that afternoon, before it was too late. I knew how early farmers tended to go to bed, since they woke up so early in the morning.

"Come on, I have some hot coffee and sweet tea. Your choice," John said, pointing at the table he had set up.

"As hot as it is, I can't say no to a good cup of coffee," I told him, and sat down at the side of the picnic table that faced the lake. He didn't waste any time in sitting directly beside me. I could feel the heat emanating off his leg, which was only mere inches from mine.

"Hey, don't go putting any pressure on me. No one said it was *good* coffee." He laughed, and I had to join him. I was usually quite reserved around new people, especially men, but John had done a good job breaking down my barriers, or at least having me lower them enough for him to get a look at the real me.

"Why are you here, John?"

"Because I'm hungry," he answered.

"I mean in Cloud Lake. What is it you do?" I asked.

"Bit of a handyman." He looked away, grabbing a sandwich. He'd made an assortment, cut into small quarters of white bread. I picked one up and took a bite, the spicy mustard sharp on my tongue. "I figured I could make a decent living somewhere like here by offering to help folks with their rental properties. I'm also trained in small boat engine repair, so that's really come in handy out here too."

"Aren't there bigger places than little old Cloud Lake to settle in?" I pressed, not feeling like I was getting the whole answer.

He met my gaze, chewing his food. "I needed to get away from home. Portland. You know how it is to need to leave and go somewhere new?"

I did, only too well. Change my name, change my hair color, and get a new line of work. I nodded absently. "Not really," I said convincingly.

"Well, I drove and drove, and ended up here to get gas.

Stopped at the diner, had a burger, and saw an ad on the corkboard about a cabin for rent for the summer months. I grabbed it, called the owner, and here we are." He motioned to the cabin behind us and the lake in front.

"It's nice," I said, my gaze lingering on the door where we'd first seen Martin turn on his lights, Grandma telling us the new retired neighbor liked fishing.

"You okay?" John asked as he poured us each a sweet tea, the glass flush with melting ice cubes.

"Fine. It's too hot today." I dabbed my forehead with a napkin and ate another quarter of a sandwich, this one egg salad. "Is it me, or is egg salad the world's most suitable after-church lunch menu item ever?"

He laughed, picking one up. He turned it as if studying it with great interest. He was handsome, and the closeness to me didn't go unnoticed. "I think you're right. I didn't know what possessed me to make this, but now I know! The Spirit of our Lord and Savior," he said with a grin I didn't match. "How about you, Eva? What are you doing in Cloud Lake?"

I decided to be half honest with him. I took a sip of the tea, finding it refreshing and exactly what I needed. The sugar coursed through me quickly. "Have you ever heard of the *Brownstone Beat?*"

"Is that some sort of music band? Sorry, I listen to country radio only," he said.

"It's an online magazine I work for. You heard the rumors about the lights in the sky, the alien visitors, the UFOs?"

His smile slipped away.

"Of course I have. I was in church today while Pastor Donnelly told us all the reasons not to believe in *them*." He wiped a bead of sweat dripping down his cheek.

"And?"

"Do I believe it? Sure. I guess I do," John said. "What are the chances we're all alone in the universe? If we are, it's pretty sad, because there's no way humans are the best the big man upstairs has in his bag of tricks."

It was a funny way of looking at it, one I didn't think about often. "I'm writing a story about Cloud Lake and the history of the sightings. They date back forty years. Did you know that?"

He shook his head. "I didn't. Some of these townsfolk are tight-lipped about a few things, but I did hear some drunk buffoons arguing about Grays at the Sticky Pig Pub a couple days ago. The things people will fight about."

"What did they say?" I asked.

"One guy was saying they took someone's brother. The brother denied it, claiming that his sibling was a loser, and probably got stuck in a culvert while hiding out from the sheriff or something dumb like that. And in classic small-town fighting over nothing, there were a couple punches thrown, but they broke it up pretty quick. I stayed at the bar, minding my own," John said, as if this made him a saint.

That had to be Mark Fisher's brother, the one the sheriff said was a lowlife druggie. "Did you catch the guy's name?"

"Which one?" he asked.

"The one saying his brother wasn't abducted."

"No. Can't say that I did," he answered.

"What did he look like?"

John paused, looking at the lake glimmering in the sunlight. "Maybe an inch or two shorter than me, denim vest. Shaggy haircut. Has to be around thirty or so. I have a feeling he spends a lot of time at the bar, so if you're hoping to interview him for your article, I suspect you'll find him there."

Things were looking up. I felt like I might have a story here after all. If I could tie in a drug and brawling backstory to the lights in the field, the inept old-school sheriff's department, and crazy local farmers, there might be something worth the clicks Barns was hoping to get out of this one. He must have been banking on it, because why else would he send me all the way out here to expense a cabin rental, gas, food, and salary for a story like this?

I pulled out my phone and scribbled a few notes about Fisher, spending the next half hour or so talking with John. He told me about the lake: some things I already knew, some that I'd forgotten. When I was about to leave, he walked me to the car, and I could tell he wanted to tell me something. Or ask me something.

"Eva?"

"Yes?"

"Are you going to be here for the big barn basher at the lake this Thursday?" His voice had a slightly hopeful edge to it, his gaze giving me enough of that playful glance he hadn't quite hinted at yet.

"I don't think so, but the way things are going, it may take me a little longer to sort through the growing list of people I need to talk with. Why, are you?" Obviously he was; why else would he have asked me? I'd originally planned on leaving by Tuesday, but that was the night the UFO troop was coming into town to gawk at the sky and get eaten alive by bugs. Even if I could be done by then, I didn't think I'd be ready to go in time to make it to the city by Thursday night.

What harm could staying another night or two really cause? Plus, Barns was paying, and if things were really crashing down like he'd told me, then I was going to be out of a job sooner rather than later. I might as well take advantage of the free cabin at the lake. I was loosening up, my breathing coming more freely than it had in a long time, and John was still staring at me with hopelessly soft brown eyes.

"I thought I'd check it out. Everyone says it's the highlight of their year," he said, wiggling his eyebrows as if it was the most preposterous thing he'd heard in a while.

"If I'm here, I promise I'll go," I told him, entering my car. I rolled the window down, suddenly feeling powerful. "In the meantime, how about you come over for dinner tomorrow night?" I watched as his eyes widened slightly before he regained his composure.

"That would be… perfect."

"Great. I'll see you at six," I said, and began to drive away.

"I don't know where you're staying," he said.

"Cloud Lake Cabins, number ten." I could hear my dad's voice in my head, warning me away from giving my location away to a stranger, but John already felt like more than someone I'd just met. He'd also been at church, so my warning bells weren't chiming.

He tapped the top of the car and smiled as I left, refraining from looking at Grandma's old run-down cabin as I drove by.

I made my way to town, heading through Main Street. I stopped at the town's main intersection and saw the same man that had swung by Buddy's to pick up his dinner. He stepped in front of my car and glanced into my window. Those blue eyes locked with mine and threw a memory I had repressed into the forefront of my mind.

July 7th – 2001

We parked our bikes in front of Buddy's Diner, and I latched mine to the metal rack with a chain lock. Zoe didn't bother, and I rolled my eyes at her, knowing how pissed

Dad would be if someone stole her bike.

Buddy's was the only place in town to get food if you were a teenager. I had no doubt Zoe would be able to get into Sticky Pig Pub if she wore enough makeup, but she wasn't brave enough to try something as dumb as that yet. I knew it wouldn't be too long before the switch flipped in my sister.

The door chimes rang as we pressed through, and I was grateful for the old window-shaker, chugging out cool air into the diner's main room. It was muggy today, one of those days when clouds hung fat and lazy with rainwater, but never built up the nerve to let the precipitation go. I could smell a storm in the air, and I hoped we'd miss the brunt of it while we hid out in Buddy's.

I liked it here, and I almost had a memory of the last time our family was all together. Zoe said she could recall it vividly. We'd sat by the window, the four of us eating fries, our parents splitting a chocolate milkshake. Things had been rough between Mom and Dad, and that night, she'd left us. No note, no goodbyes, but Dad said he'd seen it coming a mile away. Grandma supported him on that, and I hadn't seen or heard from her since.

Zoe hated Mom, and part of me did too, but I tried to think of how hard it must have been for her to do that to us. Something must have been seriously messed up in her head for her to leave us behind. And my dad was the best. He worked hard, never yelled at us or her, but she'd still left him as much as she'd abandoned us.

It had been difficult for Zoe to come in here at first, but that had been ten years ago, and she didn't bring it up anymore. "Where do you want to sit?" she asked me, letting me choose. This was something she always did, and I loved her for it. I was the youngest and didn't usually get a lot of say. Zoe seemed to understand this more than Dad did.

"By the window," I pointed to the seat where we'd last seen Mom, and Zoe didn't even blink an eye.

The diner was busier than usual, and I scanned the tables for anyone we knew. One of Grandma's friends was there, and she waved and smiled at us before lowering her voice and whispering to the other old lady with her. I had no idea what they were saying, but I didn't imagine it was very nice.

I hated getting older. I was noticing too many things that used to go over my head. The subtle nuances of adulthood were creeping through my walls, and part of me was excited, but a bigger part wanted to stay little and free forever, not having to worry about getting my driver's license or kissing boys, or wondering what I was going to major in when I went off to college.

It felt like this was my last summer before the change. Zoe's metamorphosis had come after her summer out here two years ago, and I knew, as with everything else, that I'd follow closely behind her footsteps, except on a two-year delay.

I hadn't told Dad about the creepy neighbor from the other day, and we hadn't seen him again since, but I didn't forget. Suddenly, I felt like he was watching me, and I glimpsed around the room before peering through the window. He was nowhere in sight.

"What's got your panties in a bunch?" Zoe asked.

"Gross. Nothing. Dad gave you enough for milkshakes, right?" I asked.

Zoe nodded but made an obtuse comment about how she couldn't drink that stuff anymore. It would go straight to her hips. When the waitress came, I didn't order one either and felt another piece of my childhood slip away. I glanced at my fingers, as if I could see it dissipate when the lady left the tableside.

"God, you're so weird. No wonder you've never been on a date," my sister said.

I was about to retort, telling her that the only boys she'd dated looked like they belonged in a zoo, when the rain began to blow hard against the window. It splattered down with such ferocity I thought the window was going to cave in, sending shards of glass all over us. It didn't, but I still scootched a butt cheek over to the right.

"We'll wait it out, Jess. Don't worry," Zoe said.

I eyed the pass at the kitchen, feeling my stomach grumble. I'd ordered a cheeseburger with fries, and Zoe had ordered the grilled cheese with a side salad.

"Do you think Grandma's going to be okay?" I asked her, and her eyes answered my question before she did.

"Sure. Probably."

"She's going for chemo again this week," I said softly.

"I know." Zoe stretched her hand across the table and squeezed mine. "Then I guess it's a good thing we're here to brighten the mood this summer, hey, Jess?"

Rain continued to pour down outside, and the wind howled fiercely. It was five in the afternoon, and Dad was on another one of his fishing adventures. I suddenly wished we were at the safety of the cabin, reading a book or watching bad daytime TV with Grandma.

The door opened, the chimes ringing in the wind, and Zoe's eyes widened. "Lookie what we have here," she said. I craned my neck to see the boy who'd been cutting the grass when we'd entered town. His white t-shirt was soaked, and I could see his lean chest and stomach beneath. I flushed all over and averted my eyes as the boy walked in, heading for the counter.

"What'll it be, Clark?" the lady behind the counter asked the boy.

"Clark, is it?" Zoe whispered, winking at me.

I pretended to look at the clock but stared hard at the back of Clark's head, which was dripping with rainwater.

"I'll have a chocolate milkshake, please, Izzy," he said, his voice deeper than I expected. He looked around, and his eyes caught mine for a moment. They were the bluest eyes I'd ever seen, and I witnessed the start of a grin as he turned around.

"He just checked me out," Zoe said proudly.

I nodded but knew he hadn't. He'd been looking at me, I was sure of it. Why would he bother with me when my gorgeous sister was right here? He must not have seen her.

Clark sat down at an empty stool, and the waitress emerged with our food a couple minutes later. Zoe only ate half of her sandwich, and I wolfed down my burger like there was never going to be another meal. I felt a hunger inside me that I'd never known before, and I kept hoping Clark would look over again, or even… come and talk to me.

As I was pecking away at my fries, Zoe flipped her hair over her shoulders and pouted her lips. "How do I look?" she asked.

"Fine, why?" I asked, but she was already on the move. I watched in horror as Zoe, the most beautiful girl in Cloud Lake, my sister, walked up to Clark, leaned in, and giggled.

July 12th – 2020

It was Clark. I couldn't believe it. He'd been at the diner yesterday, but I hadn't clued in. I'd only seen his reflection the day prior, and it had been so long, but I knew it was him. I flicked my visor down, pretending to look in the mirror, hoping he wouldn't recognize me. What were the chances he'd ever know it was me, Jessica Carver? I doubted they were very high.

I kept driving and looked in my side mirror to see Clark get into a truck labeled *Cloud Plumbing and Heating*. So I'd been right. Clark hadn't left town, and now he was working as a plumber. I wished I'd sneaked a better look at him. He was the boy that started it all, and the one I compared every other to in my head. There were still so many things I didn't recall about that summer, but seeing Clark had reminded me of a few of them.

Zoe had casually mentioned his kissing on our last call, and it still struck me the wrong way. She never knew about my feelings for him, though, not fully. I'd never had a chance to tell her, and after what had happened, there were bigger fish to fry than a little girl's crush.

I decided to come clean when I made it home. I knew Zoe didn't care at all. She was happily married now, with kids and a great life. She'd laugh it off and tell me I was being silly, like she always did, but I wanted to get it off my chest. I'd been living with so many secrets, it would be nice to be free of at least one.

Seeing Clark had thrown me for a loop, and I checked the time. Almost two thirty. I kept driving, away from the lake now, and toward Chester Brown's farmland. It wasn't hard to find the land, since it was the largest acreage in the county, and after a series of wrong turns down the un-marked gravel roads, I found the entrance to his house.

The home was modest but nice, with a massive Quon-set and barn settled between the house and the fields. Old run-down tractors and trucks lined one edge of the long driveway; to me, this place was the epitome of Maine farm-land. I bet if I closed my eyes, I'd be able to hear a windmill rotating, in need of some oil.

Chester wasn't expecting me, mostly because I hadn't seen a number listed for him online. There had been a sprinkling of Browns listed in the area, but I thought it would be just as easy to show up. If there was one thing I'd learned, farmers tended to stay close to home. There was a lot to oversee on a daily basis. It was Sunday after-noon, and to everyone else that meant long walks and swimming in the lake, but to an old successful man of the land like Chester, I was sure he'd be puttering around in the barn or napping on his porch.

I played the odds from the brief interview I'd read, and settled on the barn. As I parked, closer to the barn than the house, I witnessed a man emerge from the red domed structure, wiping his hands with an old rag. He squinted at me, and I seized my purse, heading over to him. The sun was so high and bright, I was grateful for the sunglasses.

Chester was in a pair of dark jeans, work boots, a plaid shirt that appeared to have outlasted the seventies, and he finished it off with dark blue suspenders. He had a green tractor hat on and a scowl over his face.

"Was I expectin' ya?" he asked, and I noticed his two missing teeth, big gaps between his downturned lips.

"No." I stuck my hand out, approaching him. "I'm Eva Heart, from the *Brownstone Beat* out of New York, and I'd like to talk to you about the other night. July sixth."

His eyes didn't show any surprise. "I've gone an' had a dozen of you pretty people show up here to talk to me. Not much else to say, ma'am."

"If it's all the same to you, I'd love to hear your take on it."

"*Brownstone?* What type of paper is that? And New York? Why'd ya come all the way out here?" Chester started walking toward his house and I followed beside.

"I have a fascination with UFOs, aliens, abductions, anything about the unknown beings that many think are watching us from the skies and beyond." I instantly felt foolish for saying it, but I saw something in his eye, something that told me I was selling him on it. "I've wanted to know all about them ever since I was a teenager."

"I'll talk, but know this. There ain't nothin' good comin' from them Grays, I'll tell you what." Chester let out a high-pitched whistle as a dog barked from inside the barn, and I laughed as the droopy-eared Basset hound lazily trod toward the deck. It was a covered porch, and stepping out of the sun cut the temperature by ten degrees.

"Why do you say that?" I asked.

He sat down on his old rocking chair, the aged wood creaking under his body weight. He petted the dog, who plopped at his feet without so much as a greeting to me, and glanced into my eyes. "Because they aren't here to make friends."

He pointed at a weathered bench, and I sat down on it. "You wan' a drink?" he asked, and I saw the cooler beside him. Classic blue and white, and he stuck a hand in, pulling out a can of cheap beer without looking. He passed it toward me, and even though I didn't want it, I accepted.

Chester grabbed another, popped the top, and sipped the chilled amber liquid before rocking in the chair slowly. "Whaddya wanna know?"

"July sixth. Tell me about it. Where were you? Where did you see it? What time was it?" I asked the series of questions, hoping he'd give me a few details. I had my tablet out and was ready to make notes.

"How 'bout I show you?" he asked, and I nodded. He stood, gripping the chair arm for support. I didn't know how old he was, but I judged at least eighty. I rose and went beside him, giving him my arm, which he waved away. "Don't need that. If I did, I'd be dead ten years ago. Now, I was sittin' in ma chair. Have a seat," he said, and I did.

The rocking chair was surprisingly comfortable, and now the dog finally acknowledged me with a glare, before huffing and lowering his head to the wooden porch slats. "It was dark, you know the kind of night you only git for a month or so in the summer. After sundown, was around eleven, but still a little light left in the day's tank."

I nodded, trying to imagine the setting from my seat.

"Crickets chirping like they like to do, an' I got some frogs makin' a racket too. Animals were asleep, but the cows woke up, few of them went to lowing out their concerns for anyone listenin'. I was, and I got up." He pointed to the front of the porch, and I took a breath, thinking of the cows' noise and the crickets in song with the frogs. He kept talking. "Suddenly, all the sound goes quiet. I tap ma ear, wonderin' if I gone deaf. But Turtle here." Chester

72

nodded at the dog. "He craned his neck so far to the side, I thought his head was gonna fall off. I knew then what was about to happen."

I pictured the silence, the dark night sky from this vantage point. From here, I could see the fields in the distance, over the barn and other structures. It was a gorgeous view, and when Chester spoke again, chills ran through me.

"They came then."

"They?" I asked, my voice a tiny whisper.

"Yes, ma'am. The light flew, faster'n any plane, jet, weather balloon, or firefly. This was the Grays, and they hovered there, light flashing for a good thirty seconds. I thought that was it for me. Ma heart beat so fast in ma chest, I couldn't breathe. Then it was gone, no warning, jus' gone." Chester was staring over his field, eyes watering. He wiped a tear away with a liver-spotted hand and turned from me. He meandered back to his chair, sat down, and drank the rest of the can of beer before making eye contact again. "That what you wanna hear?"

I was still standing, looking over the field, trying to imagine what it would have been like to witness something so unsettling. "I'm sorry if you were scared. I hope you're okay," I said, unsure what else to offer him.

"I'm fine. Went to see the doc, an' he said I ain't never been stronger." He patted his chest and smiled, grabbing another beer from the cooler. He glanced at mine, which remained sweating into a ring on the bench. I sat as well and opened it, tasting the bitter brew and finding it wasn't all that terrible in the moment.

"You told the other reporter this was your third sighting, and that they take people. What do you know about the abductions?" I asked, feeling like I was onto something here. Chester was turning out to be a gold mine.

He started to rock again, smooth short motions. It was

calming. "Nineteen sixty-seven. First year me and Bethel moved onto our own farm. Right here." Now I saw it, his emotions rising again.

"How old were you?" I asked.

"Twenty-six. She was twenty-two. The mos' prettiest lass at the ball, that one. Passed twelve years ago." He glanced over, giving me a weary smile. My heart broke a little at his expression. Twelve years was a long time to be alone on a huge farm like this, especially at his age. "Can you believe we saw the lights the first time together? Our first summer out here."

I shook my head. "That must have been scary."

"Nope. We were right here, me in my muddy boots, and Bethel in her apron making a stew, if I remember correctly. She always made the best stew in the state." Chester comforted his dog again, and continued. "We din't know what we was lookin' at, so we watched, thinking it was something special. It wan't until years later, when I seen it again, that I even considered them Grays."

My hand shook as I made the notes, and I had a feeling I already knew the answer to the next question. "When did you see them again?"

"Been a while, but I was already an old man, I suppose. Had to be twenty years ago, give or take," Chester said before taking another sip.

"Could it have been two thousand and one?" I asked with a tremor to my voice.

He met my gaze and nodded. "Seems about right. Much the same that year. Watched it over the lake in the distance, before it roamed over my land again. Bert claims it took his wife, my cousin. They lived a few miles from here. Used to see them a lot. After that night, she never came home, and Bert didn't last too long himself."

My heart raced. "You're telling me your cousin was

taken by these Grays?"

He shrugged. "Who's to say? She was in her late fifties. Happy woman, Carol was. Bert done right by her, and they had good kids, strong family. She didn't walk away, not that I can judge."

"And she vanished that night and never made it home?" I asked, nervously taking a sip from my can.

"Be right back. I'll get you the date," he said, entering his house. The old wooden screen door slammed against the frame, causing me to jump in my seat. He returned with a clipping from a newspaper, passing it to me.

I read it, and I caught the tears threatening to burst from my eyes. "July sixteenth, 2001. Unidentified lights seen over Cloud Lake." There was an article on the bottom of the page about it, but the one that caught my eye made it all the more real. There was a picture of fourteen-year-old me, smiling while I held a fish up at Grandma's dock. I read the headline: *Fourteen-year-old girl missing after the Summer Kick-Off party at Cloud Lake.*

"Are you okay, Miss Heart?" Chester asked.

"Can I take this?" I asked, and he nodded, seeing how upset I was.

"Thank you for everything. I appreciate your candor, Mr. Brown." I patted his arm.

"Call me Chester. Mr. Brown is my father." He laughed, trying to lighten the mood, but I was a wreck.

Once I was in the safety of my car, I pulled the article out again. Under the picture of the girl, I read the name, *Jessica Carver*, and burst into tears.

July 8th – 2001

"You sure you don't want to go with your dad and sister?" Grandma asked me, and I nodded. It was another rainy day, making that three in a row. It was oven hot, the humid air threatening to make everything cling as we sat on the porch. Here, we were safe from the incessant drops, and even the bloodthirsty insects were in hiding now.

"I thought we could spend some time together, Grandma," I told her, and saw her face light up in a smile. She was skinnier now, and even though she and Dad kept telling us she was going to be fine, I could see the evidence in front of me.

Grandma was dying, and quickly. The lymphoma was spreading, and the treatment had been started too late. I'd overheard Dad arguing to someone on the phone the other day, and had been obsessing over Grandma's time ever since. Grandma knew as well but was playing it off for my benefit.

Dad exited the cabin, Zoe right after him. She was in denial about the whole thing. We'd talked last night, and she said I was worrying too much, that Grandma was a superhero, and nothing but a meteor could take her down. I wanted so badly to believe it, but Zoe was wrong about this one.

"I have the list, Mom." My dad leaned in and kissed her on the forehead, and I loved that no matter how old they got, they were always mother and son. It was endearing. I would never have that with my own mother, but I had him, my strong father; the real pillar in my existence.

"Don't forget the marshmallows this time," Grandma scolded.

"Yeah, Dad, you can't make s'mores without them. Nothing to stick the graham crackers together with," I added, getting my own kiss on the head for my troubles. I still let him do that, where Zoe would say *gross* and push him away. I hoped I never grew up, if that was how I'd react to Dad's affection.

"I'll never live that one down, will I? Jess, anything

special? Root beer for floats? Frisbee?" Dad asked, and I had the urge to make a commitment I kept putting off. This summer was already special, and I could feel the walls of it closing in on us, like there was never going to be another year like this one to enjoy each other's company.

"Get me a pink ball cap? If you and I are going to go fishing this week, I don't want to get sunburned," I said, and giggled at the expression that appeared on his face. In a flash, it was gone, and he played along.

"Yeah, fishing day. How could I forget? I'll get you that hat, kid. Okay, Zoe, let's get out of here. Food run commence!" He started for the Bronco and glanced over to his mom. He ran the rest of the way to the vehicle, where Zoe was already inside. She gave me a demure wave, and they drove away. Once every few weeks, we'd make a longer trip to the neighboring city. Cloud Lake had most things, but it was a lot cheaper to hit the big chain for bulk stuff on occasion.

"What do you want to do?" I asked Grandma. It was after lunch time, and we were in the quiet part of the midweek day, where the rain made being outside impossible, and there was nothing to watch on TV except soap operas and game shows.

Grandma stood up, and I saw the effort it took. "I have something for you, dear. I've been wondering when to give it to you, and didn't want to around your father. Not yet." She went into the cabin, and I tensed up, wondering what the heck she could possibly have for me that she didn't want Dad seeing.

She returned and sat on her chair at the patio table beside me, placing a small rosewood box on the surface. "This was your mother's. She left it behind."

My heart stopped beating, or so it seemed. I eyed the box, afraid to touch it. I didn't speak… or move.

"She wasn't a bad person. Sure, she had issues, and I know there's no forgiving her for walking out on you and your sister. She and my son were never soul mates. They weren't meant to intertwine and survive the ages of existence together." I had never heard Grandma talk quite like this before, and I liked it. "But she shouldn't have bailed on you two, and for that, I'll never be able to forgive her."

"Why give me this?" I asked.

Grandma's hand found mine, squeezing it tenderly. "I'm not going to be around forever, and I'll be leaving you guys everything I own. I wanted you to know where this came from, and maybe you can have it as a reminder of her. You girls are so strong-willed, beautiful, and precious to me and your father. But part of that comes from her DNA, and I see her every day when I look at your face, you more than Zoe.

"I know your dad sees it too, and I can't imagine how hard, yet wonderful that is for him as well," Grandma added.

"Grandma, tell me the truth." I was crying now, unable to stop the tears from flowing like the rain around me. I glanced to the pathway off the porch and watched as dozens of ripples from the rain chased one another in a pool of murky brown water.

"I will," she promised.

"Has she ever contacted Dad? Has she ever tried to reach out to us?" I'd wanted to ask Dad that for years but couldn't bring myself to. Any time I mentioned Mom, he clammed up, became moody, and I hated to do that to him.

Grandma's face said it all. "No, dear, she hasn't."

I bawled then, wishing I could see her, if only for an instant. I'd been so young, and I wasn't able to process it as well as Zoe or even Dad. I tried to picture her face but couldn't, and it made me cry even more. Grandma was at my side, pulling my face to her chest, and she held me as I sobbed away at the memory of my vacant mother and the childhood that was quickly slipping away from me.

"You're going to be okay, Jess, and you know why?" she asked.

"Why?" I finally broke from her grasp, my face soaked, my cheeks hurting.

"Because you're a Carver, and we're tough. We don't let life get us down, and we move on," she said firmly, slapping her palm against the table, making the small box jump.

"Grandma," I started, and glanced at the woman beside me. Her hair was dyed red, fashioned into tight curls. She wore what Zoe always called "old lady" glasses, but they suited her, made her look distinguished. She was so much thinner than she used to be, but she was still the same Grandma underneath. I had to know. "Are you going to die?"

She smiled softly at me. "Honey, we're all going to die some day."

"You know that's not an answer," I told her.

"Then yes, I'm going to die," she said without sadness.

"When?"

"Soon," she said, and I wanted to cry again but found no tears.

"I'm sorry." I didn't know what else to say.

She laughed, breaking the mood. "What do you have to be sorry about? You're here with me now, aren't you? Spending time with your old granny. Now take the box, and don't show your dad yet, okay?"

I grabbed it timidly, as if I feared the ghost of my mother would jump out to haunt me. With trepidation, I tilted the lid open to find a necklace inside. It was the same one she wore in the photo I had on my mirror at home. I knew, because I'd logged a lot of hours staring at that image. Her with long brown hair, curled slightly, and a knowing smile for the camera. I was small, sporting a green blouse, Zoe in a blue one, and Dad had on the brown suit he wore for any special occasion.

"This was hers," I said as I pulled it out, feeling the weight of the thin chain in my palm. There was a small golden cross on the end.

"It was. Go tuck it away, Jess, and what do you say we go for a walk? I could use the movement," Grandma said. I hadn't seen her getting around much, and the rain had started to let up.

"Let's keep it to a short one, okay?" I asked, and she nodded as she looked at the water. I knew Grandma was scared; that she was only acting tough for my benefit, but she was feeling something I couldn't comprehend. Her existence on this world was nearing its end, and she couldn't do anything about it. I ran inside, placed the necklace in the box, and shoved it under my mattress, hoping Zoe wouldn't snoop under there and find it.

A minute later, I was on the porch, holding an umbrella and letting Grandma use my arm for leverage as we set off on what might become our last walk to the lake alone.

July 12th – 2020

I was eternally grateful for the small air-conditioning unit in cabin number ten. Cloud Lake Cabins was busier now; next week's traffic finally settled in. I hadn't been there since early in the morning, and I was exhausted. By the time I'd returned from Chester's, I'd been a disaster. The past had found me here in Cloud Lake, and I wanted to leave most of it buried in its grave.

I'd ended up staggering to the small bedroom, and the second I lay down on the bed, I'd fallen fast asleep, the hum of the AC unit lulling me away. When I woke, I was cooled down for the first time in days, and checked my phone. There was a missed call from my sister, and one from the office. Why was Barns calling me on a Sunday?

What startled me was the time. I'd slept for three hours, and it was now after eight o'clock. My stomach growled a little, and I realized I still hadn't picked up any supplies from the store. I'd been so preoccupied with the story that I'd been forgetting to do the important things in my daily routine. I hadn't taken any anxiety medication either, and I decided against it. If I was going to find Mark Fisher's brother at the bar, I would likely be drinking, and I hated the way it made me feel when I combined the two.

I used the bathroom and looked around a little more now. The tub and surround were one piece, a cheap plastic contraption with one of those tiny shower heads you always saw at a place like this; minuscule but powerful enough to hose an elephant off with. These cabins had been around long before low-flow and water conservation were a thing.

The shell-shaped sink reminded me of our old house, and I glanced down to the vanity knobs, which were made to resemble starfish. It was all a little kitschy, but quaint, and I couldn't deny liking the details I hadn't noticed until then.

I moved to the bedroom and stripped out of the clothes I was wearing, kicking them to the floor. What should I wear to the Sticky Pig Pub? I hadn't brought a lot of recreational clothing; most of what I had in my wardrobe was office clothes: professional attire that was comprised of polyester and muted tones.

I found a pair of jeggings and threw them on, eyeing the rest of the tops I'd moved into the compact dresser. I pulled out a black tank top, deciding that would be enough on this hot night. I finished it off with my necklace from the nightstand. The familiar gold chain hung around my neck, the weight of the cross calming me as it pressed to my chest.

I grabbed my curling iron and spent the next five minutes quickly making my bedhead presentable, before dabbing some perfume on and adding an extra layer of deodorant. I knew what small town bars were like, and the fact that I was hitting one on a Sunday didn't necessarily mean it was going to be any less raucous than any other night.

When I was confident I appeared like I might actually fit in, instead of sticking out like a sore thumb, I headed for the door, clutching my purse.

The second I stepped outside, I smelled the fire from next door. I turned to see Clare watching the flames flickering, a half empty bottle of white wine on the table beside her. I blew out a sigh and fought the desire to run past her and go on my merry way. It was something my therapists had helped me with, trying to connect with other humans. It was a process, but one I was steadily gaining traction on.

"Clare," I said, heading over to the fire. "Are you all alone? No Dan?" I asked, peering around. The lights in her cabin were off.

Clare beamed a smile at me, as if she'd recently found her best friend was home from a long trip. "Oh my God. If it isn't Eva Heart, the big city girl in the flesh," she said, sounding as sweet as syrup. I instantly knew she was half cut and wondered if I should leave her at home alone instead of inviting her along. Still, it would be good to have a friend to back me up.

"What are you doing out here all by yourself?" I asked her.

"Dan had to work, so I thought I may as well have a fire. I knocked on your door, but I guess you were busy," she said.

"I was sleeping. Haven't even had a bite to eat today," I said. "Was going to hit up the Sticky Pig, since everything else will be closed. You interested in coming along?"

She smiled at me and drained her wine glass. "I've never been one to say no to a girls' night," she said. "Can you give me five to get ready?" She was wearing a floral summer dress and looked ready to me. It reminded me of something Zoe would wear.

"Go for it. I'll see about putting this out." I pointed at the fire, which was mostly hot coals at this point.

Clare went inside, and I found a hose attached to the outside of their cabin. The hose was long enough for me to reach the firepit with a steady stream of water. It hissed as I doused it, and I was careful not to spray myself as I pulled the trigger.

"What do you think?" Clare asked from the porch, and she spun in the lantern light. She'd pinned her hair up and had replaced the dress with a pair of tight faded jeans and a blouse that showed off all of her assets.

She was more like Zoe than I'd even thought: a mixture of my teenage sister and a responsible adult. "You look great. I'll have to bat the men away from you with my purse. Come on," I said, leading her to my car.

I headed down the road, exiting the Cloud Lake Cabin premises, and we wound our way through the late evening dusk as we eventually came to the edge of town. The bar was like every small-town bar ever. Four or five Harleys were parked near the entrance, and at least half a dozen trucks: mostly older, beat-up, the kind the drivers used for real work, not just for showing off how shiny they could keep them.

As I parked, Clare leaned toward me, her breath a little sour. "Thanks for inviting me. I try to be supportive, but

Dan's never around, and it gets… old."

"Glad to have you along," I told her, and meant it.

The second I opened the car door, I heard the muted country music seeping through any cracks around the doorway and windows. I was sure the song had been popular when I was about ten. Clare was humming along, and a few seconds later, we were at the door. I pushed it open and almost turned around to leave, the sudden idea of being in a loud, cramped space threatening to overwhelm my senses.

Clare patted me on the arm and continued walking, not noticing the horror on my face, and I swallowed hard, wishing now that I'd taken my pill at the cabin. I took a step, and then another, the dread slipping away enough for me to breathe again.

There were two pool tables on our left, some men and women standing around them, playing a lazy game or two. The bar was straight ahead, and Clare was already there, pressing beside a man on a stool, trying to get the bartender's attention. It didn't take long.

I relaxed a little as I spotted other young women inside, and could pick out which were locals and which were tourists with little effort. The locals all presented a sullen disposition, like they had a slight distaste for the people visiting their little town. It was a hard balance, living in a place like this. The money all came in the summer months, and the locals had to fend for themselves the rest of the year.

I approached Clare, and she turned to me. "This is Tyson." She nodded to the man she was standing beside.

"A pleasure, I'm sure," I told the local man. He was wearing a vest with a construction company logo on it, and he grinned at me. He was at least ten years older than us.

"Tyson's buying our first round. Isn't that nice of him," Clare said, and I was seeing this new strange side to her.

"Thank you, Tyson," I said as politely as I could. The bartender was waiting for my order. I glanced at the beer options and chose the same one Chester had offered me earlier.

"Do you have a food menu?" I asked the nondescript man behind the bar, and he slid a laminated list of finger-food options across the bar.

We took our drinks, Clare thanked our benefactor, and we found a seat in a booth to the right of the bar. I chose a spot that had no one beside it, and I took the seat that allowed me to view the entire floor from it. I always did.

I glanced at Tyson and pictured him with a wife and three screaming kids at home. He'd tell his wife he had to work late, and he'd come here, buying drinks for attractive tourists, playing the odds that one day, one of them would finally thank him with sex. I usually stretched the truth in my internal game, but this one felt as close to the truth as any of them.

"What did Dan say he was doing tonight?" I asked her, feeling like whatever the answer would be was a lie.

"He had a meeting with a local lawyer from the county about zoning or something," she said.

"Sunday night at nine?" I pressed. I didn't really know this woman but could tell she was in a caustic relationship.

She shrugged. "He left at four, said he'd need a few hours. I don't ask questions anymore."

I left it at that, not wanting to delve into the deep dark recesses of Clare and Dan's rocky marriage. I had other things on my mind, and at the top of the list was Mark Fisher. A waitress saw me flagging her down, and I ordered some chicken wings. Clare added some mozza sticks to the order.

I pulled out my tablet from my purse and checked my entries. I crossed out some items and added a note.

- ~~Talk to the local Sheriff's department~~
- ~~Locate Chester Brown's address and interview him~~
- Locate Mark Fisher's brother
- Talk to Summer Kick-Off committee council member
- Locate Carly Miller family, friends, and/or parents
- ~~Go to the feed store and talk to Henry about the Tourist UFO watch group~~
- ~~Find out if Clark still lives in Cloud Lake~~
- Find out any details about Chester's cousin Carol. How many people have gone missing here?

I tapped the third line and looked around the room. If I was going by John's description of the guy, he was thirty years old, wore a denim vest, and had shaggy hair. There were several men who could have fallen under that description, so there was only one way to tell. I had to ask someone or come up to them directly.

"I see someone's on the prowl for a man," Clare said. She was in a far different mood than the first time we'd hung out, and I had to say I preferred the sad, reserved Clare more than this one.

"Hardly. I'm actually looking for someone. It's for my story," I explained.

"What does this place have to do with UFOs?" she asked, finishing her drink.

I wrapped my hand around my can of beer and took my first sip. It wasn't as refreshing as Chester's had been, but that could have something to do with the setting, or the company. "It's not this place." I leaned in and lowered my voice. "There may be some disappearances involving the sightings."

"What do you mean?" Clare's eyes widened. "You

86

really think there are aliens stealing away people?"

I shook my head. "No. But some people do," I lied. "And nothing sells a story quite like a missing family member thought to be abducted by aliens, right?" I took another drink, this one longer.

"Sounds fishy to me. What happened to the person you're looking for?" Clare asked.

"Local guy went missing. Cops think it was drug-related, but the brother might say otherwise. He was there on the sixth," I said, not sure I had the entire story. "Let's not worry about that, and get another drink, okay?"

Clare nodded, and soon we were eating our fried food and chatting like old friends. The waitress came over to clear our dishes. "Excuse me," I started, "do you know if any of these men in here go by the name Fisher?"

Her gaze darted around, and she shook her head. "You don't want to get involved with the Fishers, darling," the woman said, and the term of endearment was odd coming from someone my own age.

"And why's that?" I quietly asked.

"Because they have a penchant for ending up dead or in jail," she said, and walked away.

"You sure know how to pick them, Eva," Clare said with a laugh.

"Don't I know it. Come on, maybe we should go," I suggested, when I saw him across the room. Clark was playing pool. I watched him take a shot and stand up, laughing at his near miss. He was wearing a polo shirt and jeans, worn boots finishing off the look. His hair was blond, shorter than it used to be, styled as if trying to look messy. His gaze crossed the entire bar, and stopped as he made eye contact with me. Even from here, I could see the blueness of them.

"Hold the phone, who's that? Because I might be

willing to get into trouble if that's a Fisher," Clare said, seeming to forget she was married.

"That's… that's not one of them," I stammered. Had he recognized me? Did he know it was me?

His stare broke as a girl walked between us, passing Clark a pint glass. He looked around her, and I saw the slim thing slide her arm around his waist in a possessive move, even though I didn't think she'd noticed him looking at me. They went back to the pool game, and I decided it was time to go. I stood up, and Clare complained it was too early to leave.

The second I was about to pass a burly bouncer, the door swung open, and a man stumbled into me.

"Sorry, didn't see you there," he said. He was wearing a denim vest over a white t-shirt; he had forearm tattoo sleeves and shaggy brown hair, and a lopsided smile that was hard to get away with.

"Fisher?" I asked.

His smile faded. "Logan Fisher. Who's asking?"

"I wanted to talk to you about your brother," I said, and his face contorted.

"Are you with the police? FBI? What the hell do you want?" he shouted.

I glanced around, noticing a lot of the bar patrons watching us, Clark included. "I only need five minutes outside," I pleaded.

"Fine," he said. "Tucker, get me a beer. I'll be a minute." The bartender nodded twice.

The outside air was refreshing, somewhat cooler than it had been. Clare was behind me, and I asked her if she wouldn't mind waiting in the car. She grabbed my keys and left the two of us alone. I walked a short ways from the bar, trying to escape the noise.

"My name's Eva. I'm doing a piece on the recent

sightings, and I wanted to talk to you about Mark," I explained.

"What does my brother have to do with that bullshit?" he asked.

"You don't think the two are related?" I asked.

"Look, this town has a lot of history with strange stuff going down. Lights, and God knows what else. Sometimes things can be explained. People go missing all the time, across the country. Spouses leave one another in the middle of the night, kids get abducted, and sometimes a low-end drug dealer gets killed," Logan said, and I felt like I'd been slapped. Most of what he'd said struck home with me.

"So you think… what? The night that there were multiple sightings of lights in the sky, your brother Mark was killed on a deal gone wrong? What about Carly Miller? What about all the others over the years?" I stepped closer to him, almost daring him to deny it.

"Cloud Lake gets a lot of people moving through here in the summer. Our population triples in July and August. Lots of bad things happen in those months, so much more than the police or papers ever know. So yes, I'm saying that I think he was killed, or maybe he got spooked and bailed."

"Without telling his own brother," I said.

"We weren't that close. Now, if you don't mind, I have a beer waiting inside for me." Logan stepped away and left me standing there alone.

"There goes that lead," I muttered.

Tomorrow was another day. I headed to the car and drove us home, the whole time thinking about Clark and wondering if he had any idea who he was looking at inside that dive bar. What would he think if Jessica Carver appeared back in his life?

It didn't take long to drive to the Cloud Lake Cabins, and the porch light was on at unit nine when I pulled up.

"Crap, Dan's home." Clare pulled up her shirt at the collar in a vain attempt at hiding her cleavage. "If he asks, can I tell him we went for a drive to Florence for dinner? There's a spot called Buon Cibo there. Italian."

What could another lie hurt? "Sure. Buon Cibo. I had the fettucine, you had the lasagna." I smiled weakly at her, and she came in for a hug.

"Thank you," she whispered into my ear.

I went into my cabin, and could hear Dan yelling through both sets of walls.

July 13th – 2020

Since my fridge was still empty in the morning, I decided to freshen up and hit Buddy's Diner before heading over to the church. I wanted to talk with Carly Miller's family friend, the woman I'd seen comforting the mother on Sunday. If anyone would know what her name was, the pastor would. I considered asking around town for the Millers' address, since it was unlisted, but I knew no one would surrender it if I told them I was a reporter. Small towns like this stuck together.

Buddy's was busier than I expected on a Monday morning, but I found my favorite booth open by the window and took it. Isabelle, the same waitress from the other evening, came over with a pot of steaming coffee.

"You again. Glad to see you back at Buddy's." Isabelle flipped over a chipped white cup and poured coffee into it without asking first. She nodded to the menu. "Stick with the classics today. Earl is out sick, and his cousin doesn't know an omelette from a frittata." She leaned in to say this, and I could smell menthol cigarettes and a layer of cheap perfume doing a poor job of covering up her habit.

"Two scrambled eggs, toast, and hash browns," I told her without looking at the menu.

She nodded and winked at me before heading over the table beside mine to chat and refill their empty cups. I wished that I'd asked the priest about the Millers on Sunday, but John had been there with me, creating an unintentional distraction. He was supposed to come over for dinner tonight, and I considered calling him to cancel. I didn't know what to make, and the last thing I needed was getting involved with some guy that lived in Peter Martin's old cabin.

I tried to imagine Zoe's face when I told her. If I told her. Ever since that summer, Zoe had been overprotective of me. She blamed herself, even though she didn't know the whole truth. Neither did I, for that matter. I was missing that week, but being here again was letting the memory map expand, and I understood the events leading up better. Back then, it had been a whirlwind of confusion and horror, quickly erased by medication and therapy. Dad was so adamant about making me forget, he didn't think what that would do to me in the long run.

My food came, and I ate it slowly while watching the morning traffic head through Main Street. Families towed boats along behind their large SUVs, local road crews headed to and from their jobsites, often with their windows rolled down, loud country music playing from the speakers. It was relaxing. The noises reminded me a bit of being in New York, and for a second, I closed my eyes and even heard a honk in the distance. I could do this.

The story was coming along nicely. I had the great piece on Chester Brown, the disappearance of Carly Miller, and the angle with Mark Fisher tied in with the seedy underbelly of drugs in Cloud Lake. Something flashed into my mind, and my breath caught in my throat. It all went hand in hand with Peter Martin. The missing girl, the drugs, the same time as the lights appearing. Part of me felt like I was reliving my experience again, only from an aerial viewpoint. Maybe I could help. Maybe I could be the one to figure out these lights that had haunted the town and my own mind for so long.

"Anything else?" Isabelle asked, and I shook my head, pulling out fifteen dollars and handing it to her. "Thank you, dear."

"Tell Earl's cousin I enjoyed it," I told her, and moved for the door. As I stepped out onto the sidewalk, I knew it was going to be another scorcher. It made me feel like a storm was coming. Maybe not today or tomorrow, but soon. It used to always be like that here. A week of hot, then a few days of thunderstorms to wash it all away.

A truck drove by, a father and daughter pulling a small-engine boat behind, with fishing rods sticking out of the bed of the vehicle. The girl was smiling and chatting her dad's ear off. It made me want to call my own dad. I'd only fished that one day with him and knew he'd always longed for more time like that with me.

July 10ᵗʰ – 2001

"Shhh, don't wake Grandma," I told my dad, and he exaggerated sneaking around our living room on his tippy toes. I rolled my eyes at him when he stumbled and knocked over a garbage can. "Good work, Dad. I'm sure you woke the neighborhood with that move."

"It *is* after five in the morning. Shouldn't they all be up anyways?" he joked, grabbing some granola bars and bananas from the kitchen. Coffee was brewed, and he filled up his thermos, raising a questioning eyebrow in my direction. "Want some?"

I blinked the sleep from my eyes. "Coffee? You said I

wasn't allowed until I was twenty. Or was that dating?"

"Both. But since you're acting so grown up these days, I thought you might enjoy a little fresh brew. Just a little bit," he said. Dad started preparing it, and I went outside to grab our lifejackets from the shed. The door was stuck, and I pulled on it. The rain must have expanded the wood during the heat wave.

"Need a hand?" a voice asked, and I glanced over to see the neighbor, Mr. Martin, standing five feet away. He was in a dark green bathrobe, cinched tight around his waist. He was younger than I'd originally thought, and seeing him there so suddenly caused me to freeze in place.

"Did you get the jackets?" Dad asked from the porch.

"I can't get the door, Dad. Can you come help me?" I asked, pushing the waver from my voice.

"Sure, kiddo."

I stepped away from Mr. Martin without ever speaking to him, and when Dad arrived, he turned on his friendly neighbor routine. "Oh, we finally meet. You're up early, aren't you?" Dad asked the man.

"Pete. Pete Martin." He stuck his hand out, and I cringed as Dad shook it. The man was thin, his hair graying and receding from his forehead.

"Brian Carver. But my mom calls me late for dinner." Dad laughed.

"Kate's a sweet woman," Mr. Martin said.

"Unless she catches you sneaking out past curfew. Then she's a real killer," Dad said, and the two men laughed. I didn't like the interaction one bit. I could still see the way his stare lingered on my sister the other day, and to me, this man was never getting my trust.

"And who's this lady?" He caught my gaze and winked at me.

I wanted to run away, to get out of there, but Dad was

all too happy to chat casually. "This is Jessica. Other daughter's still sleeping."

Mr. Martin nodded, grinning at me. "Good. Going fishing, I see?"

"Yep. I'd usually be out there an hour ago, but you know how it is getting a teenager to wake up," Dad said, and that hurt a little. I thought I'd been extra fast. "Do you have kids?"

"I do. But they're past their own teenage years. My son's actually around for a few weeks," Mr. Martin said.

"Well, we'd best be off. Good to meet you," Dad said, and I turned, walking away. "Jess, what about the vests?"

"You get them. I'll meet you in the boat," I said, without turning around.

A half hour later, we were drifting along the far edge of the lake, the sun peeking through the trees, casting shadows on the water. Dad had told me this was his favorite spot in Cloud Lake, and I could see why. The air was fresh, and it was still cool enough to not feel constantly overheated.

"Pass me the bug spray?" Dad asked, and I sprayed my legs again before passing the can over. "You having fun?"

I held my rod, not sure I remembered his brief instructions, but the line was in the water now as we trolled along the coast. It didn't feel like anyone else was out on the water, just my dad and me, and I loved it.

"I am. I can see why you're always out here," I said, trying to keep an accusatory hint from my words.

It didn't work. "Jess, I know it's hard only having a dad, and that I'm not the easiest man to deal with. If you think I'm coming out here to get away from you or your sister, that's not true. Life's been tough, and now with Grandma…"

We sat facing each other on the benches, and my mind

drifted to the necklace tucked under my bed. I understood what he meant. "We're the Carvers. We'll get through it, Dad." I forced a smile for his benefit.

"You're right. How's the summer going? Did you go down to the volunteer center yet for the Summer Kick-Off party?" Dad asked. He knew we hadn't, but he was making small talk, trying to get me to open up.

"Tomorrow. Zoe hates the idea of babysitting kids, but I think it might be fun. I mean, if you can teach kids every day, we can at least help watch some for a few hours," I said, getting a laugh.

"Are you worried about starting high school?" Dad asked. He didn't often divert into topics like this, but fishing together was some really solid alone time, and he probably wanted to take advantage of that. I didn't mind.

I unscrewed the thermos and drank the coffee. "It's not what I expected," I told him, pretending I hadn't been sneaking sips from his cup for years.

"Coffee can be an acquired taste. You need to get it right for yourself. Two cream, one sugar is my go-to, but you might like it with more or less of something. And if you're starting out, stay away from the sugar. My doctor told me to stop using it years ago, and here we are." Dad took a sip from his cup before raising it in the air. He never told me stuff like that, so I decided to open up to him about next year.

"I wasn't trying to avoid the question about school. I'm nervous. Some of my friends are going to other schools, and there's the whole…"

"Your dad being a teacher thing?" he asked.

"Yeah, and Zoe already going there two years ahead of me. She's so pretty and popular." I gripped the fishing rod and stared blankly at it.

"She's your sister, and she loves you. I bet having Zoe

in the same school as you can only help your transition. She won't leave you behind, no matter what you think. That girl adores you," Dad said, making me feel better.

"What about you? Is it weird teaching Zoe?" I asked.

"I'm her physical education instructor. So for the most part, she plays the sports and does the work. Of course, I enjoy it because I get to see my kid and get paid at the same time. It'll be the same with you, Jess." Dad craned his neck backward and looked toward the rising sun. "We should get moving," he started as my rod's line began to pull.

"I got one! I got one!" I yelled, almost letting go of the rod in the process. "What do I do?"

Dad came over and showed me, giving me step-by-step instructions, never taking over, only guiding. I loved him for it. He was teaching me, and if this was how he did things, I knew having him there for my gym class was going to be fun. A couple minutes later, I was cranking the reel and pulling a fish from the water. It flapped around in the air, and I hated the idea of killing an innocent creature like this.

Dad was so proud, I could see it all over his face. He must have sensed my trepidation, because he showed me how to unhook the lure and set the fish into the water. He said it was catch and release. The next one, I decided to keep, but felt terrible for doing so.

An hour later, Dad had three of his own caught, and we were on the dock, the boat tethered to the end.

"Smile," Dad said, using a disposable camera to take a picture. I held the rod and fish, smiling for the shot, but feeling dreadful about the life I'd snuffed out.

July 13th – 2020

For a few moments, I stared at the photo from the local paper of me holding up the fish before folding the sheet up and shoving it into my purse. That had been the only time I'd ever fished, and it was the only proof I'd caught something. Dad had the roll developed and handed it to the police the day I'd gone missing, never to retrieve the picture again.

I looked younger than I had in my head at that time, still a girl.

The church parking lot was empty except one old Cadillac, and I decided the pastor was exactly the type of man who'd drive that car. I was about to head in when Zoe's image appeared on my phone's screen.

I had to answer it. I'd already ignored her calls and had replied to her worried text with an: *I'm okay*. Clearly, that hadn't been enough to satisfy her concern.

I used the car's Bluetooth to answer the call. "Hey, Zoe, sorry I didn't call yet."

"Where are you?" she asked.

"Cloud Lake. You know, for the story," I said.

"I know that… why are you there? I know I played it off like no big deal the other night when we spoke, but after you hung up, I got to thinking. This is bad news, Jess."

"Eva," I muttered.

I could hear Zoe rolling her eyes. "Goddamn it, Jess… Eva. I mean it. If you don't remember that week, let me remind you: Dad and I do. We remember the search party, the helicopters, the police dogs, the eventual arrest. Then…"

"There I was. I know, Zoe," I told her calmly. "Believe me, that time affects me every single day of my life, with every action I take, with every interaction with people, so don't tell me how it affected *you*."

Zoe didn't respond right away, and I feared I'd scared her off. "I know. I'm sorry, Eva. I didn't mean it like that. It's just… you were so frightened and messed up. What happened to you was terrible."

I cut her off, tears threatening to roll down my cheeks. "I really don't want to talk about this right now, Zoe."

The line stayed silent for a moment before Zoe spoke again; this time, there was mirth in her tone. "So have you seen Clark? Did he turn out to be a beer-bellied ditch digger like you thought?"

I hadn't thought that, but I could imagine my sister, happily married with wonderful children, wanting to know what happened to some boy she'd kissed so long ago. "He's here," I told her.

"Like in the car?" she sputtered.

"No, you crazy woman, he's still in town. I think he's a plumber," I said.

"Have you… talked to him?" Zoe asked.

"Why would… No, I haven't talked to him. What would I have to say to him?" There was so much Zoe didn't know about the days leading up to my abduction, and I wasn't about to tell her. It would only make her upset with herself, and it was a long time ago.

"Is he…?"

"Good-looking? You might say that." I thought about those eyes, and the smile, and shook my head, trying to erase the childish crush I used to have.

"How's the story going?" Zoe asked.

"Good. You remember the lights?" I asked, not needing to explain further.

"Sure. Some kids pulled a prank the same night you went missing. It was all over the paper and town," Zoe said. Only then, my disappearance had trumped the news about a silly UFO sighting. I wondered why Carly wasn't attracting more press. It was like no one knew she was gone.

I took a risk. "I'm not so sure it was a prank."

"What are you talking about? God, not this again. What's with you and this alien abduction fascination? The lights had nothing to do with you," she said.

"I know." I'd seen the evidence, read the court reports, even as an adult. But there was something to these sightings, and I was determined to get to the bottom of it.

"Jess." She said my real name, and I didn't correct her this time. "Be careful there. That place has a lot darker secrets than you'd think. Grandma felt so secure, and look what was right next door to her," Zoe pleaded. I heard voices shouting for her, and she sighed before telling them to go outside to play.

"You sound like you have a full plate. I don't want to keep you," I said to my sister.

"Do me a favor?" Zoe's voice was firm.

"Anything."

"Phone me Thursday. It can be for five minutes. I want to know you're okay," she said.

"Deal. Talk then." I ended the call with the press of a button on the steering wheel, and heard the church entrance door open. I quickly maneuvered before the man could make it to his car. "Pastor Donnelly, can I have a moment?"

He stopped short of the Cadillac and appraised me, his thick fingers intertwining around his protruding stomach. His mustache wavered as he addressed my question. "Sure. What can I do for you?"

It was hot out, and I saw beads of sweat push from his tall forehead. "I'm hoping to speak with a woman from Sunday's service. She was beside Mrs. Miller, consoling her."

"And what do you need to speak with her about?" The pastor's voice told me he wasn't so quick to sell his congregation's information.

I didn't think the truth would work on him, so I made up a lie. I'd planned it the night before, and it flowed out smoothly. "I accidentally bumped into her car after the service, and I went inside to find her. When I came out, she was gone, and the last people here didn't seem to know who I was talking about," I said with expressive eyes and guilt in my voice.

"You could have left a note with me," he said.

"I didn't think of it. I've never scratched someone's car like that, and I was flustered. It was so hot, and that poor little girl is gone. It's a trying time for the community," I said.

He was glancing over at my car, as if trying to inspect where my damage was on it. "Are you new to town?" he asked.

"Yes." I told him I lived in Grandma's house, using her address, and he didn't flinch, not that I expected him to.

"Good. I hope you enjoyed the sermon the other day." I nodded.

"That woman is Maddie Lawson. She works at the town library, and I anticipate that's where she is at this moment," Pastor Donnelly told me. He went for his car and glanced back at me. "I hope to see you Sunday, Miss…"

"Heart. Eva Heart," I said, digging my nails into my palms.

He drove off, leaving me alone in the parking lot. That settled that. At least I knew where to find my target now. It was off to the library, but first, I had to get some groceries for my dinner date. *Date.* The word wasn't one I used often, and it felt weird even thinking about it.

I wondered at John's intentions. Had he invited me over to be kind to a visitor? Or had he anticipated something more? I'd met him at church, so that gave me hope that he wasn't going to try to make a move tonight. But if he did, would it be such a bad thing?

I was in the car, driving into town, and I pictured myself at the small table in the cabin, hosting John; only when I saw the man with me, poking at a piece of salmon, it was Clark's face looking back at me.

"Let it go, Jess," I told myself, realizing I'd used my old name only after I'd said it aloud.

I had to be more careful.

The library was right off Main Street, and I mentally marked it as I kept moving toward the grocery store, parking beside the building. It was smaller than I remembered it, and before I turned the car off, I thought back to the day after my fishing trip with Dad.

July 11th – 2001

Zoe and I parked our bikes outside the market and stepped onto the big rubber mat that set the automated sliding doors off. Zoe stomped down with her Skechers, trying to get the door to work, but it wouldn't open.

Someone left through the manual door on the other side, and I ran to it, catching the door before it closed behind the man. "This way," I said.

The store smelled off today, and it was hot and muggy. It was obvious they were having some issues with their power. There was no air conditioning, and when I looked through the door, I saw the big blue power company van skid into the parking lot, like they were on a deadly mission to prevent any more ice cream from melting.

"Do you think this means the slushies are down?" I asked, Zoe who gave me a light punch on the arm.

"You could stand to skip the sugar one day in your life." She winked, and even though the words were mean, I knew she didn't intend any harm behind them. It was just her way, and I loved that she gave me that kind of hard-to-please attitude.

The store was busy. It was mid-afternoon, and everyone was trying to get prepared for dinner. This week was busy in Cloud Lake. You couldn't step outside without smelling roasting hot dogs or barbecue burgers. Or hearing kids playing as they chased each other with water guns and splashed into the lake. I loved it here. There was something special about this summer, and I was soaking it all in. It was partly because of Grandma's condition, partly because Dad and I had grown a little closer, and Zoe and I were still besties, even when I thought she might try to pry away from her smaller sis.

There was more to it as well, but I didn't quite understand what it was. Then I saw him. Clark was in the snack aisle, loading a cart up with an assortment of sunflower seeds, chips, pop, and hot dogs with matching buns. He spotted me and locked eyes, giving me a wave.

Zoe was there in an instant. "Oh, hi, Clark." She stepped around me, moving with the efficiency of a jungle cat stalking her prey.

"Hey, Zoe. What are you guys doing here?" he asked.

"Got tired of tanning in my bikini, so I thought I'd bring the kid sister to town for ice cream." Zoe's left foot was planted on her toes, and her hips swayed side to side. I wanted to tell her to shut up, that Clark had seen me first, but I bit my tongue.

Clark reached around her and stuck his hand out. "We didn't meet. I'm Clark," he said, and I thought my heart might explode.

I stood there shaking his hand, and Zoe laughed. "This is the part where you tell the nice boy your name."

"Jess… Jessica," I said.

"I like it. Nice to meet you finally, Jess… Jessica. What are you guys up to tonight?" he asked casually.

103

Zoe answered a second later. "We're coming to your party." She nodded to the cart full of food.

"Cool. We're heading to the beach for a bonfire at around eight." Clark looked around, as if someone might be listening in on our conversation. "Not the beach the tourists know about, the local beach."

My ears perked up. We'd been coming here for a long time, and I'd never heard of this local beach. "Where is it?" I asked, getting a glare from Zoe, as if I was sucking any potential cool from us by being in their presence.

"I'll draw you a map." Clark smiled, grabbing a pen from the bulk food bins behind us. He found a coupon, plucked it from under the bag of chips, and scribbled on it until black ink formed a circle. Then he drew the lake, a path leading from the main road, and marked the beach with an X. "This is it. Eight o'clock. Don't tell anyone. Especially any adults," he said with a smirk.

My heart was racing for a multitude of reasons. He was so cute, and I couldn't put an age on him. He might be as old as seventeen, but he still had that puppy-dog face that might mean he'd grown faster than his years. Luke back home had been like that. I hoped he was fifteen, and that he didn't mind the idea of kissing a girl a year younger than him. I stood there frozen in time as I watched him talking, not hearing a word, only seeing his lips move.

"We won't tell. I'll be there, but I'm not sure Jess can make it. I wouldn't want her to get into trouble. Curfew and all that," Zoe said, as if not realizing how badly she was breaking the best friend/sister bond we'd worked so long at forming.

"I'm coming too," I said, and saw a faint smile form on Clark's mouth.

"Cool. I better go. Still have to cut a couple yards today. Later," he said, and pushed the cart away.

When he was out of earshot, Zoe grabbed my arm. "What are you doing? He's totally into me. Don't be such a tagalong," she said, and walked away. It was the first time I'd really felt betrayed by her, and it hurt.

July 13th – 2020

The store was much the same, except the doors worked properly, and it was nice and cool inside as I walked in, feeling like I was entering a time warp. Everything was almost as it had been. The color scheme was dated, the linoleum flooring freshly waxed, but still worn and sun-faded underneath. It smelled like baked bread and roasting chickens inside, and if I closed my eyes, I was in Chelsea at the local market, shopping for my weekend groceries.

"Excuse me," a woman said after bumping into me. She scurried off, on a mission, carrying a too-full basket of processed foods.

Dinner with John. What to make? I needed something I was confident in preparing, without seeming like I was trying too hard. He'd made sandwiches, but that was kind of an after-church tradition to a lot of people. I walked the aisles, fingers sliding against a row of cans, searching the shelves for ideas. I pulled a few essentials for myself to live on for the next few days: eggs, cream, coffee, bread.

I'd thought about salmon earlier, so salmon it was. I could make a nice risotto with it, so I gathered some Italian rice, fresh peas from the produce section, a lemon, dill, Parmesan, broth, and a bottle of white wine; not too cheap, not too classy. That was something I would have called Zoe when we were kids, and she would have laughed and pretended to be insulted. I missed those times between us, when we were innocent and carefree. Things change; they always do.

I was suddenly bombarded with strange thoughts as I

walked toward the check-out. I imagined the lights above Cloud Lake, the sightings, the missing persons, my own history here. What if aliens were real? What if they were drawn to Cloud Lake for some mysterious reason, and they appeared, choosing people to take with them? Abductions. A subject I'd read, watched, and listened about for far too many hours.

I tried to think what would drive them to this area. There were a lot of references to UFOs near farmland, and that was abundant here. Crop circles, cow mutilations, that kind of thing usually came with the reports, but as far as I knew, that wasn't happening in this circumstance. I believed that most of that was manmade, including Chester Brown's apparent missing cows. Even after all the years of obsessing over the subject, I was still on the fence. I did believe they were out there, but were they hovering over Cloud Lake? A nowhere semi-tourist town in the middle of nowhere Maine, USA? That was where it didn't add up.

But there was something to it. There were far less sightings in the big cities. My theory was that if UFOs existed, they probably stayed clear of large populations. Why risk the exposure?

I was next in line, and I settled the basket down. On the magazine stand, surrounded by gum and chocolate bars, I spotted the *Unknown* paper with an image of a classic UFO: round base, domed top, floating over a field, with a person being beamed up. The headline read: *More sightings in Cloud Lake, more missing persons.*

The pimply kid at the check-out frowned at me, and I tossed the paper down on the conveyer before adding my few ingredients.

The whole time, I stared at the fake image of the UFO on the paper as it slid by.

Shortly after, the brown bag was settled in my back seat

and I headed for the library, knowing I'd need to be quick to keep the fish from spoiling.

The library was old, and I finally recognized that it was once the video store. We'd spent countless hours inside there as kids, arguing over whether we should watch *The Lion King* again, or an eighties classic like *Sixteen Candles*. I usually won the battles, Zoe giving in to me, and Dad would sit and watch whatever we wanted, even if we'd seen it a dozen times already. That was how he was. He wanted to be the perfect father to us, and I knew he blamed himself for Mom taking off.

As I parked on the street a half block away, I thought about the time Zoe had made Dad pick a movie to watch. He chose some lawyer movie that had no fewer than three scenes with naked women. He was so embarrassed; that was the last time he let himself pick for movie night.

I brought my bag with my tablet and entered the library, instantly smelling the old books. I loved libraries and often loitered inside one of New York's many. My favorite was the main branch of the New York Public Library: lion statue on guard, the immense pillars and ornate finishes inside. They always set my spirits on a high, and even though this place was nothing but an ancient video store with books on the shelving now, I still appreciated it.

Sunlight cascaded through the west-facing windows, and several elderly women sat in chairs, reading some well-worn paperback thrillers. I smiled at one as she glanced up at me, returning my gesture in kind. I walked past a few displays of popular items, stopping at a section of alien and UFO interest. They were playing off the sightings that Cloud Lake had a history of, and I scanned through them, finding one volume I'd never heard of before. I flipped to the end and saw it was written by a local man about twelve years ago.

I stuck it under my arm and carried on to the front desk. A woman was typing away at a computer, her glasses perched on the end of her nose, perilously close to making a jump for it.

I cleared my throat. "Hello. I'm wondering if you can point me toward Maddie Lawson?"

The woman seemed surprised. "I'm Maddie. What can I do for you?" She used a finger to slide the spectacles up the bridge of her nose.

"I'm with the *Brownstone Beat*, and I'm doing an article on the recent sightings around Cloud Lake. I was wondering if you'd be willing to talk to me about Carly Miller?" I used my friendliest voice, smiling widely.

"What a tragedy. Poor girl, poor family. What does that have to do with your story?" she asked.

"There could be a connection. I'm trying to cover all bases," I told her.

"How does a phony UFO sighting relate to Carly being taken from a sleepover?" Maddie asked.

"I'm only saying someone could have used the lights as a distraction. It wouldn't be the first time something like this happened in Cloud Lake," I said, swallowing hard.

"Did you say you're from around here?" she asked.

"No. Eva, from New York. The City." I smiled again.

"Well, I don't have much to tell you other than what you probably know already. She was over at the Uptons' house and apparently vanished in the middle of the night. The girls thought she went home, but she never made it. No sign of her anywhere. We scoured that neighborhood. Sheriff brought in dogs from the city, even. Nothing. It's so tragic. Nancy Miller is my best friend. You should see her…" Maddie was crying, tears flowing down her face, streaking the thick mascara around her eyes.

I patted her hand over the counter, and she sobbed.

"Where do the Uptons live?" I asked.

"Only five houses down from Nancy. That's why she never minded Carly walking herself there all the time. She's been doing it since she was a little girl. We're in Cloud Lake. Nothing like this ever happens."

I thought about myself, and Mark Fisher's disappearance, even old Chester Brown claiming his cousin was taken. She was wrong. Things like this had a tendency to happen in Cloud Lake, but perhaps no more often than in any other small town in America. I felt like I was grasping at straws and realized this visit had absolutely nothing to do with the story any longer. It might have begun as that, but now I couldn't even think to the future. I could imagine trudging to the office to sit in a cubicle, waiting for Barns to tell me the magazine was shutting down.

My life was here in Cloud Lake at the moment, and there was nothing past this. I'd almost lost everything in this place, and I could feel my arms tiring as I tried to tread the water now.

"Eva?" Maddie asked, wiping her eyes with a tissue. I was staring out the window like I'd suffered a hit to the head.

"Yes, five houses that direction. Do you have their house number? I wouldn't mind walking around the street, just to see it." I hoped she would bite. The Uptons might have been listed, but they also might not have been, especially after this ordeal.

She told me an address, and I made notes on my phone, thanking her for the information. "Is there anyone that would have wanted to take Carly? Are there any suspects around town? New people, offenders?"

"You sound like McCrae." She laughed and blew her nose. "Nancy can't think of anyone. No one has seen any men like that around the block, and McCrae says there are no offenders listed in the area."

"And there's no way Carly ran away from home? Thirteen is a tough age, and kids are growing up so fast these days..."

She cut me off. "No. Nothing like that. She's a kid. She loves her parents and her little brother. She was... is a great girl, from a church-going family." I smiled, as if going to church solved all of life's little problems. It didn't. I was a testament to that.

"Okay, Mrs. Lawson. Thanks again," I said. She continued at her computer without saying another word, and I left the library, still with the book under my arm. I'd forgotten to ask her to check it out, and I contemplated turning around, but kept walking instead. I'd drop it off in a couple days.

Being bombarded by the hot morning reminded me I needed to get the groceries over to the cabin, and that was where I headed next. The roads were busy, Monday in the middle of summer. I saw the public beach access from the road leading to the Cloud Lake Cabins, and the parking lot was nearly full. Through my open window came the sound of screaming kids, and Top 40 music droned through the air from a distant speaker. These were happy noises, and I found myself smiling.

What would my life have been like if we'd stayed home instead of coming to see Grandma that summer? Maybe I would have been married with my own kids now, coming to the lake for holidays, blissfully unaware of how lucky I was.

As I pulled into the Cabins, I noticed Trevor, the young guy that worked there, bringing a white garbage bag out of unit five. He tossed it into a bin and waved at me as I drove by. The place was dead at this hour, most of the people staying already departed for their day's activities. It was perfect beach weather. Hot, the sun high in the sky, with the occasional cloud roaming in like a lost puppy, giving brief reprieve before being dragged away by its owner.

I realized I hadn't even brought a bathing suit in my haste to pack. This wasn't a vacation, and I pushed the idea of lazing on the beach, reading the book I'd recently pilfered, from my thoughts. The groceries found a home inside the fridge of Cabin Ten, and I dropped the book titled *They're Among Us* onto the small table before using the bathroom to rid myself of that last cup of coffee from Buddy's.

I glanced in the mirror, wondering if a white blouse with khaki capris was the right choice for sleuthing about a neighborhood. To be safe, I peeled the top off and threw on a black V-neck t-shirt in its place, electing to throw socks and runners on instead of the flats I'd been sporting. I pulled my hair into a ponytail, sliding a black elastic around it. Perfect.

Once outside, I looked over to Clare's cabin, which appeared empty. There was no car in the parking lot, and Clare wasn't in her usual spot by the firepit or on the porch. I worried about her. The yelling I'd heard last night wasn't the normal "couple in a spat" type; it was abusive. I wanted to tell her to dump the guy, get the hell away from him before she was hurt, or worse. But I'd only just met her, and it wasn't my place to stick my nose in her business. Not yet, anyway.

Inside my car, I cranked the AC again and keyed the address into my GPS, finding it was only five minutes away. The good thing about being in a small town like this was the commute. I passed cars heading to the lake, kids bouncing excitedly in the backseats, families walking along the side of the road carrying inflatable animals, the dads all seeming to have a blob of thick sunscreen on their already burned noses.

Eventually, I turned onto Ash Street, where the trees were huge, happy, and sheltering, stretching across the roadway to make a canopy. It was beautiful, and I decided if I were ever going to move out of the city, I wanted a similar setting. Not in Cloud Lake, but this cozy idyllic idea. It made me long for a different life, something more than working and listening to New York taxicabs.

No wonder the Millers felt safe here. How could someone come onto their street, this picture-perfect row of forty-year-old colonial homes, white picket fences, and manicured landscaping, and rip their child from their lives? I slowed as I neared the address of Carly Miller's sleepover friend, counting five away from it to see where the Millers lived. I didn't have to work hard. The house was beautiful, but the grass was too long, Mr. Miller obviously unable to cut it in the last week since his daughter had been missing.

A small forested area ended the opposite side of the street across from the Uptons' house, where ash tress grew in close proximity. I drove past the house Carly had last slept over in and turned around at the end of the street, parking a few houses down beside the treed copse. There weren't many cars on the street. This kind of neighborhood kept tons of space between the homes and oversized garages to house any vehicles they cherished.

My first instinct was to head into the trees. She'd gone missing, and if there was anywhere someone would have taken her, it was into the woods. I knew the sheriff's department had done a thorough search of the area, and the community had helped, just like they had in 2001. I pictured my dad walking through the forests near the lake, screaming out my name time and time again, until his throat was raw.

I stepped into the treeline and instantly transported to

another world, one run by birds and squirrels and spiders. The grass was decimated from the search parties, which made it easy to navigate. I wanted to see where the thicket led and meandered through the trees, getting scratched by low-hanging branches and prickly shrubbery. A bird squawked at me as I neared its nest, a mother protecting her babies. I veered to the right, avoiding upsetting the bird further, and kept moving until I saw a break in the small forested area.

All in, I'd only been walking for ten minutes, and my pace hadn't been fast. We were probably only a half mile from Carly's house, and already I was exiting the trees. I stepped past them, raising a hand to cover the overbearing sun. The land beyond dipped down, giving me a panoramic view of farmland. My heart raced as I noticed the familiar structures a mile off in the distance. That was Chester Brown's house. He'd seen the lights over these fields. The very same fields that were adjacent to the missing girl's home.

I squinted into the sky, imagining Carly out here, perhaps dared by friends to walk through the trees to hang out here. I noticed a few crushed beer cans and cigarette butts on the grass, directly beside two large boulders. If I were a betting woman, this was a spot local kids came at night. It gave an amazing view of the huge sky above and would be quite the sight on a cloudless starry night. Which was similar to the night a week ago, judging by the weather reports.

So what had happened? Carly came here, and there happened to be a man waiting, sitting on the rocks, idly chatting to make her comfortable before abducting her, or… had she seen lights flicker over the black expanse of space and been taken by something entirely different? No. I was being foolish again, letting a little girl's stress-induced memories take over.

I was about to turn when I heard a sound. It was like a sick cat mewling, and the noise was coming from a short distance. I closed my eyes, straining to hear the source, and turned toward the field beyond a barbed wooden fence.

I saw her there, brown hair a mess, clothed in pink pajama bottoms and a white long-sleeved shirt that said *Princess* across the chest in glittering gold writing. It was Carly Miller, and she was alive.

July 13th – 2020

"Carly, you're going to be okay." I was kneeling beside her. The girl's hair was greasy, matted to her head. Her lips were dry and cracked, a pale version of their former selves. Her brown eyes were shut, but she was trying to talk.

I leaned in and heard the same two words, repeated over and over. "Help me. Help me."

"I'm here, baby," I said, trying to be comforting, even though I didn't know her. "You're going to be fine. I'm going to call…" I patted my pocket, seeing that I didn't have my cell phone with me. It was still in the car, a half mile of trees between us.

I wanted to slap her, to snap her out of the near-coma-tose state she was in, and ask what happened. I wanted to yell "Who did this?" at the top of my lungs. Was it the lights? Then I felt foolish for even thinking it. I thought about a crime scene and knew I couldn't leave her alone. How did she get here? A week later. A week… it was the same amount of days as when I…

"Help me," she said again, and I smiled as her brown eyes tried to flutter open. They were semi-closed by a crusty goop on her eyelids.

"Don't panic. Close them, and I'll help you," I told her. She listened, and I used my fingers to brush enough of the gunk away for her to open them fully.

She swung around with panic before her gaze met mine. She sat up, her thin gawky teenage arms wrapping around me, pulling me tightly as she sobbed into my t-shirt.

"Shhhh. You're safe now. Don't worry. You're safe." I held her like that for a minute before telling her we needed to go. I didn't ask her a thing about what happened, no matter how much I wanted to. I remembered the confusion, how scared I'd been, the series of questions being thrown at me by the sheriff, my dad, anyone within earshot.

The only thing keeping me from screaming in frustration at my own memories was the little girl in front of me. I had to be strong for her. She needed me.

I was going to ask her if she could walk, but she didn't appear to have the strength to make it the uneven half mile or so, and she couldn't have weighed more than eighty pounds, so I picked her up, cradling her small frame in my arms. She nuzzled in, not saying a word, only pressing her forehead firmly against my neck as I walked, at first awkwardly climbing over the fence before entering the trees.

We didn't speak for the next fifteen minutes as I carried her through the forest, trying hard to avoid letting any branches scrape her. My arms were turning to lead, and my legs burned with fire, and I whispered to her that we were almost home. Finally, we breached the trees once again, and I viewed her house down the block. She didn't seem to react to anything, her head still pressed into me, and I saw a woman jogging by.

"Help!" I shouted, but she didn't pay us an attention. "Help!" I yelled, and this time she stopped, running on the spot, and she pulled out her earbuds.

She was across the street, her head tilted acutely to the side, trying to decipher what it was she was seeing. "This is Carly Miller. Go to her house. Call the police!" I said, as I set the girl on the ground. I couldn't hold her any longer, not even for the half block to her home. I fell to my knees, panting, feeling light-headed in the immense heat of the afternoon.

The woman stood there like a statue. "Now!" I ordered, and she turned around, running toward the Millers' house. Someone came out from the Uptons', and I heard the man shout into a cell phone. At least someone had the sense to phone the sheriff. I was breathing hard, a combination of the onslaught of anxiety and stress behind my own memories of appearing much like Carly, and the exertion in the heat. Black spots appeared in my vision, and as the man from the Uptons' house approached, I could hear screaming from down the block, likely Nancy Miller, shouting for her returned daughter.

I smiled briefly, and fell face-forward into the grass.

———

"Miss. Can you hear me?" I was asked. I blinked my eyes open, realizing I was in the back of an ambulance, lying on a stretcher. A cool cloth was draped over my forehead, and the man passed me a water bottle. I felt my legs draped over a box, giving blood flow to my heart.

"What happened?" I asked, trying to recover the few minutes I had blanked out. It took a moment, but I remembered. "Where's Carly?"

He didn't answer that question, just the first. "You passed out. We think you were too hot, overdid it. The sheriff wants to talk to you. I told him it would take you a few. Are you ready to talk to him?"

I nodded, sitting up. I felt a little weak, but otherwise fine. Once I was perched on the rear of the ambulance, I searched for Carly. A sheriff's car was parked in front of the Millers' house, as well as an ambulance. Both had their lights on, but no sirens.

The EMT left my side, and Sheriff McCrae arrived not long after. He looked worse than he had since I last saw him, his eyes dark, his stubble grown in more than he was probably allowed. "Miss Heart. Imagine my surprise when I heard who was found beside Carly Miller out here. I'd given up all hope of ever finding the girl, and here we are, one week later, and you, a reporter, somehow managed to save her." His eyes told another story, and I wondered if he was seriously thinking I was involved in her abduction in any way. They'd gotten my ID, which meant they'd been in my car; they'd see the UFO book, maybe even the notes in my tablet… the folded article about my disappearance beside my wallet.

"I came out here to investigate the area she went missing from. I honestly didn't expect to find anything, not after you all searched it high and low. I broke through the trees and heard a noise fifty yards from the boulders." He nodded, as if he knew about the spot where kids drank beer and smoked cigarettes.

"And there she was?" he asked.

"There she was. Her eyes were crusted over. She only asked me to help her, nothing else. I had no choice but to carry her, since I didn't have my phone, which I'm assuming you already know," I told McCrae, and he nodded.

He ran a hand through his thinning hair and laughed, a sound so unexpected it shocked me a little. "She's back. I saw this miracle once before in my tenure. I was fresh-faced then, with big hopes and dreams, and when that little girl was taken, it threatened to ruin me. She returned too, and we nailed the bastard who took her."

I grabbed the water bottle and drank it down, my hand shaking so badly, I spilled it on myself. McCrae didn't notice.

"Anyway. I'm grateful the Lord has helped get another girl home safely, and I thank you for being here. Who knows how long she was outside? Maybe the perp returned her after seeing the parents' plea online." He scratched at his chin, as if trying to solve a puzzle he didn't even have the box cover for.

Relief flooded me. They weren't going to bring me in for questioning. If they did, McCrae might learn my last name, and if he found out I was the other girl he was mentioning, there would be a lot more questions, ones I didn't want to endure.

"Is she okay?" I asked.

"She will be. Still not saying much. Her mom couldn't get anything out of her. They're bringing her to County General a town over to look her over for…" He stopped and looked at me. "Anyway. Thank you. Thank God for your woman's intuition, or divine intervention, but if you need anything while you're here, you only have to ask, Miss Heart. I will need your number, though. In case we have some follow-up for you."

I gave him my cell, writing the numbers with shaky penmanship. He took the paper, smiled, and patted his stomach slowly as he backed away, leaving me in the ambulance alone.

By the time I made it to my car, it was already six. Events had caused the day to fly by, and I found John's number in my phone, texting him to say I was running behind. He replied seconds later, letting me know that wasn't a problem.

I considered calling him for a ride but felt fine. The EMT had provided another bottle of cool water, and I opened it, drinking half before starting the car. I drove by the Millers' house, and the police and ambulance were noticeably gone. That poor girl. I knew what she was going through. I might have lost a week, but everything that happened afterwards was as clear as crystal. The tests, the questions, the anger from the sheriff and my father. The accusations, the trial, all of it.

I pushed it aside, the flood of memories, like I always did, and reconstructed my barriers in my mind. *Forget the past, don't stress the future. You are here. Forget the past, don't stress the future. You are here.* I said it twice and could feel the knot of anxiety begin to melt away.

The drive was quick, and I'd nearly forgotten about my date, even though I'd texted John moments earlier. When I showed up at the cabin, John's truck was parked in my spot, and I pulled up beside it. The second I stepped out of the car, I heard laughter from next door, and John's affable voice carried over to me. I glanced at the grocery bag and hoped nothing had spoiled. I placed it in the shade on my porch.

I walked around Cabin Nine. The three of them were sitting around their picnic table, each drinking a bottle of beer in the sun. John turned to me, his eyes glimmering as he found me standing there.

"Eva! We were just talking about you," he said with a big smile on his face.

Clare waved, and I returned it. "Eva, come join us," she said, and I glanced at the man beside her. He was a few years older than her. Smaller than I'd imagined, especially considering the yelling voice he'd projected the night before. "This is my husband, Dan. Dan, this is Eva, the one I had dinner with last night." Her eyes widened in a warning, and I took the hint.

"Hi, Dan. It's nice to meet you. You're a lucky man. Clare here is a wonderful woman," I said, playing nice.

"Good to meet you too… Eva." Dan's eyes lingered on me a second too long, and the conversation lulled until John broke the silence.

"These are for you," he said, pulling a bouquet of yellow daffodils from the table. "We better get these in water. The heat's making them wilt."

John stood and left a half-finished beer on the picnic table. He thanked Clare and Dan, and walked over to me.

"Talk to you later, Clare. Nice meeting you, Dan." And with that, we were away, free from the awkward situation. I noticed John turn around, and if I wasn't crazy, he made eye contact with Clare. I wondered what that was about. Could I ask him? Maybe he'd noticed the abusive relationship she was buried in and sought a way to assist her.

"Sorry I'm late," I told him as we entered my cabin. John was wearing a nice pair of dark gray shorts with a button-down short-sleeved blue shirt, open wide at the collar. I felt self-conscious, as my hair was covered in sweat and my t-shirt was filthy from my excursion into the forested area.

"No worries at all. You went for a hike?" he asked.

"I… I went digging on Carly Miller's street. For my story," I started to say.

"And then went for a hike?" John laughed as we sat at the table.

"No. I found her," I said quietly, almost unable to believe my own words.

His eyes widened as he leaned forward, so close to my face I felt his breath. "You found her?"

I nodded. "Yeah, in the field a half mile through a treed section across from her house."

121

"How did no one see her before? Her parents must be devastated." John rubbed his temples, as if the idea gave him a headache.

"You don't understand," I whispered, feeling the tears roll over my cheeks. "Carly's alive."

John stood up so fast, the chair flew to the side. "She's alive!" He didn't say it like a question, but he pumped a fist in the air, cheering. "And you found her. Amazing. You really are a good reporter."

"Journalist," I corrected him, but it didn't matter. He hardly seemed to hear me. I was surprised by his sudden outburst and found his reaction strange. What did I know about this guy? He'd come to town only recently. An outsider. Maybe he was the one who took Carly. Alarm bells rang in my head as I assessed the man. He was handsome, perfectly groomed, polite, caring, well-spoken. I knew a lot of psychopaths were smart, cunning people.

John sat again and grabbed my hand. "You are a blessing to this community, Miss Heart." He stared at me, and I instantly felt foolish for considering him a suspect. He was just happy. He'd moved here on a whim, and only wanted to be somewhere safe, somewhere good things could happen.

"It was luck," I said, still unsure if that was the case. Something Sheriff McCrae had said about woman's intuition struck a chord with me; only it wasn't quite that, but some deeper bond I didn't understand.

"Whatever it was, it deserves a cheers." John rose and opened the fridge. If anyone else had opened my appliance, I might have been offended, but his manner made me not care. He pulled out the bottle of wine, appraised it, and found my bottle opener.

"Glasses are…" I started to tell him, but he was already grabbing two stemmed glasses from the cupboard beside the stove, like he knew where they'd be.

"Got them." John poured liberal amounts, though I didn't want to drink. My head still hurt from the dehydration and passing out, but I accepted the glass without comment. I didn't want to tell him about that part just yet. He raised his glass, and I followed suit, clinking to my discovery. The wine hit the middle of my tongue, and I let my shoulders ease towards the floor.

"I better get the food going, and I need to change," I told him.

"Tell you what. You shower and change, and I'll make dinner," John offered.

"Do you know what we're having?" I laughed at his disposition. His energy really was infectious. I took another sip of the wine.

"No, but I make a mean… whatever you bought." John smiled again, and I was disarmed. The stress of the day's events washed away with his charm, and I realized how much I'd missed this. It had been a long time since I'd shared dinner with someone in my own apartment, and this was heaven.

"Salmon and risotto." I cocked my head to the side, smiling at his reaction.

"One of my specialities," John admitted.

"Of course it is. Deal. You get that started, and I'll try to be quick." I left my glass of wine and headed for the bedroom, grabbing my change of clothes before entering the bathroom. I already heard pots and pans clanging in harmony, and I smiled in the mirror. I really was a mess. Makeup all over the place, hair a disaster, but John hadn't looked at me with anything but happiness.

As I stripped my clothes off, I had the nagging feeling I needed to protect myself. There was a man in my cabin, and only a thin wooden door away. I double-checked the lock before stepping into the tub. I showered quickly, but still enjoyed washing the grime off my body. A few minutes later, I had a summer dress draped over me, and I towel-dried my hair, knowing it would dry into a frizzy natural look in minutes in the heat.

When I emerged, the smell of grilled salmon hit me like a brick wall, and it was amazing. I hadn't eaten since breakfast, and I was ravenous. How had he done this so quickly? The risotto sat finished in the pan on the stovetop, and John added a pinch of salt to the dish before stirring it.

"You look like you've been in a kitchen before," I told him with a laugh.

"Once or twice. Some perpetual bachelors live the life of frozen dinners and takeout, and I figured if I'm going to be eating for one, I may as well enjoy it," John said. "Dinner will be served in three minutes. If you'd care to head outside to the dining room?" He had a folded towel slung over his forearm, and he gave me a slight bow as he pointed to the door.

I headed out the cabin to the picnic table. The daffodils were placed in a cup of water, since there was no vase here, and he'd found a candle somewhere. The flame flickered in the gentle breeze. My wine glass was outside, and he'd dropped a single ice cube into it in a vain attempt at keeping it chilled. It made me think of some of my friends from the city. They would never do that to a wine, claiming it watered the intentions behind the vintage down.

I sat alone, watching the sunlight glimmer off the lake, which was active tonight. The sound of motorboats cruising blissfully carried for miles, and I smiled, thinking about the people being pulled behind on water skis, wakeboards, and tubes. I missed being on the water.

When John came out, carrying two plates of steaming food, I asked him a question. "Do you have a boat?"

He grinned and sat beside me, not across, so we could both enjoy the view of the water. "I do. It's nothing fancy, just an old sixteen-foot runabout." He looked at me as if asking if I knew what that was. I'd grown up spending my summers here, so I did, but he didn't know that.

"Sounds like a boat to me," I said casually.

"Why, do you want to go for a ride?" he asked.

I did. I wanted to feel the heat on my face as we sailed through the water; I wanted to feel that special childhood moment of being on a boat with my dad, fishing for the first and last time. "If you have time."

"How about Wednesday?" he asked.

I nodded. "Wednesday." I took a bite of the fish, and it was perfectly cooked. The risotto gave me the same feeling, and I wanted to ask John if he'd been to culinary school.

"Sorry the risotto is a little salty." John poked at his food, eating it slowly, while I had to stop myself from inhaling it and fending him off with a fork to eat his too.

"It's amazing. Now I'm really glad you took over the cooking part." It was the truth. Mine was passable, but this was exquisite.

There was a bang next door, and I heard the sound of Dan's truck door closing before it peeled off, shooting rocks at their cabin. John looked over at me, eyebrows raised. "Nice couple," he whispered.

"You know them?" I asked, remembering that small look between John and Clare.

"Not until tonight. She seems okay." John didn't comment on Dan, and he didn't have to. The man was a jerk. "Would you like to accompany me for a walk around the lake after dinner?"

I was tired, but my headache had subsided, and after a shower and food, I almost felt like myself again. Carly

125

would be at the hospital or safely at home, and I considered that a good day. "I'd love a walk." As expected, my hair was dry now, and I took the plates in, along with my half-full glass of watered-down wine.

John stayed outside, and when I returned with my walking sandals, he was out by the lake, gazing out over the gentle waves. The sun was setting below the treeline, and I wondered if we should bring a flashlight just in case.

"It's beautiful here. I never knew what I was missing, spending all those years in cities. Don't you miss this?" he asked.

Miss this? "How could I miss this?" I asked, my never-ending alarm bells ringing again.

"You couldn't have always lived in Manhattan. Wherever you hail from must have involved nature." He said this with such poise, I wanted to kick myself for constantly over-reacting about nothing. I had to put my issues behind me, at least for tonight.

"You're right. Connecticut. Outside Hartford." That was where Dad lived now, and I could describe his home with ease. "There was a lake, but not as big as this. My grandma lived there, and we'd visit all the time. I do miss it. I really do." We started our walk, heading past the grounds of the Cloud Lake Cabins. There was nothing but trees and a well-worn dirt path for almost a mile. It was probably the last section of the lake that was undeveloped, and I wondered if this was one of the sights Dan had his eye on turning into a resort.

Eventually, we began to pass huge cabins, ones that hadn't existed when I was a kid. There were two-story log houses with sprawling decks, double docks with fancy motorboats. We saw two women sitting in wooden chairs, and John waved to them.

"I've done jobs for a bunch of these people already.

They were so happy to have someone local to maintain their houses. The other guys around town are either always heading out of Cloud Lake to find work or they're drunk," John admitted.

"Then you must seem like a good alternative. At least, compared to the absent and uncouth," I said jokingly.

"Only by a narrow margin," he played along. I was really enjoying the walk, and the company. This trip to Cloud Lake had become something I'd never expected. A bizarre adventure, but one with very little UFO presence. My mind drifted to the story I needed to be writing, and I wondered how Carly's story would merge into the piece.

"This is where the infill ends and the dilapidation continues." John pointed to the next cabin, which was decrepit and rotting. The roof looked near to collapsing, but smoke poured from a chimney, telling me someone actually lived there. "The county's trying to force these people out, but not all of them want to sell."

I saw a kid playing behind the cabin, kicking a soccer ball around by himself. "What happens if they don't sell?"

John kicked a big pinecone on the path. "They always sell. Money talks, and these people need it."

We kept going, passing through an opening in the trees, and I scanned the lake to catch a glimpse of the other side. From here, I could almost make out Grandma's cabin, and Mr. Martin's next to it, the one John was residing in. I wondered if the basement had been fixed, or if John had any idea whose place he'd moved into.

Eventually, we found the public section, the outer edge to Local Beach. It was where things changed for me, and when John perched on a bench near the water, I couldn't help but meander away from him to where a fire roared, people surrounding the flames.

July 11th – 2001

"Where's Grandma?" I asked Dad. He was half-asleep on a chair, a can of Coors in his hand. The TV flickered, casting shadows across the room. The drapes were closed, and it was stuffy inside the cabin.

Dad's eyes blinked open, and he looked around like he'd been asleep for years. "Grandma? She's in bed."

"How did chemo go today?" I asked, knowing the answer.

Dad didn't answer; he just gave me a forced smile in its place. "Where's Zoe?"

"She's by the lake." I held out two mason jars with lids. "We're going to catch fireflies," I said in a bold-faced lie. We used to always do that when they came out at night, as kids. It seemed to surprise him, and when he motioned to lower his recliner, I shook my head.

I took his empty can and went to the kitchen, grabbing him a fresh one. "You stay here and keep an eye on Grandma." I knew my dad was tired, and he would only have a taste before dozing off again. It felt so deceitful, and I hated myself for it.

My dad was one of only three people in the world that cared about me. I had the urge to stay and watch a movie with him while Zoe went to this Local Beach party alone, but I also felt a strange possessiveness I'd never experienced before over Clark. At least not since Lucy the elephant, my childhood stuffy I brought with me everywhere.

"Well, have fun." And just like that, Dad made my decision for me.

"Thanks. See you later," I told him, and departed out the front door. It was still warm out, but I wore jeans and a sweater, knowing it wouldn't stay hot forever. The nights could be deceivingly chilly, even in the middle of summer. Zoe was waiting a hundred yards away, wearing shorts that showed off her long tanned legs, and a t-shirt that Dad would say was too tight to have on outside the house.

"Did he buy it?" she asked, looking to the jars in my hands.

"Of course he did. Why wouldn't he believe his sweet daughter, who until tonight never lied to him?" I replied.

"Jess, listen to me. Telling Dad a few lies about what we're doing is okay. We're kids, and kids do this. And what he doesn't know won't hurt him, all right?" Zoe was already walking away, down the path that would lead us around the lake to Local Beach.

I set the mason jars behind a thick tree and followed her. We passed Mr. Martin's window, and I swore I saw the curtains jostle as we neared.

"That guy is so creepy. I think he's watching us." My voice was a harsh whisper.

"God, you are too much, Jess. I think someone's read a few too many R.L. Stine books. Would you keep it cool? I knew I should have come without you," she said, stabbing me in the heart with her words. I was seeing a new side to Zoe, one that was going to leave me behind any day now. I'd seen it coming and didn't think there was any way to stop it.

We kept onward, and I was grateful for pants as we wound our way through dense brush along narrow pathways. "Are you sure this is the right way?" I asked my sister, who clutched the coupon with the crude map like a rosary.

"Not really, but there's no other path," she said, and my uneasiness spread as we progressed further. I had to keep glancing behind me, suddenly one hundred percent positive that Mr. Martin was going to sneak up behind and grab me. I told Zoe, and she laughed, but this time, there was a nervous edge to the sound.

Minutes later, the path widened. We saw more cabins,

and eventually, a wide beach that could only be Local Beach. A fire roared beside a few picnic tables; a group of twelve or so kids lingered around it.

Some grunge rock played from a stereo, and my heart soared as I spotted Clark beside the fire. He was wearing a Bruins hoodie, his eyes dark shadows against the flickering flames.

Zoe walked over, leaving me behind, and a girl greeted her. I didn't hear what they said to each other, but they seemed friendly, and as I approached, I heard a boy offer Zoe a beer. My sister glanced at me, and I hoped she'd say no. That she'd stay a kid just for the rest of the summer, that she'd be my bestie, at least until I started at her high school.

"Sure, I'd love one," Zoe told the kid, and someone tossed her a cheap can of beer, the kind Dad said tasted like horse urine. Zoe popped the top like a seasoned pro, and foam spilled out on her hand as she giggled.

I glanced at Clark and sat by myself on the end of a picnic table, just far enough that I could barely feel the heat emanating from the bonfire on the sand. One of the kids lit a cigarette, and Zoe was in the middle of a group of five teenagers, each around her age. The oldest-looking one hovered back. He seemed like he might be out of high school. He lit a smoke, and the smell carried over to me. It wasn't a cigarette, it was marijuana. My instincts told me to leave, and to make Zoe come with me, but she seemed like she was having the time of her life.

The joint was passed around, and I was so happy to see Zoe wave it away. One of the boys grabbed a girl's hand, and they ran over toward the water. The sun was absent now, and stars littered the night sky. I caught the couple making out, and instantly, I wanted to get out of there. I wasn't ready for a party like this, even if Zoe was.

"Hey, Jess. Glad you came," Clark said.

A lump caught in my throat, and I wasn't sure I'd ever be able to speak again.

"Are you okay?" he asked, and I finally found my nerve.

I avoided eye contact with him and could feel how close he was to me as we sat there. "I'm great. Thanks for inviting us." I glanced over at Zoe, who was talking with a boy. The others had walked away from them, and she flipped her hair over her shoulder, swaying side to side, sipping her beer like a veteran.

"Your sister doesn't take long to make friends, does she?" Clark asked.

"Never. She's always everyone's friend."

"You live here?"

"No. A few hours away. It's all right, but I've been coming here for years over the summers. My grandma lives across the lake," I told him, and he moved closer. "How about you? Lived here long?"

"I moved here two years ago. From Boston."

I laughed, a glittery girl sound, and I snapped my mouth shut, suddenly aware how juvenile I sounded. "That's quite the change. Do you miss your friends?"

"I do. We talked for a while, on the phone. I visited once, then the calls stopped. You know how it is," he said, but I really didn't. I just nodded, like I was an expert at losing friends.

"I have to leave mine every summer. That's hard, but at least I get to go back to them when it's time for school. But... almost every year, something has changed. One of them has a boyfriend, or the other cut her hair drastically. Or I missed some huge event, and they talk about it all the time, almost forgetting that I wasn't even involved." I clammed up, wondering why I was talking so much. Clark didn't seem to mind.

He was listening intently, and I was aware of how close we were to each other. He jostled his knees wider, and his leg brushed against mine, once, twice, three times. My face felt crimson, and I was grateful for the dark ambience.

"I totally get that, Jess. You're really cool," he told me, smiling as he said it. I didn't smell beer or cigarettes on him, and I appreciated his character.

"You're cool too, Clark," I said, wondering if the words really came out of my lips. His hand slid over, and our fingers touched. I thought I was going to die.

"Gotta run. Five-O," one of the boys shouted, and I pointed behind us to see flashlights bobbing in the dark night.

"Jess, we have to move now. If Dad finds out we were here, he'll kill us." Zoe came beside me, glanced at Clark, and grabbed my arm, pulling me away. She tossed her beer can at the fire, and when I looked for Clark, he was already gone.

July 13th – 2020

It was a group of teenagers, and for a second, I figured I might spot myself sitting beside Clark on the picnic table, sixteen-year-old Zoe off to the side drinking her first beer. But as I approached, they paused and turned to me. John was there, and he tugged gently on my arm.

"Let's not ruin these kids' fun by being adults near them," he said.

"You're right. It just reminded me of another time in my life."

"Wait. One of these kids works for me, and I have a big job tomorrow. Let me go see if he's available tomorrow morning." John left me by the water, and I watched him head over the sand to the group of eight. I noticed two girls, and the guys were all in black, overdressed for the heat. He handed something to one of the guys, and they gripped hands for a lingering moment before John turned and came back.

"He good for the job?" I asked, and John nodded.

"Good kid. Gets mixed in some bad things, I think, but giving him gainful employment might help. I usually try to hire kids like him, ones from tough neighborhoods who could use a break. I find they always work harder than the kids that grew up with money, if that makes sense." John turned around, and I was relieved. We'd already come a long way, and I was wearing down.

"Total sense."

We were walking the now familiar pathway heading to Cloud Lake Cabins, and it was dark. A lot of the homes and cabins had their porch lights on, some with yard lights, and it added a surprising clarity to the walk. There were dozens of lights around the lake; a couple of boats still moved slowly through the water. Someone was playing loud eighties music and singing horribly, and it made me laugh.

"Tell me about New York," John said, ending the silent spell between us.

"Where do I start? It's a wonderful place. I like the amount of people always around. It makes me feel faceless," I said.

"And you want that?" he asked.

"Yes. I'm just another living, breathing body among the others, and no one stares at me or bothers me, they just let me be. I exist there like I don't feel I could anywhere else." Had I said too much? I wasn't normally one to open up so freely.

"And is it enough to just exist?"

His question hit me. I turned it over to him. "I haven't

really thought about it. Should we strive for more?"

"I don't know. Look, I'm only a guy who's renting an old cabin at a crappy summer destination, trying to do enough renovations on the locals' homes to tide me through next winter, so I may not know what I'm talking about. But there has to be more than just existing. You need to be happy, fulfilled, joyful. You know what I mean?" John stumbled on an aboveground root, and I caught his arm. "Thanks."

"I guess I understand what you're saying. I'd rather be out of the limelight, any way you look at it," I admitted.

"No delusions of grandeur growing up?" he asked.

Growing up. I wanted to tell him I almost hadn't made it, that I'd nearly had my life ripped from me. There was no "growing up" stage. I went from a kid to a scared young woman in the span of a breath for me, a week to the outside world. "Nothing like that," I said.

"What are you passionate about?" John asked.

"You're cramming it all in tonight, aren't you?" I laughed, and he joined me.

"If you're only here for a few days, I need to bogart all your time. Will you answer me?" he asked softly.

"Sure. I love bad nineties movies and have a penchant for pad Thai and long walks on the beach." I couldn't hold back the sarcasm on the last one.

"I'm being serious," he said. "What really gets your spirit going? Is it journalism? Writing? Do you want to write books? Novels? Non-fiction?"

Could I tell him about my fascination with abductions? I glanced over, and he was so endearing. Calm, collected, handsome. "This is going to sound stupid, but..."

"But what?" he prodded.

"I have a little obsession with the unknown."

"What does that mean?"

"I've read nearly every book on alien abductions, watched all the documentaries, seen all the debate from each side of believers and naysayers, and I find it all extremely interesting." It was strange to tell someone this. My family knew about it, and my dad didn't agree with it. He thought it was a transference of my anger against Peter Martin to the mystical, the unexplainable… aliens.

John let out a low whistle. "That is interesting, I have to admit. Why?"

I wasn't going to go that deep with this guy and didn't want him to know I was from here, or basically from here. "I spotted lights once, when I was a girl. It was amazing, scary, and exhilarating at the same time."

"Tell me."

"I was fourteen, at the lake… the one in Connecticut," I lied. "It was hot, sticky, like most days that summer, not far off this one, if I'm being honest." We kept walking, now past the run-down units, and we were near the expansive two-stories with path lighting and crackling firepits, where too much wine was being consumed and Cuban cigars were being smoked. I wondered what it was like to have these rich people's lives. Did it really make them any happier than everyone else?

"And you saw a ship?" John asked without a hint of mocking.

"I'm not sure. I can still remember the smell, like sulphur, strong and sudden. I froze…" I stopped walking, and I stared up to the sky, catching a twinkling satellite high above.

"What happened?"

I didn't remember. That was the last thing I saw… until my dad was calling my name. "Nothing. I snapped out of it, and it was gone. Nothing to see."

"And you think it was a UFO?" he asked.

I shrugged and moved forward. "I'm not sure, but it was strange. Ever since that moment, I've been pursuing it, you know… not academically or anything. Just an interest of mine."

"Do you believe?" he asked quietly.

Someone shot a firework over the lake. A deep red bloom spread across the sky, reflecting into the water, and the abrupt noise made my heart race. Another exploded, then another.

John and I stood there on the path, the water lapping gently against the beach, and we watched the lights over Cloud Lake.

"It's beautiful," I said.

"It is."

We didn't talk for a few minutes, while the display went off. Eventually, John broke the silence again. "You didn't answer my question."

I looked him in the eyes, and answered truthfully. "I don't know."

He nodded. "Fair enough. Let's get you home. It's getting late."

The lights stopped, and the music ceased playing across the water, and it felt like most of the porch lights turned off at the same time. A dozen families calling it a night simultaneously. It was quite spectacular timing.

We arrived at Cabin Ten, and I glanced over at the unit beside me. Dan's truck was still gone, and the lights were off inside. I silently hoped that Clare was all right. I'd check on her in the morning.

"Well, here we are," John said, walking me to the door.

My porch light cast a long shadow behind John, and I fought the urge to run inside and slam the door shut. I tried to think if I'd taken a pill that afternoon and couldn't recall. His hand reached for mine, and he held it. Did he want to come in? I was so terrible at this whole thing. I knew I should never have invited him over.

"Thanks for a wonderful time. And for cooking for me. I better get to bed. Big day tomorrow," I told him.

He nodded and pulled me in, kissing my cheek. "I have to be up early too. Thanks for everything. Have a good night." And when he was almost at his car, he turned and asked, "Still up for that boat ride Wednesday?"

I'd forgotten all about that already. "Of course. It'll be fun." I used my key and entered the unit, closing the door before locking the deadbolt and pressing my back against it.

My head was hurting again, and I drank two glasses of water before plopping onto the couch. It was only ten thirty, but it felt like two in the morning. There was no way I was getting to sleep yet. I was too wound up from finding Carly, remembering the beach like it was yesterday. I closed my eyes and could almost feel Clark's finger touch mine.

I thought about turning the TV on. It felt like so long since I'd watched anything, and I fumbled around looking for the remote. The older flat screen flicked on at the press of a button, and I searched for something resembling news. It came a few channels later. A man in a cheap blue suit, and a woman with too much blush and a frozen expression, talked about some festival going on in Bangor before going to the weather. The weatherman, a young man in a bow tie, told the audience it was going to be hot for the next few days, complete with a smiley-face sun graphic.

"Get on with it already," I muttered when it went to commercials.

My gaze drifted to the book on the table, and I stood up, my legs suddenly almost too tired to bear my weight. *They're Among Us*, written by Oscar Neville. I flipped to the end flap, catching an image of a white-haired man. His eyes were almost familiar, but I didn't know the name. I assumed I'd read a book by him at some point in my life.

I flipped to the front flap and read the blurb out loud.

Cloud Lake, a peaceful community in central Maine, only hours from civilization, is a hot spot for alien interaction. For decades, there have been extra-terrestrial sightings above the many sprawling fields, and over the iconic Cloud Lake itself.

The locals live under the active skies, and most don't even believe what so many claim to have witnessed.

They're Among Us is a testimony of a small-town inhabitant, a man who was there in the sixties when the sightings first occurred, and who was also present in eighty-seven when another influx hit and two residents went missing. He was a spectator in two thousand and one as well, when an abduction was blamed on a local man.

Oscar Neville will tell stories of faith, belief, and the Grays.

UFOs are real. Abductions are occurring. Cloud Lake is the epicenter.

I wanted to flip through the book, but I knew I'd see my name, my real name, *Jessica Carver,* plastered inside. I suspected they'd have the photo of me holding my fish, and the public shots of when I was found, disheveled and confused, sickly and skinnier than I'd ever been. I closed my eyes again, fighting the whirlwind of emotions coursing through me. I pictured myself but could only see Carly Miller's frail body in my mind's eye, my dad rushing toward her, calling my name.

"In other news, missing Cloud Lake teenager Carly Miller has been found by a sightseeing tourist, and after an extensive trip to County General, has been returned to the care of her loving family. Her parents have publicly expressed their thanks to whoever returned their child, but the local sheriff says the case is far from over." There was a picture of Carly, probably the one they'd been circulating for the entire week while searching for her.

The shot cut to McCrae being filmed outside his office. *"Whoever did this will get caught. We're testing all of Carly's clothing, hair, under her nails. We will find the perp and bring justice to this little girl and her family."*

McCrae's eyes burned fiercely in his statement, and I hoped they did find evidence. I also hoped I hadn't disrupted any proof by carrying her from the site.

The camera switched to the news anchor team in Bangor. The female anchor was shaking her head in disbelief. *"We're so happy this little girl has made it home, and our prayers are with her and her family for a quick recovery."*

I flicked the TV off; my head was spinning. I shoved the book away and went to get ready for bed. The whole time, I was trying to fight the urge to pick up the hardcover and dive in. What the hell did this Oscar Neville know about my experience?

I folded into bed a few minutes later, closed my eyes, and found sleep came easier than expected.

July 14th – 2020

The eggs fried in the pan, and since there was no toaster in the unit, I slid them off onto an old ceramic plate and dropped a slice of bread on the frying pan, flipping it a minute later. It was my grandma's old way of making toast, but she always did so after frying bacon. She said it gave the toast an edge that no toaster could, and she'd proceed to add a dollop of butter, saying no topping could beat it.

I grinned as I thought about her in her kitchen, wearing the same blue apron with white daisies on it year after year, no matter how many my dad bought her. It became a running joke, where he'd give her a new one every summer on her birthday, and she'd gush over it, kiss him on the cheek, and proceed to hang the new item into a closet full of them. I wondered what had happened to all those aprons, encased in their plastic, after all these years.

The curtains were closed, and I leaned over the sink to open them, seeing a gray overcast day outside. It never failed. A string of hot days, followed by a muggy rainy one. I expected a nasty storm and hoped my low-end tent would keep me dry tonight.

I packed up all the supplies I'd bought at the feed store, and it was a sad little pile. I'd brought a change of clothing and a sweater, knowing the nights could turn cold if it was raining. But for today, I threw on a pair of black pants, flats with no socks, and a peach blouse. I made sure I appeared like the journalist I was before heading out the door, because I was going to make an impromptu stop at the town council this morning to speak to them about the Summer Kick-Off event this coming Thursday.

Once everything was in the trunk of my car, I headed out, noticing Dan's truck in the parking spot of the cabin beside mine. It was after nine, and other families were out and about, some familiar by now, though I hadn't spoken to any of them other than in passing. I decided to chat with some visitors about the rumors surrounding Cloud Lake before I left, which gave a comprehensive perspective to the article. It would be good to have other thoughts on the talk of Grays and UFOs circulating around town. I knew the looks I'd get when asking about it, the tilted heads, the half smiles saying "really?", but it was all part of the job.

Rain drizzled from the thick gray clouds above, and I rolled my window down as it fell. Once I was on the main road heading to town, I opened it all the way, taking a deep breath of ozone and corn. The stalks here were already nearing six feet, and I glanced into the center of this field, seeing a scarecrow flapping on a post. I knew there were better devices these days, but there was something enduring about the sight of a straw man watching over the corn, protecting it.

My phone rang, my dad's number appearing on my nav screen. Ten different thoughts entered my head at the same time, but instead of trying to sort through them, I took the call.

"Dad!" I said a little too enthusiastically.

"Cloud Lake?" His voice was husky, as if he'd just woken up. I knew he wouldn't have. He was an early bird, always up by six, paper read by seven, and by now, he'd have finished his morning walk.

"I know what you're going to say…"

"Do you?" His voice was louder now, but still controlled. "You know how I'm going to tell you how Cloud Lake nearly killed you? How I know every inch of the damned town because I scoured it endlessly for a week? How you were broken by what happened, and how I blame that place for causing us to never have the relationship we were heading toward? That I lie awake at night, picturing his smug face, wishing I'd seen the signs so I could go back and kill him before he did anything?"

"Dad, stop!" I shouted, and he did. "It's not Cloud Lake's fault, and I've told you, I had my suspicions about Peter Martin. It was my fault for not telling you, telling an adult."

"None of it was your fault, honey. None of it. How many times do I have to tell you?" Dad asked.

I sighed out a breath of sour air. "I know, Dad. I know."

"Zoe tells me you're there for a story. About UFO sightings. When are you going to get over this? This dream of lights and aliens? You know your mind manifested those ideas to take you out of his power, to explain it in a way that wasn't real, so you didn't have to face the truth. How many therapists have told you that?" I could hear the pain in his voice. It had been years since we'd talked about that summer, and saying these things out loud was too much for the man.

"All of them. All of them said just that," I whispered.

"Then why are you there chasing imaginary things?" he asked. "This will only hurt you."

I wanted to tell him how I hadn't felt like drowning and numbing myself in pills since I'd been here. That I was doing surprisingly well in social situations… that I'd even met a nice man. But I couldn't. Not yet.

"It's for the *Beat*, Dad. They found the job and sent me here," I admitted.

There was silence for a minute. "That makes absolutely no sense. I've read your articles, and they're usually about a restaurant opening in a hipster neighborhood, or the history of an art gallery, not aliens in Maine. Why are you really there?"

His astute observation sent a cold rush through my veins, almost as if someone had poured ice water over my head. He was totally right. I'd been so blinded by the fact that the magazine might have been folding that I'd hopped into the story without much thought. Cloud Lake and aliens, right when the Summer Kick-Off was about to happen? But Barns knew nothing about me or my checkered past.

"I don't know. This has to be a crazy coincidence," I said.

"Jessica, you…"

"Eva. Call me Eva."

"That's not your name! See, look what this place did to you! The reporters were so invasive you had to change your name." I was using my mother's maiden name, and he hadn't spoken to me for a year after I'd made the decision to change it.

"Dad, what do you know about a book called *They're Among Us*?" I asked.

His anger dissipated with the question. I could picture him sitting inside his living room, staring at the wall, a cup of cold coffee beside him, and today's crossword half-done. "How did you find it?"

"You *did* know about it," I accused him.

"Yes. I tried to stop it, but the case was public news. They did a limited run only and kept it local. I bought most of them and burned the lot," Dad said.

"What's in it?" I asked.

"Just a bunch of nonsense. Oscar claims the Grays took you, not Martin. It was so ridiculous that I knew no one would believe it. Almost no one." His words were directed at me.

I pulled to the side of the road as heavy rain flooded my windshield, and threw my hazard lights on. I closed my eyes and saw the flashing lights, smelled the musky aroma.

"Jess?" Dad snapped me out of it.

"Yes. I'm here. I'm here," I repeated, more for my sake than his.

"Don't read it. It's garbage. And for what it's worth, I think you should leave… now." He was giving me an order: the kind only a father, especially a single father, could give after raising kids alone. He'd always felt like he'd failed me, because for a minute at fourteen, he hadn't been there at my side. It was crazy, yet still so rational.

"Dad. I love you. You've always been there for me, and I couldn't have asked for a better role model and protector. You were the one I saw when I was released, and you have no idea how many times I wake up, seeing your dirt-streaked face, hearing your voice calling my name. You need to let me do this, and when I'm done with the story, I'll stop off at your house and spend a few days with you. Maybe we can go fishing." I started crying halfway through and heard him stifling a sob.

"I just want you to be safe, honey," Dad said, and I had the sudden feeling that he was going to come to Cloud Lake. That wouldn't be good for either of us.

"Dad, tell me you won't come to this place."

Silence.

"Promise me. I'll be here until the weekend, then I'll leave. I'll be at your place by Sunday at the latest," I begged.

"I promise. I hope you know how hard this is for me, Jess." I didn't bother to correct him on my name. It wasn't worth it. He'd never look at me as Eva Heart, only as his little Jessica Carver.

"I know." I wanted to tell him about the campout I was attending tonight, and the Summer Kick-Off, even the fact that I'd seen Grandma's cabin. That brought an idea. "Dad, who owns Grandma's cabin?"

There was another pause. "We do."

"We do? How's that possible? It's been so long."

"I couldn't part with it, not after that summer. It was my mother's, and with her gone and what happened to you, I… I didn't, I couldn't get rid of it," Dad said.

"So you pay taxes on it while it rots?" I asked.

"You'd be surprised by how cheap taxes are at Cloud Lake." He laughed, but I didn't join him.

"Do you come here ever?" I asked.

"Never. I haven't been there since I packed up the truck and took you and Zoe away from there for good," he said.

"So all our stuff is still inside? Grandma's stuff?" I felt flushed and stuck my arm out the window, letting the fat drops of water splash against my skin.

"I guess so. Unless someone broke in and took it," he said.

"Dad, I have to go. I have an appointment. I'm here for a job, remember?" I finally gave him a laugh, a fake one so he thought I was okay. I wasn't going to put it past him to break his promise, not if it meant helping his youngest daughter.

"I remember. Be safe, and I'm expecting you no later

than Sunday. Message me. Stay in touch. Okay?" His voice was lighter now that the weight of years of frustration and anger were lifted.

"Deal. Dad, I love you. Thank you for everything," I said.

"Love you too, Jessica Carver." The call ended. I knew he used my real name as a reminder of who I was then, the real me, not this city girl with a made-up name.

Before I had a chance to soak in the conversation, the phone rang again, this time from an unknown local number. It had to be McCrae, looking to do a follow-up.

"Hello," I answered.

"Is this Miss Heart?" a woman's voice asked.

"It is."

"This is Nancy… Miller."

"Oh, Mrs. Miller, how's Carly doing?" I asked, the words rushing from my mouth.

"She's… would you be able to come over and talk? If you're not in the middle of anything." Her voice was small and meek.

"Of course. I'll be there in a few minutes. Does that work?" I asked.

"That works perfectly. Thank you. Thank you, Miss Heart." The call went dead. My arm remained out the window, and I drew it in quickly, shaking the rainwater off.

A few minutes later, I pulled up to their house. Here only a few drops funneled through the dense canopy of tree cover over the street, and when I emerged from the car, my gaze carried over to the area I'd stumbled over with their daughter only yesterday. Had it really only been sixteen hours ago? Somehow it felt like days as I hiked up the cobblestone walkway in the center of their yard. The oversized door opened before I reached the final step, revealing a tired but relieved mother.

She rushed forward, wrapping her arms around me. She pulled me close, and I felt the tears tumbling down her face. "Thank you so much for coming. For finding her."

"You're welcome. It was a bit of luck, but sometimes we all need a little luck, don't we?" I said, forcing myself not to fall to pieces after the flurry of her emotions clouded the entrance to her home.

Mr. Miller was waiting inside, arms crossed, a slight frown over his face. "Miss Heart."

"You can call me Eva," I said.

"Eva, this is Carly's father, my husband Terry." Nancy motioned to the stoic man, whose statuesque demeanor finally broke, and he smiled as he stuck his hand out.

"Thank you, Eva. If you hadn't found her…" He stopped himself, a layer of tears forming in his eyes.

"She's okay now, right?" I asked, scanning the foyer for any sign of the girl.

"She's… she's in her room," Nancy said. "Come inside. Would you like a cup of coffee?"

"Please."

They led me into a formal sitting space with a high ceiling, their windows stretching up along the wall. Rain dripped over the panes in long lines. The seat was hard, the arms of the chair carved ornate wood. I liked their style, though it was a little stuffy for my tastes. A fire flickered under a wide wooden mantel. I suspected the fire was more for comfort than warmth this summer morning.

"Can you tell us what happened?" Nancy asked, pouring me a cup of coffee from a white ceramic carafe.

I went into detail, telling them about my story, and how I wanted to come to the site of their daughter's abduction, because something in my gut told me to. They cried as I told them about her initial noises, the cat-like whimpers I'd heard when I overlooked the expansive farmland beyond the trees. I explained the crust on her eyes, and fact that I knew I had to carry her back since I had no cell phone on me. Terry held Nancy close, both of them wide-eyed and weary.

"You are an angel," Nancy said when it was done. I didn't tell them about me passing out from the heat and exertion, but I think they knew.

"Are you feeling okay?" Terry asked me, and I almost laughed at his concern.

"I'm fine now. Is there a suspect? Do you know what happened?" I asked, trying not to pry too much. I had to understand.

Nancy looked Terry in the eyes, and her husband gave a slight nod. "She's not telling us anything. She says she doesn't remember."

My blood turned cold again; it was becoming a bit of a habit in my return to Cloud Lake. "Nothing?"

"She only said something about flashing lights; maybe a shadow of a man, or a woman, she wasn't certain. Then you were there, carrying her." Terry picked up his coffee cup and took a loud sip.

It was all too familiar to me. "Can I see her?" I knew this was a big ask, but I also thought they might feel like they owed me any boon I sought.

"I'll see if she's feeling up to it," Nancy said, heading up the stairs.

"The hospital? Testing was done?" I prodded for details from Carly's father.

He was abashed, but he powered through. "No indication of sexual assault, and the only hair they found will probably turn out to be yours. We don't know where she was, or who took her. Do you have any idea how frustrating that is?"

I did.

148

Nancy stepped inside the room and met my gaze. "Carly says she'd like to see you. But alone." She appeared crestfallen. "If it's the same to you, I'll be right in the hallway," she whispered, and I nodded.

Terry stayed downstairs, and I walked up the flight of steps and followed Nancy to the end of the hall. She pushed the door open, and there was Carly, looking much more like a normal thirteen-year-old than how I'd found her yesterday. She was in jeans and a t-shirt, sitting on her bed, staring at a tablet with headphones on.

I entered, closing the door halfway, and I sat at the foot of the bed. Carly lifted the headphones off and set them on the comforter beside her. Her room was nice… more than nice. It was amazing. Photos of her and her family on trips around the world were in collages on the wall. A vanity with a lighted mirror and a stool held more pictures, these of her and friends. She was a popular girl, a rich girl. Bad things happened to people from all walks of life.

Her window faced the trees down the block, and I imagined seeing the two of us emerge from the forest, Carly in my weak arms.

"Hi, Carly," I said softly.

"Hi." Her hair was in a braid, obviously something her mom had done to comfort the both of them that morning.

"How are you feeling?" I asked.

"A little tired. They gave me IV fluids yesterday, and I finally ate something last night." She didn't look me in the eyes, but I was surprised by how much she was divulging.

"How did you sleep?"

Now she met my stare. "Not well."

I glanced at the doorway, wondering how close her mom was. "Carly, I know what you're going through." My voice was barely over a whisper.

"You do?"

"I was taken when I was a little girl."

Her eyes went wide, and she leaned closer to me. "What happened?"

"I don't know. The police accused someone, but I don't remember any of it. Just the lights, then being found. Is that what happened with you?" I asked, and suddenly, our foreheads were nearly touching.

She nodded. "What was it?"

"I don't know, Carly. Whatever happens, don't let this event rule your life." I wasn't sure how long I had to talk with her, but I couldn't leave without saying my piece. It was bottled up inside me, and it needed out. "Move past it, don't obsess over it. Don't let your friends or family make this your future. What just happened to you is not your identity. It isn't who or what you are." I tapped her on the chest gently. "You're a wonderful girl, and you'll grow up to be an amazing strong woman, and this will be something that happened to you, but it will not define you, do you hear me?" Tears washed over my face as I said the words, and she was crying too, nodding, and her arms flung around my neck as she pulled us into an embrace.

"Do you understand?" I asked, louder this time, and she sobbed that she did.

"What is…" Nancy was behind us, no doubt lured in by the noises.

I didn't say anything else. I just stroked Carly's hair and held her there, a victim holding another victim, bonding like no one else could, because they didn't understand. Nancy didn't bother us, but I could hear her crying from the doorway. We must have stayed in that position for five minutes before Carly finally let go, her red puffy eyes looking up at me. "Thank you. Thank you for finding me. And for talking to me."

I pulled her in again, the tears not over. I saw so much

of myself in her, and I wished for a moment that there had been someone to have this conversation with fourteen-year-old me.

July 11th – 2001

"Isn't this quite the sight," Dad said from a gloomy corner of the living room. A table lamp snapped on, casting its orange glow over him. The two empty mason jars sat on the end table beside him. "Here, now." He pointed to the couch, and Zoe took the lead, me following behind, shuffling my feet. I was so worried about being caught in a lie that I almost ran from the room.

"Tell me where you were," he said, startlingly calmly.

"We were at the beach. Fireflies are for babies, so we…"

"Don't lie to me, Zoe Daphne Carver." His voice was a low growl.

"We met up with some people at Local Beach," she admitted.

"Who? What people?" he asked, glaring at me.

I waited for Zoe to answer. She was the big sister. When she didn't, I spit it out. "Just some kids we saw in town. They invited us to come by."

Dad was leaning in close to Zoe. "Is that beer I smell?"

"You were drinking beer, it's probably just…" Zoe started.

He grabbed her face, not hard, but hard enough to startle my sister. I'd never seen Dad so upset. "Another lie. That's three so far tonight between the two of you. How often do you lie like this to me? Am I just a sad sap you fool all the time?"

"No, Daddy," I said, using a name for him I hadn't spoken in years. "I swear. We were just invited today, and didn't think you'd let us go, so we went. It's only ten thirty.

We always stay up this late!"

He slammed his hand on the coffee table. "You're fourteen years old! And you," he said to Zoe. "You're supposed to take care of her for me. You two are all I have, and there are things that go on in the dark around here that you cannot be a part of. Drugs, booze, sex."

I'd never heard Dad talk like this, and I was getting scared. "We're sorry, Dad. I only had a sip of the beer, and then we left. They weren't really that cool anyway. Plus I felt bad for lying," Zoe said.

Dad shook his head, letting out a big sigh.

"What's going on here?" Grandma asked from her bedroom door. She shuffled towards us, a robe over her shoulders. Underneath, I could see how skinny she was, wasting away before our very eyes. She didn't even look like the same woman from Christmas time.

"The kids snuck out to go to a party," he said.

"Oh, Brian. They're teenagers. I seem to recall giving you a few get-out-of-jail-free cards," Grandma said, melting my heart. She was sticking up for us.

"Do you know what it's like to have the neighbor knock on your door at nine at night, asking if I knew where my daughters were off to?" he asked.

My throat bobbed up and down. "What neighbor?"

"Peter. We're going to go fishing in the morning, by the way. So you two can help Grandma around here, and you're both grounded for a week." That was it. Dad shook his head, and I didn't blame him for the punishment. The fact that the creepy neighbor ratted us out made me want to scratch an itch I didn't have.

"Dad, what about the Summer Kick-Off?" Zoe asked.

"Is it this week?" he asked.

Zoe nodded.

"Then no. You break the rules, you pay the price." He

left the room, heading to his bed.

Grandma went to the kitchen, poured three glasses of water, and motioned us over. "Don't worry, girls. We'll butter him up. I want you there with me," she said, leaving out the fact that she knew it would be her last time.

July 14th – 2020

I left the Millers with a heavy but relieved heart. I really thought I might have helped Carly in some small way. I'd texted her my personal cell number and saved her email address. It felt important to stay in touch. I'd be that ear she could talk to when times were tough.

The rain was pouring heavier now, breaking through the canopy above with ferocity. Once inside my car, the wipers activated, and I saw it was already noon. From my experience, nothing ever got done between the hours of noon and one at a public office, so I decided to hit Buddy's for lunch before visiting Town Office.

The roads were nearly vacant. The tourists would all be nestled up out of the rain, playing games as a family around a crowded table, the kids trying to sneak that extra hotel onto their property, the moms wondering when was too early to pour that first glass of vacation wine.

This kind of weather did make me feel safe and cozy. Back home when it poured like this, I'd open my windows wide and listen to the sounds of the city in the storm. I'd have a cup of coffee in my hands while using my eBook reader to devour a thriller, often about a female FBI agent or a strong mother defending her children from some insane killer. Part of me wished I could transport myself to my apartment, to open the panes and sit on my couch with a good book.

I parked at Buddy's Diner, finding it quite busy. A family exited, running for their SUV, the mom holding a jacket above her head to stay dry. I smiled as I watched them, giggling in the rain, the dad soaked by the time the kids were in the back seat.

I didn't bother using an umbrella for the twenty feet, so by the time I was inside, water dripped from the tip of my nose. There was one table open, but it was meant for six people, so I found a seat at the counter bar. It was the one on the far right, and the stool to my left was vacant.

Isabelle caught my eyes from across the room and sauntered over to me. "You either hate to cook or you love my company," she kidded, slipping me the oversized menu. "Lucky me, here's my favorite local and favorite visitor, all at the same time."

I turned around and saw Clark standing there, his hair wet, and he was grinning at Isabelle. "How convenient. You're my favorite server on the clock, Izzy. My order all good?" he asked.

"Right as rain, pardon the pun. Have a seat. Want lunch while you're here?" she asked.

I wasn't looking at him now, just staring forward, hoping he didn't join me.

"Sure, why not? I have the day off. And it'll give me the chance to meet my competition." Clark pulled the stool out and sat, turning to face me. His eyes sprang wide open and his jaw dropped. "You…"

I knew it. He did recognize me. I should have never come here, especially when I knew he always came to Buddy's.

"Sorry. I mean, didn't I see you here the other night, then at the Pig?" he asked, and it became clear he didn't know who I was. That I wasn't Jessica Carver, just some tourist he'd seen around.

"That's right. Eva Heart." I didn't make the awkward handshake at the cramped diner bar.

"Clark Patterson. Nice to meet you, Eva. Here with your family?" he asked, and I noticed him look over at my left hand.

I almost laughed and said, 'Smooth, Clark.'

"Journalist. Doing a fluff piece on the UFO sightings in the area," I told him, trying to make it sound less interesting than I really found it.

"That's cool. Did you hear about the overnight tour this evening? I'm going. An author's running it, and Henry from the feed store's hosting on his land. Should be interesting." Clark was fidgeting with the menu.

He was going? That wasn't good for me. I really didn't want him around for this, but he didn't seem to be putting two and two together. I didn't look much like that little girl from nineteen years ago, so I couldn't blame him. He was a lot different too, but the eyes gave him away; the smirk as well.

There was no way around it unless I wanted to bail on the event, which I didn't. It was going to be the central piece of my article, the writer taking part in a ceremony of watching the skies during sighting season. It was gold. "I'll be there too."

"You will? That's great… I mean, that'll be great for your story. Where are you from, if you don't mind me asking?" Clark flipped his coffee cup over, and so did I.

"She's from New York, Clarky boy," Isabelle said, interrupting us as she poured the coffees. "And if you don't think a beautiful woman like that has a rich man in the city, you have to be kidding yourself."

I couldn't help but laugh, and Clark did too. "Don't expect a tip today, okay, Izzy?" Clark lifted his menu up, blocking the waitress from our line of sight. "So, as I was saying, where are you from?"

"New York, and no, there is no rich man waiting for

me back home," I said, regretting it. Remembering the lithe arm snaking around his waist by the pool table the other night, I had to ask him, "Is your girlfriend going with you tonight?"

He looked stunned but composed himself quickly. "Becky? Oh, the bar, you saw us… She's a friend, that's all. Do I know you?" he asked, sending my heart racing. He was going to call me out, point at me, knocking his stool over, and he'd tell everyone I was Jessica Carver, the girl who'd vanished the night of the Summer Kick-Off in 2001. But he didn't; he just stared harder, as if sheer will would provide the answer he was seeking.

"I'm sure you don't. It's my first trip to your little town," I said, more playfully than I normally would have.

"And how are you liking it?" he asked.

"It's… quaint. I'm staying at Cloud Lake Cabins," I said, unsure why I gave him the added information.

"I like those guys. I did their hot water tank retrofit last fall. Fast payers," he said, and I returned to my menu. "I hope you weren't saving this seat for anyone."

"Just the local plumber," I said.

He looked worried. "How did you know…?"

"Clark, you just told me you did the hot water tanks at the Cabins." I laughed at him, and he rolled his eyes.

"You've caught me on an off day. I swear I'm far more put together than what you're now seeing," he said.

"You two kids ready to order?" Isabelle asked from behind us, startling me.

Clark motioned for me to go first, and I asked for the soup and a turkey wrap. Clark ordered a clubhouse with fries, and for a moment, we didn't talk, just sat in silence as we each sipped our coffees.

"How crazy is it that we'll both be at Henry's tonight. You have a tent?" he asked.

I nodded. "I do, but if it's raining this bad, I'm not expecting to get any sleep."

"It's supposed to clear by late evening. Tell you what. We can buddy up. These things always have a safety protocol. They don't want anyone wandering off into the trees or the fields alone, especially not after what's happened in this town before."

"What do you mean?" I asked, wishing I hadn't, but needing to.

"Cloud Lake has lost a few people. Unsolved disappearances, and even some of the solved ones haunt us." He stared into the mirror beyond the bar. "Sometimes more than the open cases," he whispered, and I didn't press him.

"So we buddy up?" I asked. I knew this was a bad idea, but being here with Clark again felt right. He was my first love, the first boy I really wanted to kiss, to have hold me, to tell me I was pretty, and I thought about that time at Local Beach; while the others smoked and drank, making out, he sat with me, our knees grazing, his finger touching mine, and the electricity I felt.

"I mean, if you want to," he said.

I nodded. "Can't be any worse than some random crazy alien hunter, I guess." I smiled at him.

"Only time will tell," he admitted. "I do have a fifth wheel. Lots of room, beds, kitchen, bathroom. It's better than using the porta-potties Henry rents."

The idea of going into Clark's private trailer concerned me, but I didn't say so. "That's great. I'll park my tent outside. If I see the aliens descending, I'll be sure to throw a rock at your window or something," I joked. For some reason, I couldn't stop playing with Clark. He was making it really easy to kid around, in a way not many people could do. John was nice, kind, but he didn't have this playful side

157

to him, nor did most of the people I spent time around back home. It was endearing. For a second, I wondered what might have been if I'd never disappeared that day. Maybe Clark and I would…

"I have a grill too. Izzy's hooking me up with twenty burgers and buns for everyone. I thought it would be nice to do the cooking," Clark said.

"How many are signed up?" I asked.

"Think with you, there'll be around twelve. Less than last year," he told me.

"This has happened before?"

"This isn't the first one. No, Mr. Neville has done five, I think. I've been to two of them," Clark admitted.

Neville. I knew the name from somewhere. "Neville. You mean Oscar Neville?" I recalled the borrowed book from the library in my cabin.

"The very same. Wow, you've really done your research for this story," Clark said.

"Why do you go, Clark? To the UFO event?" I asked him curiously.

He shrugged. "Because I find it intriguing. Life on other planets. It's fascinating to think there could be beings from different worlds coming to see us, to view us from their ships, and Cloud Lake of all places. It makes it a little easier to get up and go to work for me, if that makes sense," he said, and I nodded.

"Have you ever seen any lights?" I asked him, and was surprised when he said one word in reply.

"Yes."

Isabelle came over with a smile and dropped our plates off, winking at me as someone called for her attention.

I wanted to grab Clark by the collar and throw a barrage of questions at him, but I paced myself and took it slow. "Where did you see the light?"

"By the lake, years ago. I was trying to chase… never mind." He looked away, and Isabelle came with our lunch. I wanted to bring up his memory, to hear more about it, but I sensed it involved me. How had he seen the lights? He said he was chasing someone.

"And at this Oscar Neville's thing? Has there ever been a sighting?" I asked.

"Not that I know of, but he says the chances are slim. It's more about sharing a mutual belief, and you know… grilling burgers and having some beer with friends," he said, picking away at his French fries.

"Have you been married?" I asked out of the blue, and couldn't believe I'd said it.

He laughed, dropping a fry on my plate. "I saw you eyeballing these," he told me, and I took the offered food and dipped it into his puddle of ketchup before eating it. "No, Miss Heart. I have never been married. But what a great question to ask a stranger at a diner."

"It's my go-to. Shall we discuss religion and political views next?" I asked, taking another fry off his plate.

The chimes rang, and I noticed the uniform before I heard the voice. "Can I get a cup of coffee, Izzy?" McCrae boomed. He sauntered over to the register and glanced at the bar, meeting my gaze. I saw the corners of his mouth tilt up, and he made straight for me like an arrow to a bullseye. "Miss Heart. I didn't expect to see you here. Are you feeling all right?"

Clark was watching me from his peripheral as he turned to McCrae. "What happened, Eva?" Clark asked.

McCrae didn't seem to think it was odd I was sitting there having lunch with the local plumber, and he answered for me. "Eva here is the one that found Cloud Lake's missing treasure and brought her home."

Clark paled, and I heard utensils drop around the diner.

159

The entire room seemed to get quieter, and I wanted to hide under a table to avoid the stares. "That was you? Why didn't you say something?"

"I… I didn't want to make a big deal over it. Plus, we don't really know each other. It's not my personality type to go around shouting all the things I managed to do, especially when it was pure and unadulterated luck," I said quietly to Clark.

He grabbed my hands. "This is amazing. Carly was found by you? You're a damned hero, that's what you are."

"Enough. I'm just glad she's home," I said.

"Either way, Carly is safe because of Miss Heart here, and the town is eternally grateful, as are the Millers. I hear you were over there today." McCrae grabbed an offered to-go cup of coffee from Isabelle, and she waved away his bill.

I nodded. "I saw her today. She was doing surprisingly well. She's a strong girl," I said, almost daring someone to deny it. The diner returned to normal, and people began eating again. A few looked my way and gave me a thumbs-up. A woman was leaving, and said *thank you* quietly as she passed.

"Clark, tell me you're not going to that foolish thing at Henry's again this year," McCrae said to the man beside me.

"I am, Sheriff. But don't worry, we won't start a fire or shoot any guns off at midnight," Clark said with a smile.

McCrae didn't return the gesture. His radio went off, and I couldn't make out the unintelligible crackling voice. "Goddamn drugs. I gotta go. Thanks again, Miss Heart. Clark." He nodded at us and left, heading out to the wet afternoon.

"You're amazing," Clark said instantly.

"Your lunch is on the diner," Isabelle came over and

whispered in my ear. I wanted to deny her, but she was already gone, filling up another table's coffees.

"Really, Clark. Let's not make a big deal of this. I was doing some investigative stuff and stumbled on her. I'm glad I was there, that's all. She is a sweet girl," I said.

"Maybe it was them," he said, before biting into his double-stacked sandwich.

"Who's *them*?" I asked, but he had too big a mouthful. I slapped him on the arm, and said, "Clark, you can't drop a bomb and then bite into the world's biggest sandwich."

A full minute later, he raised a finger and drank a mouthful of coffee. "Sorry. Them. You know. The Grays, or whatever."

"Explain," I said, slurping some soup while he started.

He lowered his voice and glanced around like a crazy conspiracy theorist. "July sixth, Chester Brown witnesses lights in the sky, the very same day that Mark Fisher and Carly Miller go missing. A week later, Carly is found. Do they know who took her?"

I shook my head.

"See. It's all so clear. They've been coming to Cloud Lake, taking people, and for some reason, they spit Carly back. I know, it's out there, but who knows. Stranger things have happened… maybe." He kept eating, and I didn't press him anymore.

Someone entered, and people turned to the door. I joined them. He spoke in a low, gravelly voice, his farmer's hat nervously clenched in his gnarled grip. The farmer addressed the diner. "Lake's closed for those of you thinkin' of heading there."

"How come, Carl?" a woman asked from her seat.

"Body. They been combing it this week. Found a body," the old man said.

July 14th – 2020

The rain had let up, and Clark had offered me his number, making me promise to be skywatch buddies with him. He was so sweet and still as handsome as I'd remembered. I liked how young I felt around him, as if his very presence plucked a decade from my weary mind.

The Town Office was only two blocks away, and I decided to walk the short distance. People were out already, the streets becoming busier as the sun emerged from behind the dense clouds. I found the building without issue as I pushed through the glass entrance door, and was greeted by a happy smiling girl at the receptionist's desk. She couldn't have been out of high school, but I appreciated the friendly disposition in a world of cranky customer service.

"Hello, I'm Eva Heart from the *Brownstone Beat*, and I'd like to speak with the mayor or town council about the Summer Kick-Off for an article. Would someone be available?" I asked.

"If you'd like to have a seat, I'll check and be right with you," she said, her voice calm and professional.

I did just that and grabbed my phone, deciding to email Harry. I'd meant to call in to the office but didn't want to talk to Barns right now. Harry would have the scoop on the status of our workplace, and I was curious if word had gotten out that the magazine might be finished. I kept it simple, letting him know the story was going along well, taking longer than anticipated, but that I should be home by next Monday. I also asked just enough about the morale of the office that he'd know what I was digging for. I sent it and sat there, waiting on the comfortable chair.

The space was dated but inviting. A ten-foot-tall rubber tree was stretched up alongside the window, and I polished one of the leaves between my fingers, seeing if it was indeed real. It was. I liked to sit without staring at a screen like the rest of the world. It was nice to remember what life was before smart phones and tablets, portable streaming channels and social media. As much as I used all of those things, I still resented them.

I watched the girl behind the desk as she intercepted phone calls, each time with a bubbly disposition. I imagined she was a cheerleader, captain of the squad, dating the local football hero most likely, but she was starting to have to think about colleges and majors, and there was an underlying tension to her life, an imperfect family. Sunday dinners that ended in arguments more often than hugs. I heard a dog bark outside, and I drew my attention away from the girl. I needed to stop daydreaming like this. I tried to think when that had begun, and suspected I'd been doing it my whole life.

"Eva Heart?" the girl asked, as if she were a nurse at a doctor's office with a full waiting room. It was only me in the room with her.

"That's me," I said with a smirk, and followed her past a scattering of offices with closed doors. She waved me inside one that had the name *Caroline Fowler* in lettering on the glass window, and left.

"Hello," the woman behind the desk said. "Please, have a seat." Caroline was roughly my age, her strawberry-blonde hair sun-bleached, and her fair skin littered with pronounced freckles.

"Thank you for seeing me on such short notice. My assistant in the city was supposed to call for an appointment, but you know how they can be," I lied, and she nodded absently.

"You're here to do a story on Cloud Lake's Summer Kick-Off party?" She leaned forward, tapping her chin with a pen.

I nodded. "Sort of. I'm travelling around the Northeast, researching different summer events. You should see the party they had outside Bridgewater, New Hampshire," I said, not elaborating.

"What would you like to know?" she asked.

I set my recording device on the desk and pulled out my tablet, taking notes. "What's your position here?"

She smiled. "I'm the Head Councillor, and that puts me in charge of a few things, one of them the annual summer event."

"And how long have you been a resident of Cloud Lake?" I asked.

She smiled again. "My whole life. Born and bred."

"So you've been to a lot of these Kick-Offs, then?"

"Probably all of them. My parents took us every year. It was the best time of our summer."

"What do you like best about the event?" I asked.

Caroline's posture changed. She relaxed, and I pretended to make notes, tapping nonsense on the screen. "The ambiance. We've added some features – live music, parasailing, hot-dog eating contests – but the one thing that's always the same are the smells. That scent you get in a crowd when it's hot, near the water, motorboats in full swing on the open water, music playing, kids laughing and playing. It's the best thing in the world, and I'm so blessed to be able to run this now, and share my passion for it with the next generation."

I looked around her desk for picture frames. "Do you have children of your own?" The question might have been a little awkward, but I always talked about kids as an ice-breaker.

"I have two. Dane is five and Holly is two," she said, beaming the entire time. "And you?"

I shook my head and lowered my gaze, not saying a word, as if implying I couldn't have them. It was my way of stopping the questioning about why a woman in her thirties wouldn't want the miracle of life. I pressed on. "Can you tell me how the event is funded?" I asked, not caring in the least. It was something a member of the town council would be obligated to tell me about, and it would help disarm her.

She talked for five minutes, citing various fundraisers and private donations they did throughout the year to fund events, and how they relied on volunteers for a lot of it. I made more fake notes, smiling as I did so.

"Why are you having it on a Thursday instead of a Friday this year?" I asked.

"It's grown so much, we decided to add a second day. With the local musicians filling the stages, and so many people coming through on one day, it made a lot of sense to add the extra day. Twice the fun," she said with an exaggerated smile.

It was time to shift gears. "How do you feel about continuing the event after the disappearance of three of the town's residents?"

She looked taken aback but probably knew I was just doing my due diligence. She remained fairly poised, and I liked her more for it. "Well, as you might not know, Carly Miller has been found safe, and she's now at home with her family recovering."

"I've heard."

"And word just came in they've found a body at the far corner of the lake."

Word came quickly to the town office, but it made sense, considering a farmer had told the entire diner only a half hour ago. "Who do they think it is?" I asked.

"Mark Fisher," she answered.

"The missing man? How do they know?" I asked, actually surprised by the news.

"Tattoo. He had a fishhook on his arm, big one with his ex's name down the side of the barb. Apparently, the body has the same tattoo," she said.

I lost my train of thought. I don't know what I'd expected to have befallen the man. The sheriff and Mark's own brother suspected foul play. Had I really thought it could have been anything but?

"Will that affect the event?" I asked her, and she shook her head in response.

"No. The beach is four miles from there. No reason to stop it. Now that the loose ends are tied up, we can move on," Caroline said.

"Tied up? You have a dead body and a girl who was abducted by someone, with no answers on either case," I told her, my voice growing louder than intended.

"That's for Sheriff McCrae and his team to handle, and I suspect they will."

"They sound like a good department. What about all these rumors around town?" I tried to read her expression as I asked the question.

"Which ones?"

"I think you know." I laughed lightly.

"The UFOs?"

I shrugged. "You bet."

"I've lived here my whole life, and have never once seen anything out of the ordinary."

"But? I sense a but," I told her.

"But… a few people I admire and trust have claimed to be witnesses to some strange occurrences."

I leaned toward the desk and flipped my tablet on its face, into my lap. "Strange occurrences?"

"Lights. Flashing lights. Farmers claiming animals have vanished in the middle of the night. People disappearing with no recollection of where they were," she admitted.

"And what do you think it is?" I asked her.

"I think it's electrical storms, and maybe some mental imbalances. Could be diet-related. Maybe their well water has too much lead. I really don't know," Caroline said, tapping her pen open and closed against the desktop.

"So you don't believe in life from other planets visiting you here in Cloud Lake?" I asked.

She looked at the recording device and smiled at me. "No. I don't believe in aliens or UFOs. Do you have any further questions regarding the Kick-Off?"

"No, I think we've got it all," I said, and stood up. We shook hands, hers warm to my always cool touch.

"Will we see you there?" Caroline smiled widely, actually seeming to want me there.

"You will. I'm going to be there to witness the whole thing. I like the idea of the sounds and smells, and will try to soak up the vibe you were explaining. Thank you for meeting with me, Caroline. It was really nice to meet you," I said.

"You too. Enjoy the rest of your time in Cloud Lake,

Miss Heart."

I walked by the closed offices and past the young bubbly girl, who I told to have a great day. I walked the few blocks to the diner where my car was waiting, thinking about Mark's body being located. My mind drifted to Carly. Would they make her go under hypnosis like they had me? Would they find her results as confusing and terrifying as mine? I wished I could stay here to find out, but it wasn't my place to pry. Plus, I had her email.

I could still remember the look of horror on the therapist's face after my first session. Dad had changed after that day. He'd started walking on eggshells even more, and when he wasn't being fake kind to me, he was angrier in all other parts of his life. At the time, I wished I could have given them what they were after. They wanted me to explain being taken, being trapped in a room somewhere, they wanted evidence and my conviction of the man arrested for my abduction, but I couldn't give them that, and neither could my subconscious.

The diner was nearly empty when I arrived at my car. It was three in the afternoon, that magical witching hour that allowed restaurants to switch workers, and to prep for dinner service. To clean the tables and have a smoke break. I saw a thick man in a white apron in the alley, talking loudly on his phone while puffing away at a cigarette.

Isabelle was inside, sitting at a table, drinking a coffee and reading the paper. I waved at her, and she smiled gingerly, a bone-tired look on the hard-working woman's face.

Once I made it to my car, I checked my phone, startled to see Harry had already replied. I opened the email and read it.

Eva,

This place is bonkers without you. It's like there's no one to talk to, at least no one sane. Barns is losing his shit. I went to talk to him about the magazine, and he tossed a stapler at me, telling me I'd never have had the job if my dad hadn't bribed him into hiring me. Needless to say, I'm looking for work... actually, that's what I'm doing right now, on company time. Lol.

Good to hear the story is going well. It may be your last. I brought you up to Barns and he was pissed, his face turned red and he told me to get out of his office. What happened? Did you talk to him or tell him off or something?

Anyway. I'm going to expedite a few more résumés and hit the gym. I'll run off any frustrations I have with my uncle. Hope you're having fun at Sun Pond, or whatever it's called. Don't forget bug spray!

Talk soon,
Harry

I scrolled up, trying to understand what Barns was so upset about. I knew he was probably being forced to call it quits, but I was determined to finish this piece and move on when I returned. I had the urge to call Barns and went to my contact list, finding his name and number. My finger hovered over the icon, but I exited out, not wanting to deal with his crap at that moment. I needed to get ready for the night's festivities.

Clark had told me not to worry about the food, but I decided to stop at the store to pick up a few drinks and snacks. It wouldn't hurt for me to bring offerings to the other sky watchers, to start off on the right foot. I hit the market for the second time that week and grabbed far too many beverages: pop, wine, beer, and a Styrofoam cooler with four bags of ice to keep it all cold. The rest of the cart filled up with various chips and pretzels, and when I knew I'd overdone it, I checked out and had the teenage kid load the stuff into my back seat.

It was four by the time I made it to the cabin one last time, to change and make sure I didn't forget anything.

Some of the families were already setting up for the evening, and I could smell food being cooked even at this early hour. Dan's truck was noticeably missing, and I decided I should check on Clare. I hadn't seen her since John had come over, and I couldn't help but worry about the woman. Her moods were all over the place, and Dan had "abusive husband" written all over his face.

"Clare?" I called as I rounded the cabin, and I noticed her by the water. The Cloud Lake Cabins had one long dock with various canoes tethered to it. They bumped the wooden dock lightly as the waves bounced them around.

Clare was at the end, feet dangling over the edge. She didn't even look up when I arrived. She had a bottle of wine in her hand, and it was almost empty. Her nose was red: a combination of too much drink and sun. "Do you ever wonder what it's like to drown?" she asked.

I didn't know what to say. "No, I don't."

"I do. All the time. I think it's the best way to go. You're surrounded by it, the water means you no harm, it just envelops your body in a brutal hug, every square inch of you is covered, and that's not enough. It needs inside you. It needs to slide into your mouth and down your throat. It needs to fill your stomach, and most importantly, your lungs. Water isn't evil. But it kills so many people. That I can understand. Water, I get." Clare lifted the bottle to her lips and tilted her head back. The remaining red wine flowed, and she dropped the bottle to the dock. It flipped to its side and rolled off into the water with a splash.

"Clare, I think you should go to your cabin. Maybe have a nap," I suggested.

"I've slept enough, Eva. I've slept enough. I feel like my eyes are open for the first time in years," she said, and I saw the glint of the steel beside her.

"What's that for?" I asked, knowing full well it was

either meant for her or her husband.

"Protection. I didn't want to be out here by myself, and Dan can't understand that. He leaves me alone at this cabin day and night, just like every town we go to, and I've had it up to here." She lifted her arm high above her head, her hand flat, making a line in the air, a unit of an unmeasurable portion.

She pulled a small plastic pill bottle from her pocket, popped off the cap, and placed it in her mouth, swallowing in a gesture that told me she was used to it. I would know. I hadn't had one of my pills today, but still felt I could manage. Dealing with Clare now made me regret my choice not to medicate. Her energy was unnerving, and I couldn't become caught up in her sweeping emotions.

"What are those?" I asked, holding my hand out.

"Why not take one? Dulls that edge we all get," she said, passing the vial to me.

I flipped it around, reading the label. Vicodin. Take one tablet every four hours as needed for pain. Janice Quinn.

They clearly weren't hers. "Where did you find these?" I asked her.

Clare's glassy eyes slowly glanced over to me. "They were in the cabin."

I didn't believe her, not one bit. "How many have you had?" She was looking worse for wear, and I thought that probably hadn't been her first bottle of wine either.

"Don't worry about me, honey. I'll be fine. It's just another Saturday for old Clarabelle," she said, and I wondered if that was even her name.

"It's Tuesday," I corrected her.

"Po-*tay*-to, po-*tah*-to." She laughed, and gone was the morose, death-enthralled woman. She was replaced by happy Clare, the one who drank too much wine, had too much sun, and enjoyed popping some pills to, as she said, dull the edge.

"Come to the cabin. I need to use the bathroom and pour a drink," I said, knowing the second ticket item would get her attention.

"Sounds good. Do you want to play cribbage?" she asked, her words slurring deeply.

"As long as you don't mind being skunked," I said, helping her up. She took a step toward the shore, her bare feet slapping against the graying wooden slats.

I let go of her arm, and she nearly fell sideways. I caught her, and she leaned into me, laughing at the motion. I didn't know what to do. Did I leave her in her own place for Dan to come and find her, or would it be safer for her in my cabin? That would open up all sorts of other issues, and I really didn't want them inside my cabin snooping through my things. I didn't know Clare. The woman seemed friendly enough, but she was trouble. Still, no one deserved to be abused.

We made it to the beach, then up the small stone pathway leading between our cabins. Clare steered me to her place, and I didn't stop her. She opened the door and I stepped inside. It was messy; not overly dirty, just disheveled. Dan's shirts hung from the kitchen chairs. Dishes piled in the sink, and the garbage was overflowing.

Clare went to the kitchen, and I poured her some water, pushing it into her hand. She glanced up at me with a thick sadness in her eyes. I nodded; a look that told her 'I know, it'll be okay'. She smiled, and I led her to her bedroom. I removed a sprawled-out dress and a bathrobe, draping them over the dresser, and Clare flopped down face-first into the pillows. I turned her and stroked her hair.

"I'll help you if you want," I told her. It was a promise, and I meant it. "We'll talk before I leave. I will help you."

She mumbled something and drifted off, already

snoring lightly, her lips half an inch apart. She looked younger there in the dim bedroom, the curtains closed. It could have been midnight inside that room, and I watched her sleep for a few minutes, wishing there was something I could do.

I glanced at the clock, realizing it was after five. I also didn't want to be here when Dan came home. I had no idea if he was violent, or what he would do if he found me inside their place. Leaving her here alone was difficult.

After a quick change at my place, I was ready to go in sneakers, jeans, and a sweatshirt. I grabbed the umbrella in a basket by the exit and threw it into the backseat before heading for Henry's farmland. I had the map he'd drawn on the reverse of his feed store flyer, and headed out, ready for my very first Alien Adventure evening.

I immediately knew which turnoff to take, but there were also helpful cardboard signs pegged into the roadside, with arrows pointing to the long gravel driveway. Henry had a picturesque farm, cornfields with old rooted trees behind them. Between his home and the fields was at least three acres of grass: a massive yard. I imagined Henry out there himself on a riding mower, chewing sunflower seeds and wearing protective ear-muffs for the sound.

The corn stalks were extraordinary, taller than the others I'd driven by, and I assumed Henry, being the owner of the town's only farming store, had access to the best fertilizers at a low cost.

Already there were rows of tents set up, and I pulled up to a line of seven various vehicles. The second I parked beside an old mid-nineties pickup, someone honked behind me. Clark was there, pulling his trailer behind his work truck.

It was insufferably hot now that the clouds had dissipated and drifted away. The recent moisture added to the heat, making it muggy, and I immediately sloughed off my sweatshirt, setting it aside for later.

The group of people were gathered around one man, and they created space for me as I approached. The man was Oscar Neville, the spitting image of his backflap picture from the book, only fast-forwarded ten years. He was a little whiter-haired, heavier, and more desperate.

He was performing roll-call, and when he got through the ensemble cast, his eyes lingered on me.

"I'm sorry, ma'am. I don't see you on my registration list?" He made it a question.

"Sorry, I only heard of it a couple days ago. Is it okay if I join and pay the fee?" I asked, trying to sound like a happy-go-lucky woman.

"Of course, of course. The rest of you, get settled, and we'll meet up in ten minutes for the first part," Oscar said. The group meandered away before I could meet any of them, and Oscar pulled me to the side. I had a lot of questions for him, especially since he'd been so vocal about my case, even though I hadn't discovered this until I found his obscure book.

"Can you fill this waiver out?" He pulled a clipboard from his van, which turned out to be a rusted Econoline with *Alien Adventures* stickered on the side. Both A's were peeling off, the red color worn to a burnt orange.

I filled in my name, Eva Heart, made up a local address, and gave my secondary email account.

"Sign here." He pointed to a missed page full of paragraph blocks.

"What's this?" I asked.

"Just lawyer-speak, mumbo jumbo. Basically says you

can't sue me if you're abducted by aliens, or if you stare at the UFO lights too long, that kind of thing," he said, and I fought the urge to roll my eyes and sign it *Minnie Mouse*. I used my Eva signature and drew a heart over my last name for emphasis.

"Thank you," he read the name, "Eva. Now there's just the matter of the fee. Normally it's only one hundred dollars, but because we have to make room, and there's the fee to Henry per head, and the food…"

He was fishing me for more money, and I opened my wallet, slipping out two hundred dollars. "There you go. That should do," I told him.

He didn't even count the twenties, just slid them into his breast pocket with a big smile. "Great. Thank you for coming."

Clark had parked his trailer about a hundred yards from the tents and was working on setting it up. I decided now was as good a time as any to build my own tent, especially since the others had already finished. All in, there were eight tents of varying shapes and sizes out, and one sleeping bag on the grass. A man was perched on a fold-out chair, holding binoculars beside it.

"Going all out, aren't you?" I asked him, and he turned to me, pushing his black plastic glasses up his nose. He was wearing a baseball cap, the words *Trust No One* stitched across the front.

"I'm here to see them. Kind of hard to do inside a tent, isn't it?" he asked.

"I guess so." I stepped forward and stuck my hand out. "I'm Eva."

"Frank. Nice to meet you. I haven't seen you around. You from out of town?" he asked.

I considered telling him I was a reporter, but thought it might worry Oscar that I was there to defraud his little scheme, so I didn't quite lie about my occupation. "In town from Portland. Doing a story on the Kick-Off for the *Times*, and wanted to do something like this while I was here. I've always been fascinated with UFOs."

He hoisted himself up and stretched his back. "That's great. It's always good to have new blood around here. This is my fourth one. So far, zilch, but I take a week off work every year to come down. Live a five-hour drive from here. I'm feeling lucky tonight, though. I think we're going to see the show," he said, staring at the blue sky.

"I hope so," I said, but really wasn't sure what to believe. If I saw something, it would reiterate a lot, but the rational part of my mind told me I was being crazy, that there was no such thing as aliens, and definitely not over Cloud Lake. "I'll be back. I'm looking forward to talking to you more."

"Likewise," he said, plopping into his seat.

I pulled my gear from the car and headed over to Clark, who was sweating as he cranked some levers on the trailer, leveling it. "I see you made it," he said as he wiped his brow. "Jeez. I thought it was supposed to be cooler today."

He smiled at me, and I felt my heart bang inside my chest like a bird in a cage. There was something about this man that removed my barriers, just like he had as a boy.

"You okay?" he asked, and I nodded.

"Yeah. You're still good with me setting up camp here?" I pointed outside his trailer to a lush patch of grass.

"For sure. Make yourself at home, Eva," he said, and for a second, I thought he was going to call me Jess. But he didn't, because he didn't know that was me.

I dropped my stuff and opened the tent packaging. Soon I had lengths of sticks attached by rubbery strings. I looked at the pile of tent guts and found the instructions, blowing out a sigh.

"Need some help?" Clark was behind me, hands on his hips.

"If you don't mind," I said, feeling pathetic.

"Not in the least. I used to have one just like this when I was a kid," he said, and started to fit the pieces together, making one long section. He pushed it through slits in the tent, and jammed an end of the stick into one corner of it. He repeated this two more times, and I made an effort to help as we bent them, creating a dome in the material. The whole thing only took five minutes, and before I knew it, we were hammering in the pegs with a tool from his truck and standing back, admiring our handiwork.

"Who knew it was so simple?" I asked, showing him the twenty-step instructions with a stick man making the tent.

"I'm a man. We can't be bothered with that kind of stuff, but save it," he said.

"Why?"

"For a fire starter later." He laughed, and I crumpled it up, throwing the paper ball at him.

Clark ducked and avoided being struck. "Looks like Oscar's ready for us. A quick itinerary scan and we're making burgers and swigging beer in no time." That reminded me of the supplies in the car. I hoped the Styrofoam cooler hadn't leaked on my leather seats.

As we walked over to the circle of people again, I fumbled through my bag, finding my sunglasses, and wondered why I hadn't been wearing them.

"Good, everyone is here," Oscar said. I glanced around the circle, and there were fourteen of us, including the man in charge. Someone materialized from the house, and I recognized Henry from the other day at his store. He was still wearing his red work shirt and waved as he neared the group.

"Howdy, all. Don't worry, I won't be sticking around, but I thought I'd hang out while Oscar laid out the rules," Henry said.

Oscar looked at him and frowned. "There was an… incident last year. Someone went into his house and used the washroom. Let's make sure that doesn't happen again, okay, people?"

Everyone agreed, and I saw Clark was snickering. He cleared his throat and went straight-faced as Oscar stared in his direction.

A woman with a high-tech camera around her neck raised a hand. "I've used the porta-potty and it's clean, so no one should have to worry," she told us.

"Thank you," Oscar scanned his clipboard, "Blaire. I wanted to do a rundown of what's going to happen. It's almost six. We're going to eat, and Clark, you all know Clark, right?" He waited for the gathered people to nod before continuing. "Clark is going to grill for us, and you all should have brought your own drinks."

I raised my hand now. "I brought enough to feed a high school party, as long as someone helps me carry it out of my car."

A guy across from me stuck his fist out to me, waiting for a bump. I tapped his knuckles with mine, feeling awkward about it. "You're the coolest," he said. He looked to be in his early twenties. The girl beside him had short black hair and blunt bangs. Her nose was pierced, and she was chewing what appeared to be a whole pack of gum. Her lips smacked loudly.

"I thought since I was coming late, and I'm the newbie, that it would be nice," I told them, and they all seemed to brighten up.

Oscar continued his itinerary talk. "The sun sets around eight twenty tonight, so we'll gather at eight, and

I'll go over the history of encounters with the flying saucers in the region. Many of you have read my book, or have heard it before, but there are some new faces." Oscar glanced at me and pointed with his pen at the photographer woman he'd called Blaire.

"And then it's party time?" a bearded middle-aged man asked, sparking a few laughs.

"Clay, if the Grays come and take you away tonight, they're going to think humans all smell like an old sock in the bottom of a gym locker. Do you mind rinsing off? I can give you some deodorant," a woman told the man. "I think I saw a hose by Henry's house."

"Your pit stick probably smells like flowers," Clay said.

"Better than rotting meat," she retorted, and he shrugged, nodding along.

Most of these people knew each other, and it was obvious I was one of the only strangers here. Even the photographer appeared to know some of them.

"As I was saying." Oscar tapped his clipboard with his pen. "At eight, I'll discuss my experience with the lights, and we'll go around the circle talking about our own. Then the sun will set, and we'll wait, hoping to catch a glimpse."

"We never do," Clay said under his breath.

"Maybe this year," Oscar said hopefully.

I leaned toward Clark. "What do we really do from eight thirty on?"

He smiled. "Mostly drink beer. We end up having a fire, even though Oscar says it might keep them away. But it gets chilly, and I don't think any of us really expect a flying saucer to show up," he admitted.

"Okay, everyone got it?" Oscar asked, and before anyone answered, he kept going. "Good. Food will be starting in a few, and let's be nice, keep it clean, and whatever you do, don't…" Oscar paused, adding dramatic effect, "go into Henry's house."

Henry nodded and unfolded his arms. "Everyone have fun. Stay safe, and may you see the light you seek." With that, the feed store owner trudged toward his home, leaving me beside Clark.

"Need some help with that cooler?" he asked. Frank ambled up behind him, and the two men carried the heavy ice cooler full of beer and beverages out of my car and set it on the ground beside the picnic tables, near the barbecue.

The grill was soon heating up, and minutes later, the smell of freshly-ground homemade diner patties spread out around the grass patch between Henry's house and the cornfields. I helped pass out plates and organize the sides, and before we knew it, the group of us were eating like family, scattered around the two picnic tables. It was a tight fit, and I was sandwiched between Clark and the woman with the camera.

"I'm Eva," I said to her between bites.

"Blaire. First time too?" she asked, setting down half her hamburger.

"Yep. You live here, though?" I asked.

"Not right in town, but I'm here often enough to know some faces. I'm also one of the only photographers for hire in the area, so believe it or not, I've done shoots for Frank's website, Oscar's pamphlets, Henry's store, and Clay's brother's wedding last summer," Blaire explained. She was likely my age and had a nice carefree demeanor. Her long hair was wavy, puffy in the humidity, and she wore it well. I noticed the mala around her neck, one hundred and eight beads with what appeared to be a black onyx stone at the center.

"Meditation?" I asked, eyeing the necklace.

"Sometimes, but each stone has a purpose, and onyx can be for protection," she said.

"Do you think you need to be protected tonight?" I asked her quietly.

She picked up the remains of her dinner and smiled. "I think we always need a little protection, don't you?"

I nodded slowly, unsure exactly what that meant.

"What do you think?" Clark asked from the other side of me.

"It's good." I took a bite, fresh juices dripping down my chin, and I jutted my head out to avoid grease on my clothes. "Buddy's doesn't mess around."

"No, they don't. I'm getting a beer. Need anything?" Clark asked.

I hadn't even considered a beverage. I didn't really have any favorites. "Sure. Surprise me."

While I had a moment of privacy, after Frank had excused himself, I whispered to Blaire, "Would you mind taking a few shots of this for me? I'm a reporter and I'm doing a story on Cloud Lake."

Her eyes widened, and she looked excited. "Sure. You paying?"

"Of course."

"What kind of shots do you want?"

"Ideally a UFO," I laughed, "but we can start with one of the people eating, the camaraderie, the fire later. Maybe one of the cornfields at dusk, one of Oscar talking to us later, and one of his van, please," I said without really thinking.

"Perfect. I'll do some more, and you can choose from them." She slipped me a business card from a back pocket and kept eating. "You don't want the others to know?"

"Not Oscar." The UFO enthusiast was chatting with Clay as they ate a second serving of potato salad.

"I get that. He's a little out there, hey?" Blaire suggested.

"I'm not sure. I haven't read his book yet. Do you believe?" I didn't have to expand on the question.

"No."

"Then why are you here?" I asked.

"Something to do. You'd be amazed at how boring it can be around here at times," she said, sticking her tongue out the side of her mouth like Zoe used to do. I knew exactly what she meant. "How about you?"

My gaze drifted to the deep blue sky above. An idle cloud hovered in the air, slightly circular in shape. "I'm not sure if I do. Part of me thinks they're real, but the rational part, the deep-seated me, thinks there's no way. That people may just make them up, convincing their brains of what they saw, only because they're pushing something else away. Something they don't want to surface about themselves." My voice lowered. "Or something that happened to them."

"Who ordered a beer?" Clark asked, and set a wet can of beer on the picnic table, placing a half-full bottle of white wine near Blaire. Her cup was empty, and she glanced up at Clark.

"Why, thank you. I don't believe we've met," she said, grabbing hold of Clark's hand. She stood, pulling herself close to him, and I kept staring away from them, feeling uncomfortable at their sudden intimacy. "Blaire," she said, her voice an octave lower than a moment ago.

"Clark. What brings you…" The rest of the conversation turned to mush in my ears. For some reason, I became jealous. I was a mess sitting there at the table while Clark merely talked with another member of the Alien Adventures group. I knew it was completely out of hand, and out of character, at least for the thirty-something version of myself.

Somebody tapped me on the shoulder and I turned to

see Clark's grinning face. "What's gotten into you?" he asked, and I swung my legs around the bench to see Blaire was already gone. Had I made that whole scenario up, exaggerated the contact in my mind? My therapist used to say I did that all the time.

"Oh, nothing. Thanks for the beer." I drank from the bottle, finding this one bitter. I set it down and began helping clean up the tables, making sure every speck of garbage ended up in a big black bag. One of the men stayed put on the bench while I grabbed at a plate, and his eyes followed my every move. I hadn't caught his name, and I felt uneasy with his demeanor.

"Who's that?" I asked Clark afterward.

"Jeremy Cross. Used to be the best mason worker in the area," he told me.

"Used to be?"

"He had an accident. Pile of bricks fell on him. Lost some functions in his brain. If you see him staring at you, it's not his fault." Clark smiled and cinched the last garbage bag up.

I peeked over at Jeremy, and was brought back to another time.

July 12th – 2001

Zoe and Dad had snuck into town to buy a treat for Grandma. She wanted something sweet, and Dad wasn't about to let his sick mom go without. Zoe took the opportunity to have Dad let her drive, since he'd promised he'd help her this summer. I'd watched her slowly reverse out of the parking spot, narrowly missing a tall pine tree, before jerking forward and away from the cabin.

Grandma was inside, and I had too much pent-up energy – from being trapped at the cabin for the last couple days since the grounding – to stay put. I walked out the door onto the porch, past the firepit, and over the ten-foot bar of sand between our yard and the lake. The sand's temperature had lowered along with the sun, and I stood on it barefoot, watching the tiny specks pour down as my toes sank below the surface.

A loon called from the lake, and I decided to sit on the dock and watch the sun set. The wooden structure was firm beneath my bare feet, and I loved the feeling of walking around in the summer without shoes. Back home, we always had socks on, shoes, boots, always fighting the never-ending elements. Here I could avoid socks for the summer, and I took the opportunity to run with it, literally. I jogged over the long dock, laughing as my hair bounced around my face.

For a moment, I felt free: like I wasn't under house arrest for a simple lie, like Grandma wasn't sick, or like my mother hadn't abandoned us when I was a little girl. It was me, the lake, and the sunset.

The lake was quiet tonight. I couldn't hear any boat engines or music careening across the air. It was nature and me for a few special minutes as I sat at the end of the dock. My feet hung over, toes just far enough to dip into the still water. I closed my eyes and breathed it in. I was suddenly overcome with loss, and the grief of something that hadn't even happened yet.

Grandma was about to die. I could see it, and then what? She was gone, and we'd lose our respite from the city, along with one of the three people in the world that truly loved me. It was as if a third of my heart was being ripped out as I contemplated life after... after Grandma.

A sound from my left startled me from my thoughts, and I wiped tears I hadn't known were falling from my cheeks as I scanned for the source. Mr. Martin was standing at the end of his dock, and in the dusk, it was hard to see if he was facing me or not. Either way, alarm bells went off once again, but I couldn't bring myself to stand. I didn't want him to think he had that kind of power over me, so I stayed put.

He didn't move, and now I was sure he was watching me. He lifted a hand, a gentle wave in the darkness, and I froze, petrified of interacting with him. I glanced past the dock, toward the cabin. Could I make it inside before him? Was he fast? The thoughts crossed my mind without preamble, and I finally unfroze, pushing myself up. At first I walked naturally, choosing not to glance over to the neighbor's dock, but when my feet hit the sand, I ran.

I moved quickly. As I neared the porch, I finally broke my own rule and looked back, only to crash to the wooden deck. Lights cut through the treed driveway, and I had to put my hand over my face to keep from being blinded. What was that? My leg ached; I crouched into a seated position and heard the familiar rumble of my dad's old Bronco as it pulled into the driveway. The lights cut off, and Zoe hopped out of the driver's seat, a huge grin on her face.

"What are you doing down there?" she asked.

Before I said anything, I stared at Mr. Martin's dock, but no one was there.

July 14th – 2020

The fire crackled as we surrounded it in a variety of folding chairs. Clark lent me one of his, and judging by the look of it, he'd donated the nicer of the two. He didn't seem to mind as he grinned at me, sipping away on another beer from the cooler.

The sun was lowering behind the treeline on Henry's property, casting long shadows over the cornfield. From here, I could see a scarecrow perched high on a stick, arms wide like he was being crucified. I asked Blaire to take a picture of that for the article. At this point, I doubted the story would ever be told, especially after the email from Harry at the office.

But since I was here, it wouldn't hurt to snap the images and details anyway. Maybe Barns had been onto something: my own account of Cloud Lake and the truth behind my past. I wasn't sure I was ready for that quite yet, but the fact that I was considering it was a huge step forward for me.

Oscar proceeded to talk; the dusk, combined with the newly started fire, cast an orange glow over him. "Nineteen forty-three, four years before the flying disk would capture news headlines with Roswell, New Mexico, one Albert Jackson spotted something above this very town. He was mending a fence that had been damaged in a storm. Some of you may recall hearing about this once-in-a-century storm; a hurricane blowing from the south pushed so much water over Cloud Lake, the entire town seemed to merge with our namesake.

"The calm after the storm had occurred, and the townsfolk and farmers alike were preparing to rebuild. The old library was blown away, and the First Presbyterian Church lost its roof."

I looked around the crowd, the people all nodding and chatting about their memories of family tales about the storm. Grandma hadn't mentioned it, but she wasn't a resident here at the time. I was sure she'd have heard plenty about it over the years. I suddenly wished I could call her and ask about it.

"As I was saying, old Albert was out there, banging away at fence posts with a sledgehammer in the dark, when he spotted the unidentified flying object. Testimony shows him describing it as a circular object in the sky. At least a dozen individual lights shone from below the dome, progressively brighter as they neared, until he could only see them as one solid beam. It hovered over his farm, pausing for at least ten seconds before flashing for another few seconds.

"It then proceeded to vanish. Not into thin air, but it raced away with a speed that boggled Albert's mind. He called the police but was laughed at. He was told it was probably lightning from the storm, and they suggested he see a doctor in case he'd been struck by it."

"What happened to Albert?" I asked, having never heard this story before. There were elements that felt right about it to me, and it reminded me enough of Chester Brown's take. Deep below the pills and hypnotherapy lay a feeling that I'd witnessed this as well, but it was like trying to think of a word that was on the tip of your tongue but couldn't be recalled for the life of you.

"He sold the land. He couldn't stay. A lot of people bailed from Cloud Lake that year. It had started to become a real town, but after that storm, many people lost everything and hung up their hats. Third-generation farm owners like Albert called it quits," Oscar answered.

"Where was his land?" I asked, and he pulled out a laminated map, with Albert's name in a legend. It showed our side of the lake, right where Grandma's cabin was… sitting empty. I swallowed hard.

Oscar didn't wait; he kept talking. "There were a few more sightings over the next two decades, and in nineteen sixty-seven, the lights returned. This time, a young man vanished that night. It was out near Chester Brown's farm. He and his wife witnessed it, nearly scared them half to death."

I chuckled to myself, remembering how Chester had given me a different account. A sweet one, involving him and his new bride sharing the sights, not knowing what it was they were seeing.

"Someone vanished? What do you think it was?" I pressed, since no one else was asking questions. Oscar seemed annoyed at my constant interruptions, but he hadn't asked us to stay quiet.

"Billy Hershfeld. Good kid. Great baseball player. Folks think he could have made the big leagues, before the world became the MLB's picking pool. He was out hitting balls out behind his folks' barn when the lights came. His parents went to check on him around eleven to find his bat and lucky penny on the packed dirt mound." Oscar paused for effect, and it worked. The hair on my arms rose.

"Was he ever found?" I asked, my voice barely a whisper.

Oscar's eyes met mine as he shook his head. "No. Some say he ran away. That the pressure was too much, but he was a fifteen-year-old kid. Loved his family. Apple pie, everything Americana. He didn't run away, mark my words."

Clark was watching me intently, and I avoided looking at him, like my expression might give me away.

"What do you think happened to him?" I asked, genuinely curious.

"He was taken."

"Taken?"

"By the Grays. He was abducted by aliens and never returned." Oscar's gaze was serious. If he was putting on a show for the thousand and a half dollars our head count was bringing him, he was doing a damned good job of lying.

"Why do you call them Grays?" Clark asked, finally taking some of my heat.

"They're thought to be humanoid, about five feet tall, long limbs, wearing a dark uniform over their gray-tinged skin. Large black eyes and sucker-tipped fingers," Oscar said, fumbling through his paperwork to pull out an eight-by-ten sheet with a printed drawing. The alien stared at me with those menacing eyes, and I had to look away.

"Has anyone in Cloud Lake ever seen one?" Clark asked.

"One, so far. She was taken, and returned, and her off-the-record hypnosis treatment after the events was wiped away, but I heard them... once. She described the very same beings," Oscar said, and my blood froze. My heart slowed, and an instant thrumming in my ears began to beat in perfect timing.

I rose, walking from the firepit, sure everyone was staring as I went. I didn't care. I had to leave before I heard any more. Before I heard the name of that young girl he was recalling.

The sun was completely set, and the big Maine sky was darkening, stars becoming more visible with each excessive beat of my heart.

I stopped a couple hundred yards away from the group, standing at the cornfield's edge, and observed the stars.

July 12th – 2001

I was still shaken by the time Dad and Zoe called it a night. So far, I hadn't seen Mr. Martin again, even though we'd been outside for the several hours. I hoped he'd just gone to bed, and I kept telling myself that he hadn't even been watching me, that it was all in my head, and he was a nice man who liked fishing like Dad did.

"He's not so bad, you know. I haven't talked to him much, but I don't think you have anything to worry about, honey," Grandma said, fully aware I'd been looking over toward Mr. Martin's house all night.

"I guess you're right. It just… creeps me out," I told her.

She wasn't wearing her wig tonight, and it exemplified how sunken her face had become, how *thin* she'd become, but her eyes were still alive, dancing around the firelight. "Your father has ingrained in you girls how scary it is out there, and he's not wrong. You're right to be cautious, dear. Always look out for yourself."

I felt her leave out the "when I'm gone." She'd been doing it a lot recently. I'd overheard them talking earlier,

Dad and Grandma. Dad wanted her to come home with us in the fall, but she told him there wasn't going to be a fall. I heard Dad crying through my door, and couldn't remember the last time he'd done that. He was always so stoic when it came to her health, and now that he was seeing what I finally saw, which was a dying woman, he couldn't handle it.

"Grandma, what do you think it's like?" I asked her, poking at the charcoal logs in the pit. A flame sputtered to life as I rotated the burning piece of wood.

"Death?" she asked. She wore a silk scarf, covered in roses, over her head to keep it warm.

I nodded.

"I'm not sure. I could go on talking about the bounties of heaven, the glory of God, but I just don't know. Your grandfather was a good man, you know?"

I smiled and nodded, though I couldn't remember him. He'd died when I was three, not long before Mom left.

"I used to imagine him in heaven, playing cards with his friends, spending time with his own father. They didn't have a great relationship in life, and I prayed they'd make amends in the afterlife," she said.

"But now? What changed?" I asked her.

"I don't know. My own mortality, I guess. I don't feel anything. There's no pull to heaven; just a sore body, a tired husk, even though I still feel like myself, at least when the drugs haven't taken over," she said, her eyes glimmering in the fire's light.

"Are you ready?" I asked, feeling foolish for the question.

"I have my will sorted, and I've said goodbye to some friends, if that's what you mean. Honey, if I don't wake up tomorrow, you know how much I love you, and I know how much you love me." She reached over, placing my hand in hers. She gave it a strong squeeze, and I felt the affection ooze out of her and fortify my heart.

"I know."

"Did I ever tell you about the time I saw the lights above Cloud Lake?" she asked, and the statement startled me.

"No. What do you mean, the 'lights'?" I asked her, feeling a change about to enter into my life. Grandma wasn't going to be around long, and soon everything would be different.

"It was nineteen seventy-seven. Your dad was fifteen years old, and quite the little hellion. God, that boy could argue with the best of them," she said wistfully.

"I didn't know Dad was a troublemaker." I laughed, trying to picture Dad when he was my age, talking back to a headstrong, younger version of Grandma.

"He was, but he was still a good boy. You know why he was so hard on you kids the other night?" she asked, and when I shook my head, she answered, "Because he sees himself in you. He wants you to stay smart, stay strong, and receive great educations. He thinks he's failing you somehow because it's only him raising you. Why do you think you come here every summer?" she asked.

"To visit you," I said.

"That's part of it. He wants a woman's influence in your upbringing. Your dad loves you girls so much."

"He could just find a girlfriend like a normal human," I joked, but Grandma's eyes turned misty at this.

"He thinks your mother was the one shot he had, for some reason. Her abandoning him broke him, in a way. Don't tell him I ever said any of this, okay, dear?" Grandma met my gaze, and I told her I wouldn't.

"What about the lights?" I asked, wanting to get into the story.

"Nineteen seventy-seven. I was in my mid-thirties. A great age to be alive, I have to admit," she said. "Your grandfather was on the road for his sales job, and it was just Brian and me."

"Were you here?" I asked, meaning the cabin.

"No. This was being developed, so we were inland a ways, close to town on an acreage – not a farm, mind you. It was nice, and I sneaked outside with a glass of your grandfather's whisky after a long day. Your father was in his room doing schoolwork, and I sat in my chair and gazed at the stars, like I did when I wanted to relax.

"I never understood people wanting to be in the big cities when you could live like this. It was so quiet outside, and then I realized it was too quiet. I couldn't hear the Browns' cows mooing, or the crickets chirping. Nothing. Silence." Grandma leaned forward, and so did I, enthralled with her retelling of the tale.

"What happened?" I asked, wide-eyed. There was a nervous feeling in the pit of my stomach that I got when I read a good book and wanted to know the outcome of the big conflict.

"They came. Lights flickered in the field beside our house. I could see it clear as day. A domed shape, moving unlike anything I'd ever seen. It was… spectacular. I cried. I stood, knocking over the drink, spilling it on my dress, and walked toward the vessel. I reached my arms up, almost begging to be taken, even though I don't know why. I was a happy woman, but seeing it, knowing there was more out there, changed me." Grandma wiped tears from her cheeks, and our eyes met.

"The lights left as quickly as they came, and when I went to tell your father, he thought I was losing it. Your grandfather came home, and I told him, and he smelled the whiskey I'd spilled and laughed, telling me to take it easy on his spirits, that they were made for a man's tolerance. I never spoke of it again, until now."

I was flabbergasted. We'd all heard rumors, but until recently, I hadn't paid any attention to them. But now, my own grandma had spoken of her own encounter and admitted having seen them. I had to believe too, didn't I?

"I didn't mean to scare you," she said, patting my hand. "I just wanted to share it. You're my special girl, Jessica, yes you are. Don't forget that, okay?"

It was like Grandma knew she wasn't going to make it long, and it was painful to hear the words coming from her mouth. We both cried for a few minutes and found comfort in each other's embrace. There are few special things in life, and the love between a grandparent and a child can be one of the best. I was beginning to learn this as we sat there holding each other.

"What's going on out here?" Dad asked.

"We're having girl talk," Grandma told him, inciting a laugh from her son.

"Are you ready to come inside? It's after midnight," Dad said to both of us.

"Yes, Brian. Would you mind?" She stuck her arm out, and he helped her up, and I watched them go to the house before dousing the last remaining coals. I stared up to the sky, finding the Big Dipper among the plethora of distant specks, wondering just what my grandma had seen all those years ago.

July 14th – 2020

The Big Dipper hung in the sky as it had for ages, and as it would continue to for a long time to come, whether we were here to see it or not.

"Are you all right?" Clark's voice arose from behind me.

"I'm okay. Think I had too much sun today," I lied.

"I haven't really told many people this, but I saw the lights once too," he admitted, and I turned to face him. In the dark, he was a stranger, and I realized I really didn't know much about him other than the fact that he'd been nice to me that summer long ago, and then he'd betrayed me.

"Tell me," I said, preparing myself for what he was going to say.

He ran his hands through his hair and blew out a sigh. I could smell beer on his breath. "There was a girl. She thought she saw me doing something wrong, but it wasn't my fault, and I chased after her."

He'd come after me? He said it wasn't his fault? I wanted to press him, to explain in detail what he meant, but Eva Heart couldn't. I wasn't Jess Carver, the girl that Oscar's book put far too much focus on, and I knew my name was an urban legend now in Cloud Lake. Zoe was right; I never should have come here.

"It was during the Summer Kick-Off, a long time ago. Can you picture me as a dorky teenager?" He laughed, and I wanted to cry, because I could still see him through my young eyes, and I wanted to touch his cheek and kiss him; the kiss we'd never shared.

When I didn't answer, he kept going. "I wandered the public beach, which was too crowded, and when I couldn't find her, I asked her sister where she would have gone. She pointed me to their cabin, and I ran there, hoping to find her. To tell her what she'd seen wasn't real. When I arrived, the lights had beaten me. I saw them from a half mile away, and they were terrifying. I turned and ran from them, worried they'd come for me. I was a kid, I didn't know it wasn't real."

"So you don't believe in them?" I asked.

"I don't know. This girl, she's the one Oscar was talking about when you left. She… something terrible happened to her, and if I'd been braver, I might have been able to help," he said, and I could tell he actually meant it.

I didn't know what to say to him. I fought the urge to jump into his arms, to kiss him and tell him it was me. "We better go back to the fire. It's chilly over here," I said, leaving Clark standing at the edge of the cornfield, staring into the sky.

———

The screaming woke me some time later.

I'd gone to bed before most of the others. That hadn't been long after midnight. I'd listened to their stories, and luckily, no one brought up my name for the rest of the evening. It really was more of a campfire chillout, and Clay broke out the acoustic guitar after drinking eight or so beers, surprising us all with his deft fingers. They sang old country songs, and I sat there among them, feeling like an alien myself.

As soon as Blaire announced to the group that she was heading to bed, I took the chance to excuse myself as well. As I lay in my thin tent, I tried to sleep through the sounds from the firepit. It had to be after two by the time Clark walked past the tent toward his trailer. His footsteps stopped not far from my space, and he lingered there for ten seconds before I heard his door open and close.

I drifted off. Then someone screamed. I saw the flash of light through the canvas, and I tried to listen for any other sounds. Other than the woman's shriek, it was total silence.

I ripped open my tent's zipper, and the sky was totally dark. Random flashlight beams jostled around toward the other group of tents, and Clark rushed out in his boxers and a t-shirt, grabbing my arm protectively.

"Are you hurt?" he asked, and I shook my head.

We ran over to the others. "What was it?" Clark asked, and we got five different answers.

"Did you see the lights?"

"Where's Frank?"

"They came. The Grays came!"

That was when I saw the empty spot where Frank had set up camp outside. His hat was on the pillow, his car keys in the middle of the sleeping bag.

Oscar plodded out of his van, eyes bugging out. "Were they here?" he asked, looking at our group in the darkness.

The woman who'd made fun of Clay's body odor the night before spoke up. "They took Frank."

Oscar was panicked, and Clark stood right beside me. "Surveillance. I have cameras!" Oscar shouted, rushing to his van. Clark and I followed, leaving the others to discuss what they'd seen.

Oscar waved us inside, and there was a plastic table set up, a mattress on the ground, with dirty clothing strewn about. I hoped he didn't live in here full time. He flipped open an old laptop and activated a program.

"There we go. It clicks on with movement." Oscar didn't seem as concerned with losing one of his tour members as he did with capturing an image of the object. He scrolled through video, and on one frame, there was a bright flash; then it stopped, the sky dark once more.

"Why didn't it work?" he asked, staring at the screen. He rewound it and tried again.

"Come on," Clark said. "We'd better call the police."

July 15th – 2020

I was exhausted by the time I got to Cabin Ten and didn't

even bother to unpack my tent and other supplies. We'd been unable to find Frank, and Sheriff McCrae and the rest of the department were working on it now. After asking me and Clark a few questions, they sent us on our way. It was nine in the morning when I fell to my mattress, wishing for sleep.

Part of me thought it was all a ruse, one to give Oscar some publicity. It had to be. This Frank character was wearing a *Trust No One* hat, and was the only person sleeping outside a tent under the open skies. It was a big publicity stunt, and that was what I was going to write it as. I pieced together the night's events as I tried to sleep, but just when I was about to fall asleep, I remembered I was supposed to meet John for a boat ride today.

I had a few hours left, but no desire to play around on the water any longer. This town was triggering all sorts of emotions and memories to flood in, and I didn't think it was wise to be here any longer than possible. The Kick-Off started tomorrow, and for some reason, I felt it was a mistake to leave before then. I was going to get my damn closure on Cloud Lake, and I couldn't do that without making it through tomorrow.

My thoughts drifted to Clark, standing there close to me, telling me about a girl he'd wronged, and I pictured him there that night, kissing me instead, and fell asleep with a smile.

When I woke, the sun had moved to the other side of the cabin, and I rolled over, grabbing my phone. I had a text from a friend in New York, asking if I had dinner plans. Obviously, I hadn't mentioned where I was headed before I left. There were numerous emails in the inbox, and the time showed two in the afternoon. My head ached slightly, but it subsided as I closed my eyes and took a few deep breaths.

My bare feet carried me into the living room, and I opened the curtains, letting in sunlight. It was stuffy in here, and I cranked some windows wide, letting fresh air inside. I saw Clare by the water again, this time with a cup of coffee. I wanted to go talk to her, to see how she was after yesterday, but I couldn't bring myself to go out there quite yet.

I was ravenous, and I quickly whipped up scrambled eggs, consuming them in minutes and making coffee before having a shower. I texted John, asking what time we were supposed to meet up, hoping that he hadn't been waiting for my call all day. He was a busy guy with a business to run, so I doubted he had the day off anyway. He didn't reply right away, and I set the phone down, pulling out the laptop.

I scanned my inbox for anything of interest, finding a new one from Blaire. She'd already sent me about ten edited photos from last night: everything I'd asked for, and more. The last image was of Clark and me talking beside the cornfield, him chasing after me after I avoided listening to Oscar talk about Jessica Carver.

I zoomed in, seeing Clark standing near, leaning toward me in a protective manner. What would he say if he knew I was Jessica from that summer? He'd probably be furious I'd lied to him, but I was okay with the consequences. I'd be gone in a couple of days, and Clark would remain in Cloud Lake.

I replied, thanking Blaire for the images and asking her to send an invoice, hitting send. The next message was from Barns. I opened it and read the short but sweet message.

Hi Eva,

I hope everything is good with the story. I'm sorry I haven't been in contact. It's been a busy week here at the office.

I'm sorry. For everything.
Chris Barns

I read it again and again. It was nothing like his usual emails, and I focused on his last four words. What was he apologizing for? The magazine closing? I was way past that. I was going to reply, but after reading it one last time, I left it in the inbox for future contemplation.

Oscar Neville's book was still sitting there unread, and I pushed away the urge to comb over what he'd said about me. I got the gist. It was almost three thirty when I figured I may as well head over to John's place, since I knew where he lived. He'd probably be off work in an hour, and he'd have the pleasure of arriving home to find me waiting for him. It wasn't stalkerish at all.

Dan's truck was noticeably absent from Cabin Nine, and I felt bad I hadn't gone to talk to Clare. I just didn't have the energy for her drama today, not after last night. I knew I had to call the sheriff's department later to follow up on Frank's situation, and fully expected it to be revealed that Oscar had set the whole thing up. On my way out, I saw Trevor, the young guy who worked there, offer a wave, and it was only after I saw him in the rearview mirror from the road that it clicked that he'd wanted to talk to me. I'd just stop by later, or in the morning, to see what he wanted.

The drive to John's didn't take long, and I knew the roads like the back of my hand. I avoided looking at Grandma's cabin as I parked outside John's. It was almost hard to think of it as John's when I knew Mr. Martin had owned it. Each time I glanced at the porch or the dock, I saw Peter Martin staring at me.

I texted John once again, letting him know I was at his place; I didn't want to startle him. After sitting in the car with the windows all rolled down for five minutes, I decided to stroll over toward Grandma's. There was a definitive line in the grass where John stopped mowing. Grandma's old yard was covered in knee-high weeds and thick, unruly grass. It deserved better. At that moment, I wished Dad had sold it instead of ignoring it. Grandma would have hated to see it like this.

The grass draped over the cobblestone pathway, weeds erupting from between the bricks, making the walk uneven as I meandered to the porch. Several of the windows were broken, and someone had been there to board them up. I wondered who'd taken the time to do it. The water called to me, and I made my way through the unkempt beach to the dock. I slipped my sandals off and stepped up, feeling the wood beneath my bare feet for the first time in nearly twenty years.

The dock was a little rickety, and potentially rotten, but the water wasn't deep. My purse was in the car, and I left my cell with my sandals as I carefully walked to the edge of the dock, taking in the view. It looked much the same, but I could see the big houses across the lake shimmering in the distance. Other than that, it was almost like being transported to a different time at a familiar place.

I sat at the end, my toes dipping into the water. My feet swayed through the water, and I closed my eyes, almost hearing my grandma's voice, smelling her cooking. God, I'd lost a lot that summer, and Grandma would always be the biggest absence. If only I could have seen her one more time, been able to say goodbye like Dad and Zoe had. It wasn't fair.

But instead of wallowing in self-pity, I made my way to the shed and found the old lawnmower. Dad had taught me to use it, but this one was too old, too rusted out to fire up, so I moved over to John's rental and opened his shed. Inside, the tools were aged but pristine, and after pressing the choke and pulling the cord twice, the engine rumbled to life. I brought it over to Grandma's and started to cut the lawn. I regretted not having the sandals, my feet and ankles decimated by the roughage, but in twenty minutes, the small yard was cleaned up. I found some garbage under the brush and borrowed a bag from John's to toss it into.

It was an hour later by the time I'd watered her old plants and hosed the sidewalk off, picking weeds from between the stones. Before I knew it, I had half of John's shed contents spread out, and Grandma's place appeared almost liveable, at least from the outside. I dumped the remains of the firepit into the garbage bag and stood to appreciate the scene. I saw the large ash tree on the side of the property, separating her from the other neighbors, and found the lines cut into the trunk.

I laughed as I recalled my dad carving them when Zoe and I were only five and seven. He told us he had to, because our last name was Carver. The lines depicting our heights were deep, and Zoe and I had been so small, even though the tree had grown since then.

The house started to draw my attention, and I decided to look inside. When I stepped on the porch, I peered through a window, which was greasy and dirty. I used a hand to wipe away a clear spot, and it was a disaster. I was sure there had to be a few rodents and God knows what else living inside, and I left the front door closed. There wasn't anything left here for me.

I checked the time, seeing that it was well after eight already. The sun was descending in the sky, and John still hadn't texted. It was time to go. I touched the lawn mower handle and pushed it over to the shed, beginning the cleanup process.

July 13th – 2001

Dad finally gave in and let me go out on my own. It was Friday, the day of the Summer Kick-Off party. I think Grandma had something to do with his leniency, because he told us our grounding was over with, as long as we proved what grownups we could be today. He was sunburned from a trip on the water the morning before, and he sent me to the market to buy some sunscreen. Dad slipped a ten into my palm and told me to order a slushie with the change. What, was I ten? I was surprised he didn't try to ruffle my hair while he said it.

It felt great riding my bike, the wind blowing my hair around my face, the smells of the season thick and heady today. Everyone looked like they were in good moods. It was the perfect summer day: tourists were out spending money, the weather was at its peak, there wasn't a cloud above Cloud Lake, and it didn't hurt that it was Friday.

I kept my eyes peeled for Clark, hoping I'd run into him before resorting to hunting him down, but he was nowhere in sight. Buddy's Diner was packed, cars of all sorts parked along the street and across the way in the gravel overflow lot that was rarely used.

There were balloons along the windows, celebrating the Summer Kick-Off, and now I finally understood what the fuss was about. They were doing a pancake breakfast sponsored by the town of Cloud Lake, with all proceeds going to fund the party. I saw a few familiar faces among the line-up and went by the door, poking my head inside, my bike leaning against the wall of the building.

I recognized some of the kids Clark had been hanging out with inside, all overdressed in the blistering morning. I felt like an outsider in my white shorts and pink tank top as I pressed through the line, heading over to their group.

"Hey, guys," I said, and a girl glanced up, her eyes expressing nothing but disinterest.

"What do you want?" she asked.

A nervous bead of sweat dripped onto my forehead. "Have you seen Clark today?" I glanced around, thinking maybe I'd missed him in the crowd.

The girl eyed me with distaste and scoffed. "Is that a no?" I asked her.

One of the boys replied, the one Zoe had been chatting with. "Where's your sister?"

"At home. Have you seen Clark or not?" My hands went to my hips, like a scornful mother.

"He's working," the boy said. "Your sister going to be at the beach later?"

"Do you know where he's cutting grass?" I asked.

"Answer me first," he said.

"Fine. Yes, Zoe, my sister, is going to be at the party this afternoon. Clark?"

The boy grinned, and I could see all the adolescent thoughts threatening to hurt his brain as he likely started to picture my sister in a bikini. "Clark's cutting the park across from Town Square. Tell Zoe I'll be looking for her."

I nodded and started for the door, when I heard the waitress call for me. She was young, pretty, and I heard someone call her Izzy, though her nametag said Isabelle. "You. Did I see you on a bike?" she asked.

I fidgeted with my necklace, the one Grandma had given me. I'd put it on that morning when I left, feeling the need for a connection to my mom. I'd slipped it on after leaving the cabin and tried to remind myself to take it off again before seeing Dad. "Sure. My bike's outside."

"We're out of syrup, can you believe it? None of us can escape to grab some more. Would you be able to run to the market for me?" She had a look of desperation I couldn't ignore.

"What kind?" I asked as she slipped me fifty dollars. My eyes went wide. That was a lot of syrup.

"Whatever they have, the bigger the better. Can you ride with bags on the handles?" she asked, as if suddenly seeing how dumb it was to ask a girl on a bike to buy groceries.

"I'll be right back." I ran out the door, onto my bike, and rocketed down the sidewalk, heading for the store. It was only two blocks, and the doors were wide open, the AC issue still not solved. I shoved my bike in the rack and walked inside, feeling the wind of large floor fans blow against the skin of my bare legs.

I quickly found Dad's sunscreen and grabbed a cart, loading as many cans and squeeze bottles of syrup as I could. The check-out woman eyed me oddly as I pushed the cart up.

"I like to bathe in it," I said jokingly, but she didn't even crack a smile. I threw a pack of gum onto the conveyor and waited for her to double-pack them all. Soon I left with three dollars of change and five heavy bags of syrup.

Balancing them wasn't easy, and when I started forward, my knees kept hitting the bags.

"Need a hand?" a voice asked.

A glance over my shoulder showed me it was Clark. He was on a bicycle himself, and he was covered in small green blades of grass, especially his ankles. He had on plastic sunglasses and a sideways grin that meant trouble, but made me want to reach out and kiss him.

"I'd love some help." I pushed three bags toward him, and he peeked inside.

"Should I ask?" he laughed.

"Nope. We're going to the diner," I said, taking the lead.

In a minute, we were leaning our bikes beside each other along Buddy's exterior wall, the line-up outside the door now. Even from here I could smell the pancakes, bacon, and sausages frying away from inside. Clark took all five bags, not letting me carry any of it, and I held a finger up, searching through the bags for my gum and sunscreen.

"You work here?" he asked, raising an eyebrow.

"Just part time. I think I'll hand in my resignation today," I joked, and he grinned again. I liked it when he smiled at me. It made everything in the world feel all right.

Isabelle noticed us and came over, taking the bags. "And you even found backup. Good work, kid." She dropped the syrup off at the kitchen and returned, slipping a twenty-dollar bill into my hand. "You saved our butts. Thank you."

I left it on the counter. "Consider it a tip."

"At least let me feed you." She hesitated but took the twenty back with the grace of a royal and maneuvered to the front of the line, where a cook was flipping flapjacks onto the next patron's plate.

"Want to eat?" Clark asked me.

"I could eat," I replied shyly.

A few minutes later, we were outside, on a bench across the street, each with a Styrofoam plate full of meat and cooked batter.

"I didn't know if I was going to see you again," Clark said before taking a bite of pancake.

I poked at a sausage. "My dad found out we sneaked out, and he smelled beer on Zoe's breath. It wasn't good."

"I'm sorry. I shouldn't have invited you. Most of the kids around here can come and go as they please, as long as they're home by eleven."

"How about you?" I asked him. This time, it was me who inched over, accidentally touching his leg with my knee. If he noticed, he didn't show it.

"My parents are pretty cool. I don't really like to drink or smoke or any of that. There aren't a lot of choices in friends around here. It's a small town. When the summer's over and the tourists leave, school starts, and it's slim pickings there too. I kind of just hang with whoever's my age, I guess."

"You can hang out with me. I'm here all summer," I said, wondering when I'd gotten so brazen.

He finally glanced over at me, and I lifted a finger, wiping a speck of pancake from his lips. "I'd like that. Speaking of which, you heading to the beach today for the Kick-Off?"

"I sure am. Wouldn't miss it for the world. It might be my grandma's last one," I said quietly.

"Is she moving?" he asked.

"No. Cancer. She's supposed to be at the hospital, but she knows it's the end. I can see it in her eyes. I heard my dad arguing with her, but she wants to be at home. She wants to live a normal life for her last few days, instead of being surrounded by scrubs and beeping machines. Her words." I stared at my feet as I spoke, and Clark's arm settled around my shoulder, pulling me closer. It felt… right.

"I'm so sorry, Jess. That must be really hard for you," he said, and we sat there in silence while we pretended to eat, but mostly moved our food around our messy plates.

Eventually, Clark patted his knees with his palms and cleared his throat. "I have four more yards to cut, but I'll see you at the beach?" His eyes were blue and expressive. I wondered if he might kiss me, but the mood was sullen since bringing up Grandma.

"You bet. What time are you getting there?" I asked, maybe a little too hopefully.

"Around four. My parents are coming too, but I'll be able to blow them off," he said with a smirk. "Want me to ride home with you?"

I thought about it and took the opportunity. "Sure. That'd be nice." We headed over to our bikes, and soon we were racing down the side roads, making for the lake and Grandma's cabin. We arrived ten minutes later, and Clark pulled up short of the driveway, skidding to a halt on the gravel.

"I'd better go. See you later," he said, and I noticed his line of sight steer to the cabin, where Zoe was standing in her bikini. She lifted a hand and waved at us, at Clark, and before I knew it, Clark was gone, dust kicking up as he pedaled quickly.

July 15th – 2020

John wouldn't answer his phone, and I wasn't about to be a desperate Betty about it, so I took off, deciding to stop at the sheriff's office to see if there was any news on Frank. It was quiet there, only two marked cars in the parking lot, and I doubted McCrae was around. I went inside after the streetlight flipped on, the daylight sensors activating the bulbs as the sun crept beyond the treeline.

McCrae was occupied in someone's office, his back to me, and I stood there patiently waiting for him to finish his conversation.

"We have to let Teddy Martin go," he said, and the room began to spin. Teddy Martin. Peter Martin's son. What was he doing here? I listened, taking a step farther into the room and trying to stay undetected.

The other voice was muffled, and I couldn't hear their side.

"There's not enough proof, and we searched the place a week ago. Squeaky clean. He's got a business, and there are a few testimonies of his character these days. We can't take every anonymous sighting of the guy trading pills for cash that we hear. We just don't have the resources," McCrae said.

I managed to hear the other man in the room. He must have stood up and walked toward the door. "What about Mark Fisher? His brother's blaming Teddy. He said they were in it together, and things went sour."

"Scott, you know we need proof. Evidence. Something we don't have in this case. We'll keep an eye on him, but there's not enough to detain him any longer," McCrae said, and I cringed as he turned, seeing me.

I tried to look nonchalant, like I hadn't been listening.

"Miss Heart. What can I do for you?" he asked, unable to keep the annoyance from his voice.

"I wanted to follow up on Frank. Have you found him?" I asked, still reeling from the news on Teddy Martin being in town. I hadn't even considered that a possibility. I could recall the few times I'd seen him; the first when he was smoking weed at Local Beach behind Zoe, while she drank her first beer.

"Turns out Oscar Neville is a devious man. Frank was

inside Henry's house the whole time. Thought it was a good way to add some excitement to the whole Alien Adventure thing." McCrae sighed and crossed his arms across his expansive chest.

I wasn't surprised. "Good. Well, you know what I mean. Sorry to come over here so late," I said. I wanted to ask about Teddy, but what reason did I have? I decided to try. "Is there a drug problem in Cloud Lake?"

"You find any small town, big town, city, or otherwise in the world, and tell me there isn't a drug problem. We have weed, even a bit of heroin sneaking up on us, but mostly pills. They're easier to obtain and far more dangerous than the old days of homegrown pot," he told me.

"Who's Teddy Martin?" I asked, using my reporter voice.

"Just a local man. Been here a long time. Spent some time in the slammer, like his old man before him. Not a great lineage there. Again, every town has a family that messes up the community. Ours is the Martins," he said, regret forming deep lines on his forehead.

I wanted to ask more, but his expression told me he was closed for business. "Have a good night, Sheriff. See you tomorrow?"

He looked confused, before a light bulb went off. "Summer Kick-Off. I'll be there. I thought you were leaving town?"

"Friday. Going to stick around for this last day of fun in the sun," I said, my light tone sounding fake even to me. McCrae didn't seem to notice.

It was dark by the time I drove to the Cloud Lake Cabins, and when I pulled up, my beams shone on my porch, bathing Clare in their bright light. She was sitting there in a white bathrobe, holding a coffee cup. I turned the engine off, and the lights dimmed, leaving her to form a dark shadow.

I hesitated but left the car, throwing a smile I didn't feel across my face. "Clare, what are you doing here?"

She held the cup with both hands, and I saw she was barefoot. "I wanted to apologize for yesterday."

I considered her erratic behavior. Drinking far too much wine, taking pills that weren't hers, and talking about drowning. It was all unnerving. "Don't. You're in a tough spot." I glanced over, seeing Dan's truck gone… again. "Where is he tonight?"

"Celebrating. Probably the Sticky Pig Pub."

"Did he secure the land?" I asked.

She nodded. "Looks that way. Guess he'll be here a lot more."

"And you?" I asked, not wanting to outright say it.

"I'm going home. Tomorrow. I told him we were through." Clare set the cup down, and I sat beside her, grabbing her hand.

"Are you okay? Do you have somewhere to go?" I asked, thrilled she was leaving the man, but worried she wasn't in the right frame of mind to deal with it.

"My mother's in Ohio. She's a good woman. Kind of feels like I'm heading home with my tail between my legs," she said.

"It's the right call. I can already see the change in you, Clare," I squeezed her hand, and she finally broke a grin.

"Thank you. Thanks for being there for me yesterday. I don't think… I don't want to think what I might have done," she admitted.

"Do you want to stay with me tonight?" I asked, unsure if that was the right move. I tried to imagine Dan coming home from the bar, angry with Clare. One last beating before she left him for good.

She shook her head. "Dan said he was going to find a

room at the motel. He took his stuff already."

"How are you getting to your mom's?" I asked.

"Bus, I suppose," she said.

"At least let me drop you off at the station tomorrow," I offered, and she nodded.

"That would be nice. Thanks again, Eva," she said.

I had to know. "Clare? I know this might be in bad taste, but I have to ask you something," I said, the words sputtering from my mouth.

"What?"

"Where did you buy those pills?" I asked, and she stood up.

"A local guy."

"Who?"

"I guess he was found in the lake," she said quietly.

"You bought them from Mark Fisher?" I asked, thinking about what I'd heard in McCrae's office.

"Yes."

I didn't push her any further. I could tell she already felt like a terrible human, somehow mixing herself into the affairs of dead homegrown drug dealers.

"See you tomorrow?" I asked her, and she agreed before slowly walking home. Her cup was still on my porch, and I thought about calling to her, but picked it up instead. There was a note taped to my door, and I snatched it off and unlocked the cabin, turning on the interior light.

I flipped the deadbolt, suddenly not feeling safe in Cloud Lake, not now that I knew Teddy Martin was still lurking around. It all rang a bell in my head. The Martins, the drugs… his father dealt them too, and was only caught because of me. I shoved the thoughts away and read the note, scrawled in messy handwriting.

Miss Heart,

Please stop by the office at your earliest convenience. There is an issue with payment.

Trevor

I lowered the message and immediately assumed Barns had gone bust and his credit card was no longer any good. Worst case scenario, I pulled out my own card to pay for the nights, and I'd have to fight to get reimbursed. I was sweaty after spending hours in the sun cleaning up Grandma's cabin, and I slipped into the shower, brewing a pot of coffee while I did so. By the time I was finished, the mirrors were fogged, and I wrapped a towel around my wet hair, smelling the fresh brew. It instantly perked me up, and I opened my laptop, reviewing my notes. I scratched out the completed items from my to-do list, and only one remained.

- ~~Talk to the local Sheriff's department~~
- ~~Locate Chester Brown's address and interview him~~
- ~~Locate Mark Fisher's brother~~
- ~~Talk to Summer Kick-Off committee council member~~
- ~~Locate Carly Miller family, friends, and/or parents~~
- ~~Go to the feed store and talk to Henry about the Tourist UFO watch group~~
- ~~Find out if Clark still lives in Cloud Lake~~
- Find out any details about Chester's cousin Carol. How many people have gone missing here?

Chester Brown claimed his cousin had been taken by the Grays, but there was no supporting evidence. Just like the fact that Frank's disappearance was a hoax, and Jess Carver, a scared fourteen-year-old version of myself, had been returned. So had Carly Miller, and no matter what my own faded and blocked memories said about that week, people were behind our abductions, not lean gray aliens.

It made me think about my mother, and I fiddled with the chain around my neck. I held the small golden cross, and for a moment, I let myself imagine that she'd been taken by a flying saucer against her will. That she'd never intended to leave Zoe and me, even our father, alone and behind, but she'd had no choice. Maybe she was still out there somewhere, thinking about me.

"Stop being so stupid," I told myself out loud. *She left you, and you were taken into a dark room by Peter Martin. You were kept there while he drugged you; the very same drugs that were found in his house could have done that to your body.* I mentally scanned the toxicology reports that had come up inconclusive so long ago, the very same ones the judge chose to ignore. They saw a girl taken by a self-proclaimed drug pusher, and threw the book at him.

I closed my eyes, the light of my laptop suddenly too oppressive, and I recalled my dad's face when the verdict came guilty. He was so elated, and I'd only watched him with a knot in my stomach and detached emotions.

My fingers found the fresh Word document, and I stared at the blinking cursor before typing.

Cloud Lake is a seemingly perfect tourist location for the summer months. The beach is idyllic: clean sand, and big open skies. Skies that many claim to have seen flying saucers hovering over in the last few decades. Stories date back to before the great Roswell conspiracy of the nineteen forties, but evidence is lacking in the mysterious sightings, as usual.

While Cloud Lake looks calm on the surface, below the gentle waves, we find a tumultuous past, full of drugs, abductions, and abuse. Not from aliens, or Grays as the locals call them, but from the tangled web the tourists and residents weaved.

I sat there, staring at the words, hating every one of them. With one fell swoop, I highlighted and deleted the batch, closing the document. This was one story I wasn't going to tell. Barns was going to have to suck it up and accept my resignation from the *Brownstone Beat*. That life felt so far away at this moment, like it was someone else's, and all I had was myself and Cloud Lake.

My coffee was hot and dark, all the cream used up throughout the week. I could leave right now. Pack my things and head home, away from this place that somehow felt like I belonged here. It wasn't real, though. It was all a trap, one that I was leading myself into knowingly.

I grabbed my phone and found Clark's number. He'd given it to me at Henry's, and I had the urge to ask him here. To explain everything to him. He would understand why I couldn't tell him who I was. He'd hug me, hold me tight, and keep me safe from this place.

My phone beeped, and I almost dropped it in surprise. Maybe Clark decided… Nope. It was from John's number.

I'm so sorry about today. I got caught up on a job, and there was no power out there, so I couldn't charge my phone. Forgive me?

I read it, feeling relief that he was indeed okay. I couldn't be angry with him; it was, after all, only a boat ride during the week. He was busy trying to make a name for himself in Cloud Lake, and there was no faulting him for that.

No problem at all. I was busy too, I texted back.

Was that your handiwork?

He could only be talking about Grandma's place. *I hope you don't mind. I borrowed some stuff, but put everything in its place when I was finished.*

It looks great. I don't mind one bit. Kick-Off tomorrow?

I wasn't sure if he was implying we go together, or if he was just asking if I was still going. I didn't have room to complicate my life anymore. I was going to stop by, make my peace with Clark, and leave. *I'll be there for a bit. See you if I see you?* I hoped the text wasn't too dismissive.

Perfect. Casual cool.

I laughed. I really did like John. He was handsome, hard-working, had a sense of humor, and he really seemed like the type that would dote on you. In another lifetime, I suspected we'd make a good pairing, but not in this one. In this one, my heart was a teenage girl's, and it belonged to a young man with blond hair, blue eyes, and a sideways grin.

Talk later.

I set the phone down. The compulsion to call Clark and spill the beans had passed. I'd tell him tomorrow. I had to. It was the only way I could leave and never feel the need to come back to Cloud Lake. I needed to end my affair with the place; the trauma was too deep-rooted, and it was time to cut it out and move forward. Texas was sounding better and better.

Scrolling through my contacts, I found Zoe's number, and I knew she'd be heading to bed if she wasn't already in it, reading a worn paperback romance.

Ready to talk about visiting. Still have that spare room with my name on it? My finger hovered over the send button, and I bit my lip as I tapped it.

Zoe must have had her phone beside her, because the response came quickly. *I'll wash the sheets tomorrow. Just tell me when. I love you, dude.*

This brought a smile to my face. Everything was looking up. *Love you too.*

I left the words I was thinking out of the text.

I forgive you.

July 16th – 2020

It was Thursday morning, the opening day of the Summer Kick-Off and my last few hours in Cloud Lake. I felt good, better than I had in years, but coming off medication wasn't an easy feat. I glared at my bottle of pills, almost unable to believe that I'd functioned for most of the week without them. I left the lid on and shoved them into my open purse.

For once, I had a future staring me in the face, one that was unknown but positive. Cloud Lake and what had happened as a kid were going to be put to rest, and this trip was doing what a half dozen therapists and medications had never been able to. It was freeing my memories and barriers.

My clothes didn't take long to pack, and I threw on capris and a plain white tee with a deep V neck. My hair was loose and frizzy from the humidity, and I left it that way, trying to have it feel as free as I did at that moment. There was a new Eva Heart... Jessica Carver in town. I wondered what it would be like to change my name back. Maybe I'd find out.

My computer was charging, and I gathered all my things into a pile by the door. I'd come for them later, after breakfast. My fridge was all but empty, and I took a moment to collect the last egg and an old apple from the counter, throwing them into the garbage, which I tied up and brought with me outside.

I grabbed the note from Trevor and headed toward the gravel road. Families were already outside, and I waved to a couple of kids, who ran for the cabin shyly as they saw me. My shoes crunched against the rocky road, my steps lighter than they'd felt in years. I tossed the garbage bag into the communal bin before changing my direction to the entrance of Cloud Lake Cabins.

The office had an open sign, and I knocked before pressing the door open. Trevor was there, sitting behind a desk, and he glanced up when I entered.

"Sorry to leave a note like that, Miss Heart," he said,

eyeing the paper in my hand.

"No problem at all. What's the issue?" I asked, wallet already zipped open.

"You were prepaid for four nights, but not last night. Are you sticking around for longer?" Trevor asked, clicking away at the keyboard.

"No. I'm leaving today."

"Do you mind paying for last night, then? I can give you a great deal, it's just, I can't do any gratis… management likes to see sold-out bookings or else I lose my bonus," he said, and I laughed, letting him know there was no problem with me paying.

"My boss can reimburse me later." I slid my card over to him, and he smiled as he took it, keying in the digits before printing the receipt on a clunky old laser printer. It jammed, and he went over to it, pulling the damaged paper out, and soon another sheet flowed out freely.

"Do you mind?" he asked, holding the torn paper up.

"That'll do just fine," I said, and he had me sign my name before handing me the receipts. I looked at the first sheet, the one Barns had paid for, and my world crumbled in. The name on the reservation stood out like it was in flashing lights. *Theodore Martin.* "What… what…" I couldn't find the words, and Trevor stared at me, blank-faced.

"What is it, Eva?" he asked, finally using my first name.

"The booking. Who made it?" I asked as my pulse raced through my body, the heavy pounding filling my head.

He returned his gaze to the computer and shrugged. "The guy didn't say who he was, specifically. He only gave yours, and spouted off a credit card."

I stared at the name, trying to understand how this could be. It didn't make any sense, and I stumbled backwards, looking for a seat. I plopped onto a sofa behind me and stared at the paperwork. Trevor was saying something, but I couldn't hear him.

My hands fumbled into my pocket for my phone, and I pulled it out, searching for my work contacts. I found Harry's number and dialed it, taking deep breaths alongside each ring, my head beginning to clear.

"Hello," Harry answered.

"Harry. Is Barns in the office?" I asked without preface.

"Eva, what is it? You're scaring me," he said.

"Is Barns in the office?" I asked again, this time yelling.

"No. He didn't come in today. No one knows where he is," Harry admitted.

"Do me a favor. Go into his office. Search everything for this name. Theodore Martin. Teddy Martin."

"What's this about? You want me to break into my uncle's office and search through his things?" Harry's voice was incredulous.

"Harry, if you've ever cared about me in the least, do this for me. Now!" I shouted, and the other end of the line was silent for a few seconds.

"I'm on it. I'll call you when I have something," Harry said.

I seized the papers, and Trevor called my name, but I ignored him and stalked to my cabin, feeling the need to escape it. There was no coming back to this place. I tried to think if I'd seen a strange man around the cabins over the last while, someone with the eyes of Peter Martin. I knew those eyes well.

I drew a blank. Could Dan have been him, playing a ruse with Clare? Was that where she got the drugs from? Teddy Martin? That kind of made sense, but there was no evidence there.

It didn't take long for my bags to end up in the trunk of my car, and I sat in the driver's seat. I glanced at Cabin Nine as I drove away, remembering that I'd offered Clare a ride into town. That could all be part of the setup. Lure me inside the cabin again; this time, Teddy would be there, ready to slit my throat.

What did he want with me after all this time? How had he tracked me down? There were so many questions floating around my head, but I had none of the answers. I drove, my hands shaking on the steering wheel. I gripped it tighter, trying to stop the movement, to alter my fear and turn it to anger.

Should I go to the police? I wondered if McCrae would listen to me, or would that paint a bigger target on myself? If Teddy was in town after luring me here, he'd be trying to make a move. He'd only booked me for four nights, but he'd been detained yesterday. I knew that because I'd heard the sheriff mention it.

I needed to act normal. If he'd tracked me down in New York under my alias, I couldn't leave and risk further encounters. It was too risky to visit Texas and bring danger to my sister's family. I had to face this now. I'd go to the Kick-Off, where there were a lot of witnesses, and find Teddy. I was sure I could recognize him if I saw the man. He was likely a burnout, a useless dredge on society, maybe a creep like his father. I suddenly was so certain that he'd been the one to take Carly Miller that night, only to return her, like his dad had done with me.

Carly needed closure too, and I was going to find that for her. I'd call the police at the right time; they always had a strong presence at the Kick-Off. It was a foolhardy plan, but I felt good about it. As I neared town, my belly grumbled, reminding me I hadn't eaten much in the last day or so. I wasn't sure I'd be able to stomach any food, but I had to try.

I drove by the Town Office and remembered finding Clark there, cutting the grass on the morning of the Kick-Off back in the day. There was a pancake breakfast. I had the impulse to stop and pulled over at the market, venturing inside to buy one maple syrup squeeze bottle. After finally letting myself think about that summer, I knew Isabelle was the very same waitress who had sent me on the errand that led me to Clark.

With the syrup in the passenger seat, I drove to Buddy's Diner, parked across the street in the overflow, and left the car. I looked around, feeling like someone might be watching my every move. It was unnerving. I honestly couldn't recall having that sensation since… since Peter Martin. Like father, like son. I was anxious to hear from Harry and checked my phone. Still no text, email, or call from him. I knew Barns liked to lock his door, so Harry was probably struggling to gain access.

The parking lot was half full, and the street parking was jam-packed full of early risers. It was twice as extravagant as I remembered it as a kid; far more people were here, and now there were tables set up in the empty lot beside the diner. Isabelle was serving pancakes and sausage to the happy line-up of people. A food donation box up front was already swelling with gifts, and a massive old pickle jar sat beside the pancake station, flush with green bills and change settling on the bottom.

There was a huge sign above it. *Buddy's Diner's Fiftieth Annual Kick-Off Breakfast.* My gaze shifted from face to face, trying to determine if Teddy was among the crowd. So far, I hadn't seen him. I had the syrup tucked under my arm as I slid into the line behind a young family. The wife had a tiny baby in her arms, a bonnet covering the child's eyes from the incoming sunlight. It reached a hand out at me, and clenched its fingers.

What was I even going to do if I saw Teddy? Confront him? Let everyone know who I was? It really didn't matter anymore. I wasn't the one who'd been in the wrong. I had to protect myself, and knew just where to go to ensure my own safety. I had a feeling the old farmer would be on my side, maybe not even ask any questions.

We moved slowly through the line, and by the time I arrived at the serving station, Isabelle was gone. I set the syrup down. "In case you run out," I said to the young man flipping pancakes, and he stared at it, unsure of what to do with the bottle. I slipped a twenty out of my purse and pushed it through the opening cut into the pickle-jar lid with a smile. Since I didn't see the waitress, I took my food, slathered in sticky goodness, and crossed the street, sitting on the exact same bench Clark and I had shared back then.

I wished he was here now. I wanted to talk to him. To hear his side of the story, since he'd let it slip that he'd followed me to the cabin, even though I'd never known that. To him, I was Eva Heart, not Jess Carver.

My stomach was hungry, but my brain was telling me not to eat. I tried to find a happy medium, and ate half of the food methodically as I thought about this week. I needed to know how Barns figured into this.

"It *is* you," a voice said, and I looked up quickly to see Isabelle there. "Do you mind if I have a seat?"

I wanted to deny whatever accusation was coming, to tell her she was mistaken, but I didn't. I motioned for her to sit on the bench beside me.

"Just who do you think I am?" I asked.

"The syrup. You remember me, don't you?" she asked, and I saw the same woman working her tail off, looking more than twenty years older.

I nodded. "I didn't at first, I swear. This place… it's all

coming back to me. Well, most of it," I said.

"Why are you really here? A story? What's with the name, Eva?" she asked.

"I changed it a long time ago. Do you know how strange it is to have someone in your college class Google you and find out you were abducted by a creep when you were a kid? It was absolutely terrible. Word ran through the entire college within days. I couldn't go anywhere without someone making a bad joke, or even worse, staring at me with those sad, pity-filled gazes. I'm fine. I don't even remember that week. I never have," I said, as much for her as for myself.

"Oh, honey. I'm so sorry. For all of it." Isabelle stared at me with the same sad expression I'd mentioned, and she seemed to become aware of it.

"You didn't do anything," I said.

"But this town… this town did. You weren't treated fairly. I can't imagine how you felt. Your father… your grandmother passing away while you were… I'm just sorry," she said, with convincing empathy.

"Thank you, Izzy." I used her nickname, and she smiled.

"Why are you here?" she asked.

I didn't know why I should tell her anything, but it was nice to finally be myself, even for a few minutes. "It *was* for a story, but I think I was manipulated into coming," I whispered.

Her eyes went wide. "Who would do something like that?"

There was no harm in telling her. Actually, it was probably smart to make someone else aware of it. "Teddy Martin."

She made a *tsk* sound with her mouth. "You poor girl."

I explained everything: the assignment, the cabin being

223

booked under his credit card.

"You do know Teddy, right?" I asked.

She nodded. "Don't see much of him. He went away for some time; busted for possession. I heard he's back in town, and that he's cleaned himself up a bit."

"What does he look like?" I asked.

She shook her head. "I'd know him to see him, but it's been at least ten years. People can change a lot in ten years."

"You recognized me," I said plainly.

"Only with the subtle reminder. How's that sister of yours?" she asked.

"Good. Married, kids, living the dream life she always had, I guess," I told her.

Isabelle nodded slowly. "You have to leave. You can't be here if Teddy is after you. Or go to the police."

"He'll be at the Kick-Off. I know it. I have McCrae on speed dial. This is going to end today. If things go as planned, I'll have enough evidence of his entrapment by this afternoon," I said, hoping Harry was getting somewhere with Barns' computer.

The cook was shouting at Isabelle. The line was huge, and I could understand the frustration on the waitress' face. "Will you wait here? I want to help," she said, and I nodded, knowing that I wouldn't.

We both stood, and she pulled me in for a hug. Isabelle had tears in her eyes. "Jessica Carver. I can't believe it's really you. And you found Carly Miller. What are the chances?"

"Sometimes the universe works in remarkable ways," I told her.

"Yes. Stay put. We can figure this out," she said, and ran off, crossing the street only to receive an angry honk from a bald man in a convertible.

I waited until she was busy, her attention on the task at hand, and I proceeded to my car, before driving down Main Street toward Chester Brown's farm.

I pulled onto Chester Brown's driveway and was surprised to see the old farmer emerge from his barn almost intuitively. Turtle plodded along beside him, never more than four feet from his master. I parked near his house and made my way to the door, wondering exactly how to ask for what I'd come for.

"You again. Thought you'd gone an' left town. Finish the story?" he asked, hands on hips.

"Not quite, but I'm close. Are you heading to the lake for the Kick-Off today?" I asked, as if this was nothing more than a casual conversation.

"Don't get around much, specially to those things. Not comfortable for me an' Turtle down there in the crowds any longer," he said. If he was curious why I stopped by, he didn't ask. "Besides, they think I'm a bit of a loon after talkin' 'bout them Grays to the media."

"I believe you," I told him, and I did. If there was one living person I trusted, it was Chester Brown. If my grandma believed, so would I. Up until this point, I'd been so sure that my subconscious had tricked me. My dad had convinced me that my memories weren't real, without calling me a liar to my face. He just couldn't understand why I wouldn't fess up about what Peter Martin had allegedly done to me.

Allegedly. I'd allowed myself to think he was guilty for so long. Now, standing here talking with Chester, I wasn't so sure. Images were trying to break through from behind my mind's walls, old sturdy barriers, with dusty pictures

225

stacked neatly of that night; that week, ending with my dad's face as I saw him running to me. Picking me up, his wet tears splashing on my confused cheeks.

"You do? Well, that's a good girl. I s'pose you'd done gone and seen the lights too." He didn't ask, he stated.

I nodded, unable to keep lying to myself or others. "I did. I did see the lights."

He didn't mention anything further, just forced a smile. "Careful out there today. Weather's changin'. Use to feel it in my right knee. Now I feel her everywhere." He stretched, something skeletal popping inside him.

I glanced up at the perfectly blue sky, dismissing his concern for inclement weather. "I need to ask a favor," I said quietly.

His eyes were rheumy, cataracts looming in the sunlight. "Fer you, anything, dear."

No sense in tiptoeing around the request. "I need to borrow a gun."

He waved me toward the house. "You wantin' a rifle or handgun?" Turtle let out a low bark, and nudged my leg as we walked up the porch steps.

July 13th – 2001

I pulled the trigger, water spilling from the gun toward the porcelain clown's mouth. The buzzer sounded, but I was only halfway to full.

"Want to play again, little miss?" the man behind the game counter asked.

I shook my head, searching for Zoe in the crowd. Finally, the big party night was upon us, and it was even more grandiose than ever. There was a giant Ferris wheel set up at the base of the parking lot, and I hadn't gone for a ride yet. I wanted to find Clark first so we could sit together, isolated for a good ten minutes. I thought about what it would be like to halt at the top, waiting for people to be loaded into the cage, the two of us looking out over the lake. Maybe he'd kiss me. My stomach released butterflies at the idea.

It was busy, still before five o'clock. Once all the locals were off work, it would turn even crazier, and I knew Dad was hoping Grandma would be ready to leave before too long. She was worse by the day, weaker by the hour, but she'd demanded an outing here.

Zoe was near the water, sitting on a stump while a local artist sketched a caricature of her. Even though it amplified her eyes and nose, she still looked stunning, as if anyone could make my sister look bad.

"What's up, Jess? Find anything fun to do here?" she asked. The truth was, I was enjoying myself, but clearly she wasn't. She likely thought she was too grown up for all of this merriment and games.

"Kind of bored," I lied. "I'm going to find Dad and Grandma. Have something to eat. You want anything?"

She shrugged. "I should be there soon. Grab me a hot dog?"

I ran toward the spot where I'd left Dad. The deep sand tried filling my sandals with each step on the beach, the granules hot in the bright sun. People were still milling around the lake, suntanning, playing frisbee, and people rode by on their big motorboats, blasting music.

The entire area was vibrating with energy, and I soaked it all in, loving the feeling. But when I found Grandma and Dad, his posture was slumped in defeat, and she was on the brink of tears.

"What is it?" I asked, grabbing her hand.

"Nothing, dear. Your father's worrying too much," Grandma said. She slipped on her oversized black glasses, the kind with lenses along the sides to keep the sun from entering.

Dad looked ready to defend himself, but the wind blew from his sails. He resigned himself to sitting down, and he cracked a beer. His first, from the looks of it.

"I was thinking of eating. Do you guys want something?" I asked, hoping to be helpful.

They glanced at each other, a silent transfer of thoughts I didn't understand.

"Uhm, grab me a burger, please, honey. Mom?" Dad

was being so polite. I felt the time ticking away from Grandma, as she didn't respond. "Get her a water."

"I'll take a burger too. Cheeseburger," she said, her sights set in my direction.

"Mom, are you sure…"

She grabbed my wrist with a firm hold. "Extra pickles," she added with a smile.

Before Dad could argue, I ran off, heading for the large commercial grills set up in the center of the beach. Smoke cascaded from the cooking meats, and already there was a small line-up. Dad had slipped me some money earlier, and I pulled out a twenty, ready to pay for dinner when the group of kids from Local Beach came into view. They were sitting on a picnic table – not the benches, but the top, smoking and loudly cracking jokes at people as they casually strode by.

Clark wasn't with them, and I turned away, moving into the line, not wanting them to see me. After a minute, I peered over, seeing that the older one was with them. His hair was shaggy, even a little noticeably greasy from this distance. Still no sign of Clark.

"Next," a voice said, and a gruff woman smiled as I placed my order. "That's a lot of food for a little girl."

I wanted to tell her I wasn't a little girl, that I was going to kiss a boy tonight, and we would go steady. Instead, I smiled, accepting the food. There was a table of optional sides, and I threw some baked beans on Dad's plate and potato salad on Zoe's, grabbing some salad for my own. I saw the jar of pickles and added them on Grandma's bun until they were pouring off the sides.

By the time I made it over to my family, Zoe was there, showing them the beach artist's rendition of her, and Grandma was admiring how beautiful her granddaughter was in pencil.

229

I took the image in, unable to shake the feeling that this was going to be one of our family's final meals as a four-some.

July 16th – 2020

My phone rang as I drove toward town, and I didn't recognize the number. I answered it despite my gut telling me to leave it be.

"Hello," I said.

"Is this… Eva?" a small voice echoed.

"It is…" I tried to think of who was on the other line. "Carly?" I asked, finally cluing in.

"I need… can you… can you come over?" she asked.

Panic started to well inside me, but the girl's voice was too calm to be an emergency. "Sure. Are you okay?"

There was a pause. "I'm not sure. I tried to talk to my parents, but they don't understand," she said.

I had an inkling what it was about. She was remembering. Could this all be real? Could Oscar Neville have been right about me? The more I was in Cloud Lake, the more I felt the truth seeping from the lake and into my blood. If that was the case, Teddy Martin had every right to be upset with me, but the evidence… there was real, legitimate evidence. I gripped my necklace as I drove, making the turn toward Carly's.

"Are you there, Eva?" Carly asked. I'd been so caught up in my own thoughts, I'd forgotten we were still connected.

"I'll be there in a few minutes. I was close. Are your parents home?" I asked.

"My mom is, but she's having a nap. Meet me in the back yard? We have a swing set," she said.

"See you soon." I hung up, anticipating the conversation with Carly. I also was acutely aware I had a gun in my glove box at that moment. A borrowed weapon from an old farmer, and I doubted it was registered to anyone. Showing up at the abducted girl's house with a gun in my car was probably a bad life choice, but I didn't have a lot of time.

I parked a couple houses down, glad for the tree cover from the sun as I walked onto the sidewalk and toward the back fence of the Millers' expansive yard. Huge trees stretched at the rear of the house, and I found Carly swinging on a wooden slat, chains hanging it to a thirty-foot branch overheard. There was an empty swing beside her, and she motioned to it when she saw me. Her face broke into a weak smile as I approached, and I was surprised when the timid girl got off the swing to wrap me in a big hug.

"Thank you for coming," she said, sounding so much like an adult. Traumatic events often caused kids to grow up too fast, and I wished she could rewind her life and reclaim her innocence. Only there was no use trying to find that place. The "before it all happened." I knew from experience.

"Is it the lights?" I asked, before she said anything.

Her eyes opened wide. "I saw them flashing. I only went outside on a dare from Tina. We were playing truth or dare, and Katie had just told us she wanted to kiss Kevin on a truth. I chose dare, and they told me I had to run into the forest barefoot. I didn't think it was a big deal, but when I stepped out there, I saw something past the trees.

"I wanted to leave, but with all the rumors around town about aliens, I had to see. I needed to know, to be one of the special ones who got to see the lights." Carly's face contorted, and she began sobbing. I reached over, taking her hand.

"It's okay to be upset," I told her.

Carly gave me the saddest smile, wiping tears from her ruddy cheeks, and kept talking. "I cut my foot, but the lights were flashing faster, closer, and by the time I came out the other side, they were right above me." She stopped talking, her feet planted in a worn-out spot in the grass directly below the swing.

I'd been expecting something like this, but it still hit me in the gut like a sucker punch.

"You must think I'm crazy. I told my mom and dad, and they told the sheriff that a truck must have been out there, that I saw headlights before I was taken. Only, I heard the sheriff say there were no tire tracks in the area. What happened to me?" she asked, looking at me like I somehow held all the answers.

"What else do you remember?" I asked.

"Nothing. I've tried really hard, but I've had some dreams. I was alone in a room. At least, I think I was. There were tubes in me." She patted her arms and neck, and I leaned in, seeing no sign of punctures.

"Keep this to yourself for now, okay, Carly? I'll try to help you, but you mustn't tell anyone else. Believe me, it will only be harder on you and your family, and they won't ever believe that's the truth," I told her.

"Why? That's what happened," she said.

"Because if you weren't taken by a bad man, then the answer is too scary for their minds to understand," I said.

"If it wasn't a bad man, then who took me?"

"I don't know."

My nerves were fried when I pulled away from Carly's. We had talked for a while longer, and by the time I left, I hated that Carly had to deal with the fact that she might have been abducted by aliens. I hoped my presence helped her and wished I'd had a mentor to carry me through my own pain.

I checked my phone at a stop sign and tried calling Harry, but my call went to voicemail. I left a message, asking him to contact me right away. It was three in the afternoon, and I didn't want to arrive to the Kick-Off too early. Every piece of me knew Teddy would be there looking for me, and I had one more place to visit before heading over there.

The drive to Grandma's house was fast, and I parked in front of it, hardly feeling like it was the same cabin I'd arrived at yesterday. With the grass being cut and the weeds all pulled from the garden, it looked like someone might actually live there for the first time in forever.

I peered over at the Martin cabin, where John's truck was absent. He'd still be working, and I was glad he wasn't there. I didn't want to have an awkward goodbye with a man I wasn't meant to be with.

The porch steps groaned under my weight, the rotten boards threatening to fold under the pressure. I tried the door and found it was locked. Without any guilt, I found a rock and bashed through the small pane above the door handle, using it to brush any remaining glass shards free before I stuck my hand inside and unlocked the door.

It swung open with an angry creak, the old hinges rusted and unused for so long. I made for the kitchen first, thoughts of my grandmother pouring over me. I opened the drawer where she used to put the aprons Dad bought for her and found them mostly intact, safe in their plastic wrappers. I smiled as I touched the top one, fuzzy bunnies in various positions covering the white backdrop. I remembered him giving her that, and she'd told him she was more of a duck person. I laughed at the memory and moved toward our old bedroom.

There was evidence of rodents everywhere, and I tried not to think about the walls being filled with rats as I pushed my and Zoe's bedroom door open. It was just as we'd left it, with the exception of a thick layer of dust, and water damage spread out on the ceiling.

Beside Zoe's bed were stacks of old paperbacks, ranging from western romances to classic fantasy books. Anything Grandma had read over the years ended up in here for my sister to cycle through. I read them on occasion as well, but with far more prudent taste than Zoe.

We had only stayed in Cloud Lake until August of 2001, but that had been enough time for me to dwell on things and start to remember. I knew there were drawings in my dresser, and when I opened my drawer, there they were, stacked in a neat pile. Truth be told, I was surprised my dad hadn't destroyed the sketches, but he'd been so sure it was my mind tricking myself. He preferred my strange drawings to the truth, or his version of reality.

I went to the small desk tucked into the corner of the room, dusting the wooden chair's seat off before sitting. The first picture was of a dark night sky, angry black lines scratched across the white sheet. I'd drawn in yellow stars; then the glowing circular vessel hung above a sketch of a girl. She wore the same clothing I'd had on that night.

Then there was a face, and I dropped the sheet, finally having a recollection of drawing this image. The eyes were black, wide and oval. A lipless mouth, potentially a product of my lacking artistic ability. I sat down on the old wooden chair, plopping firmly as my knees gave out. My hand shook, and tears fell freely as I grabbed the next piece of paper.

It showed a girl in a bed, and just like Carly had mentioned in her dreams, there were tubes running to her arms.

I stared at the sheets, their implications causing me to finally believe the truth of that week after years of trying to believe that Peter Martin had indeed taken me. Without thought, I ran my left hand over my right arm, checking for puncture scars.

If Peter hadn't, why was Teddy after me? Did he blame me for wrongfully sending his father to prison, because it hadn't been my fault at all? I'd never implicated the man, but the evidence had pointed to him in an indirect manner. They'd used my fear of the man against him at the trial. Zoe admitted he'd watched us at the beach, in the water, in bathing suits. Dad expressed the concerns Grandma had told him about regarding the man, concerns neither of them had told Zoe and me about.

I kept looking, but the drawings became more obscure, the ramblings of a girl with extreme trauma. Shadows on walls, small rooms with people inside. I didn't know what it was I was looking at, and after a few tense minutes, I restacked the pages, shoving them in the dresser. I changed my mind and took the one of me inside the hospital-like room, one figure watching from beyond a window, and folded it, shoving it in my back pocket.

I remembered my dad seeing these drawings, and that was when he made the call for hypnosis treatment as soon as we got home. He hadn't liked those results any better. I wiped tears from my cheeks as I stood about the room, remembering all the fun times we had, and how much I'd missed my grandma since then. She would have been so frightened when I went missing, and I couldn't believe her body wouldn't let her hold on until I was found.

She died on the fourth day of my abduction. Dad somehow blamed me for it; I knew that without a doubt. The rational part of him knew she was on her way out regardless, but because it happened while I was gone, the two events were forever linked in a devastating knot.

Walking around the place now, I felt and saw her everywhere. The couch we'd watch game shows on at night, wheels spinning and answers in the form of questions. We always made her change it to something we liked afterward, but she never complained. I swore she spent as much time peering at us as she did the TV, especially near the end.

It broke my heart that I'd never been able to say goodbye to her, and that she'd passed on without knowing if I was dead or alive.

There was nothing I could do to change the circumstances, and that was one of the hardest things about losing someone. You can't go back. You can't say goodbye. You can't have that last talk, that last hug, that pressing of forehead to forehead while each of you cries.

I checked my phone and saw it was after five. Somehow I'd been here for two hours, wallowing in my past. It was time to face the music and head to the Kick-Off. The last time I'd been there was almost twenty years ago, and I was hardly the same person. This time, I was ready.

I drove toward the public beach, centered on this side of Cloud Lake. A banner stretched over the road from treetop to treetop. *Cloud Lake Summer Kick-Off '20*. It was surreal being here, and I nervously glanced at my glove box. I hadn't thought this through very well. What was I actually going to do? Use myself as bait in the middle of a thousand people, carrying a gun? Dad had made sure I knew how to use a gun; Zoe too. He'd put us through some rigorous self-defense. He couldn't risk us being harmed in any way, not after I'd been abducted by a man.

Sounds of children playing, live music, and the smells

of carnival foods wafted into my open window. If I weren't so terrified, it would have harbored pleasant memories. There were far more vehicles parked than I could have ever imagined in the small town festival, and I had to double back, parking across the road in the dirt patch that had been fenced with Kick-Off signs.

I glanced around me, making sure no one was watching, and shoved the 9MM into my purse, making sure the safety was on. Once outside of the car, the heat felt overbearing, like the temperature had risen ten degrees. My skin flushed in the warmth, and I flipped on my sunglasses as I walked toward the sounds of the Kick-Off event.

People were everywhere, many more still parking. An impatient man in a truck honked at an SUV in front of him, trying to illegally turn, and I stayed to the side of the road. It only took five minutes to be into the thick of it, and there I was, at the Kick-Off in Cloud Lake. The same Ferris wheel was spinning between me and the water, and to the right, a stage was set up just off the beach. A man was playing an acoustic guitar, singing a country ditty about summer and chasing girls.

There were a few deputies from the local office, and even more volunteers wearing bright green security t-shirts. I could help myself right now, and talk to the deputies. They might even know who Teddy Martin was, and McCrae could hear the whole story, bringing him up on some charges. But what if they didn't stick, what if he hadn't done anything wrong? All I knew was that he'd paid for my cabin. It wasn't much to go on. No, I needed something more, substantial proof. I'd been hoping Harry would cover that end, but it was almost the end of the day and he hadn't returned my calls; the office lines were going to voicemail as well.

I stood there, peering over the crowds of people, my

heart thumping in my chest like a bouncing ball trying to escape captivity. With all the faces, the eyes flickering about the area, I lost my nerve. Thunder boomed in the distance, and dark dense clouds began blowing toward Cloud Lake. Chester had been right about the looming storm. I made up my mind and tried winding my way to a deputy. What had I been thinking? I couldn't do this on my own.

The woman in uniform was twenty yards away, but the throng of people entering the festival was too much, and I couldn't push towards her. I watched with a disassociated coldness as she grabbed the radio from her shoulder. Her eyes went wide, and she nodded to the officer across from her. They took off, moving away from me. I spun, suddenly hearing sirens in the distance. Something was happening, maybe an accident. The local law enforcement was leaving the Summer Kick-Off. I thought about leaving, jumping into my car and leaving, when I saw John.

He stood near the beach, a single rose in his hand, and his gaze locked with mine. I felt relief at the sight of him. I wasn't a helpless woman in need of being rescued by a man, but I'd also be lying if I didn't feel strength in numbers. He walked toward me, and I wound through loitering families, meeting him in the center of the open square.

He extended his arm, pressing the lone flower into my palm. I grabbed, it, a thorn poking into my skin. "I'm so sorry about yesterday. I just need the work around here, and they caught me off guard by not having power. The generator…" John was saying, but I stopped him.

"It's okay. It was only a boat ride. Work trumps recreation," I said, using a line from my dad's book of fatherly quips.

He smiled and turned to take in the festivities. "Where to first?" he asked, and I didn't know. I was about to ask him if he'd ever heard of Teddy Martin, but he was new to town.

The clouds were rolling in, and I saw a flash of light, the first lighting strike of the evening above Cloud Lake. "Looks like it's going to storm."

"That puts a damper on the night, doesn't it?" he asked. "I think we can at least order some food first. Shall we?" He pointed toward the grilling station, which was thinning out as fat drops fell lazily from the clouds.

My phone rang, and I unzipped my purse, painfully aware there was a gun sitting inside. I turned from John and grabbed the device, lifting an apologetic finger to the man beside me.

"Harry! What the hell took you so long? I've been calling all day," I told him.

"Sorry, Eva. This was messed up." Harry's voice was tense, nervous.

"What do you mean?" I asked, walking away from John.

"His door was locked, so I had to call the building super, telling him I thought there was something burning inside. Barns must have changed his own locks, because we couldn't open it, so they called the fire department and vacated the building. With my phone inside," Harry said. "I didn't know your cell number to call you."

"Well, did you get in or not?" I asked, anxiously awaiting the response.

"I did." He paused. "They busted open the door. They were also really angry about the waste of time. I told them Susan burned some toast in the lunchroom, and we got a fine. But Barns' door was open, at least. I sent everyone else home, and started digging. Good thing I know my uncle, because he let it slip one time that he uses his favorite sports team for passwords. I found it."

"What did you find?" I asked. The rain started pouring,

and I glanced up at the ominous black clouds directly above. People were scattering, heading for shelter.

"There were emails from a TM27. They were vague, but they explained enough. He told Barns to send you to Cloud Lake for a story on the lights, the flying saucers. He paid my uncle ten thousand dollars. Gave him the name of the Cloud Lake Cabins, and said the money would be transferred when you arrived in town. Eva, this is bad. You need to leave. I don't know who this guy is, but it sounds serious," Harry said.

"Why would Barns do this?" I asked, thinking about the email he'd sent me, apologizing.

"I found a lot of other emails too. Creditors. He's broke. He sank his money into this business and was desperate. I've called the police. I didn't know what else to do," Harry said, and I imagined him explaining the suspect emails to a street cop.

"I'm leaving as soon as I can, Harry. Thank you for the help," I said.

"Get home. Call me on the way. I need to know you're all right," he said.

"I will." I hung up, tucking the phone in my purse.

Thunder boomed again and again, bright forks of lightning flashing around the lake. The crowd of a thousand residents and tourists alike was moving away from the festival in a horde, and they pressed against us.

"Everything okay?" John asked, his hair wet and plastered to his forehead.

I shook my head, fighting against my stress. We were being pushed now, forced to move by the crowd, and I fell, my ankle shouting out in agony as a man behind me stepped on it. He kept moving without even looking down, and a large woman tripped, righting herself as her foot landed on my forearm.

John was there, shoving people away from me. His eyes met mine, and he grimaced as he pulled me to my feet, my ankle protesting the weight. "Can you walk?" he asked.

"Not well," I answered. My purse was flung on the ground, and I watched as someone kicked it forward.

"Stay here," he said, cutting a young family off, a little girl wide-eyed in fear in her father's arms. People turned to monsters in a crowded area, even for something as trivial as a downpour. John arrived at my side, slinging the purse over his shoulder before gripping me around my waist. "My truck is right over here. We'll find some shelter and return in a bit for your car," he said.

"Sounds good," I grunted, each step painful. I wondered if Teddy was in the crowd, looking for me. Had he shoved me?

We arrived at the edge of the beach parking lot, and John was backed into the end spot, so he was able to drive out before most of the crowd. He must have parked awfully early to claim such a coveted spot. I limped to the passenger door, and John opened it for me, helping me inside.

"This is insane," I said, meaning more than the storm and the mob mentality. He still had my purse over his shoulder, and his expression faltered for a moment before he passed it to me.

Ten seconds later, his engine was rumbling, the belt squeaking in the warm rain, and he threw it into gear, honking at a pedestrian standing in front of us.

I saw him then. Clark was standing at the road's entrance, covering his eyes, scanning the crowds as if searching for someone. Our gazes locked as John ripped out of the parking lot, rear tires barking as they slid on the pavement.

Clark had been looking for me.

July 13th – 2001

Dad had left over an hour ago, just as it was almost dark, and he'd told Zoe to watch out for me. I didn't need her babysitting, but it was really annoying that she'd abandoned me a few minutes after Grandma was packed up, and Dad's taillights were down the road.

I blew the rest of my cash on carnival games and candy, feeling the sugar rush of overdoing it. I wanted to leave now, but I had to find Zoe first. Clark had been M.I.A. and I was angry at him for promising to come, then ditching me. It sucked. Was this what dating was like? It was obvious he was too good-looking for me, too popular to want to be with a girl younger than him, especially when there were girls around like... well, Zoe.

I trudged around aimlessly, unable to spot Zoe anywhere; then I bumped into someone.

"Sorry," I said, and looked up to see Peter Martin staring at me.

"Hello, Zoe," he said.

"Jess. I'm Jess." I wished I'd just kept moving.

"My apologies. You two are so much alike," he said,

and I wondered if that was his feeble attempt at flattery. He gave me the creeps, and I tried to excuse myself when someone arrived at his side. It was the older kid from Local Beach, the one with the joint in his mouth. I could smell it on him now, a mixture of weed and stale cigarettes.

"Have you met my son?" Mr. Martin asked with a hint of distaste.

I shook my head.

"This is Theodore. He's… here for the summer."

"Teddy. Dad, don't call me that." His eyes met mine, dark brown, aloof, like he'd just told the world's biggest joke and didn't care.

"Nice… nice to meet you." My skin was crawling. Mr. Martin made me want to throw an oversized coat on and hide.

"Are you having fun?" the older of the two asked.

"Sure. My dad's over there. I'm just going to…"

"Your dad's at home. I passed them on the way here," Mr. Martin said, and Teddy chuckled.

"Bye," I said, attempting to swerve around them. I could feel their eyes on me as I went, heading for the Ferris wheel. I wanted to ride it with Clark, and instead I was here alone, ditched by both him and my sister, while strange men disturbed me. I hated Zoe with a passion at that moment. She was supposed to be there for me, but she'd bailed. I felt like shouting her name at the top of my lungs and making her call Dad to bring us home. *Home.* The cabin felt like something far from home at that moment. It was temporary. A place for us to watch Grandma die, and somewhere Dad could forget he was ever married.

Dad was supposed to come at ten, and I asked a lady what time it was. Nine ten. That left fifty minutes to wait. The Ferris wheel line wasn't too long, so I walked over to it, pulling my last four tokens from my shorts pocket.

People filed onto the ride two at a time, when I heard Zoe's laugh. I glanced to the source, and saw my sister standing there talking to a boy. They were at a popcorn vendor; the smell of kernels oversaturated with butter and salt carried to me as I started for them.

The boy's back was to me, but it clicked when I saw his white tennis shoes. It was Clark. Zoe laughed again, and I saw her arm pull Clark toward her, lifting on her toes to kiss him. They turned as they kissed, and tears flew from my eyes before I registered what I was seeing.

I ran. Ran from my traitorous sister, and from the boy who was supposed to like me. How could I ever have thought Clark would choose me over my older sister? She was gorgeous, developed, and apparently more apt to put out than I was. I let out a screech of frustration, and thought I heard someone calling my name as I ran. I'd competed in track the last two years, and I used the skills now to soar from the Kick-Off grounds.

Soon I was in the forest, dashing toward our cabin. Betrayal burned in my chest, anger fueling each step. Branches caught my arms and legs, slapping and slicing into me as I ran. I didn't care. I let the sweat, tears, and blood intermingle, but eventually, I had to stop. I jerked my head up, locating the moon in the sky, and tried to determine where I was. The stars reflected into the water beyond, and I made my way to the lake's edge, knowing that if I followed it long enough, I'd arrive at Grandma's.

July 16th – 2020

Those eyes. Peter Martin had introduced his son to me once, and as John flashed me his effortless grin, my memory filled in the blanks. It was him. John Oliver was Teddy Martin. How had I been so stupid? It was obvious now. He lived in the same damned cabin! I'd bought what he was selling so easily.

He was handsome, short styled hair instead of shaggy locks. Dress shirts and designer jeans instead of torn pants and oversized hoodies. But the eyes. I should have remembered the eyes. Dangerous brown eyes.

"What is it?" he asked me, sensing a shift in my posture. I'd gone rigid, petrified.

"My ankle hurts." It wasn't a lie, but it wasn't the full truth either. I had to get out of the truck. My hand dug into my purse, and I heard the truck doors lock with a click.

Water was bucketing onto the windshield, making the visibility terrible, and when John looked over at me, I was worried he was going to veer off the road.

"Don't do anything irrational… Jessica," he said, not even sounding like the man I'd spent time with this week. Hearing my real name off his lips sealed the deal...not that I had any doubts.

"What do you want with me, Teddy?" I barked out, fumbling through my possessions. The gun was missing.

"Looking for something?" he asked, pulling the gun from somewhere beside him. "You didn't think I'd bring you here to let you shoot me, did you?" He laughed; at first it was a normal sound, then the pitch rose, and his eyes danced wildly in their sockets.

I stared at the gun that I'd been foolish to bring with me. "You didn't answer my question," I told him, unable to hide the fear from my voice.

"All in due time, Jessica Carver." My name was spat off his tongue with distaste. I was wearing my seatbelt, and I saw he wasn't. If I could take hold of the steering wheel, maybe I could crash the truck, send him flying. But other headlights were up ahead, and I couldn't risk hurting anyone else on the road. The streets were full of families, coming home from a long day, tired, soaked kids screaming in backseats.

My hand felt my cell in the purse, and I tried peeking into it, seeing if I could send a message out.

"Pass it here." Teddy motioned the gun toward me, and I offered it with a shaky hand.

He rolled his window down and tossed my phone onto the road. "Good girl. I'm surprised it took you so long. I've been following you for years, you know. Reading all your articles. Cute stories about puppy adoption in the city, best cronut spots in Manhattan. Secret rooftop bars you don't want to miss. It's so good to know you've made the most out of your life." His last comment dripped with sarcasm.

"How did you find me?" I asked.

"Records like that are only sealed to the outside. People are easy, Jess. They like money. I give them money, they give me things in return. Like your old friend Chris Barns. He was only too happy to sell you down the river for a few bucks," John said. I corrected myself. *Teddy* said. John was as much who he really was as Eva was me. I almost laughed at our interactions, each using an alias, thinking we were smart enough to trick the other; only he had bested me, and I was at his mercy.

I played the one card I had. "Barns has been arrested. I found out about it all, the email trail from TM27, the money transfer. It's all on record, and they'll come for you."

He laughed again; this time, it had a maniacal tinge to it. "You really think I paid him from my bank account? Didn't you do a piece on cryptocurrency this year? Didn't you also allude that it was a way to launder money, drugs, prostitution, et cetera? You hit the nail on the head, my dear."

I'd taken the shot and missed. He was driving fast, and braked hard, as if realizing too late he'd missed a turn. He cranked the steering wheel, sliding to the side as he corrected the truck's path, and the vehicle glided on the wet gravel. We were heading toward Grandma's cabin, toward Peter Martin's cabin.

"Where are you taking me?" I asked.

"To the place you claimed my dad kept you. Only he didn't, did he? You made it all up. You're a pathetic liar." The truck lurched to a standstill, and he threw it into park. Teddy pushed out of his driver's side door and ran around the truck, already soaked by the time he arrived at my window. "Get out!" My own gun was pointed to the window, the barrel aimed at my face.

I did as he said, without any options. After a glance around, I saw there was nothing to use as a weapon. Dad used to always say you never brought a stick to a gunfight, unless there was no other option. The door flung open, and Teddy stepped over, far enough away that I couldn't lunge at him without being shot for the effort.

"Get inside," he shouted over the booming thunder. If it was possible, the rain was coming down in droves, even heavier now. I plodded forward, my ankle swollen from before. I couldn't go inside. It was a sure death. I knew this, could feel it with every inch of my being. I heard my Dad's voice call to me, the overprotective man that I'd known since the summer of 2001. He warned me. He told me to run. To fight.

We were nearing the porch, right by the shed I'd poked around in for yard equipment the day before. The door was still open, and a shovel leaned against the exterior walls of the structure.

I waited for the right moment and shoved Teddy as we stepped onto the dirt path in front of his cabin. The rain had turned it to mud, and he slipped, the gun going off just as a thunderclap echoed over Cloud Lake. I heard him cursing me as I ran, limping to the shed. My fingers grabbed the wet handle, and I gripped it as tightly as I could as Teddy wiped mud off his pants. The gun had fallen to the ground, and I took my chance.

We were twenty yards apart, and I moved as quickly as my injured leg would let me, hobbling over to him as he leaned down, trying to get hold of the 9MM. He found it just as I arrived, the shovel raised high in the sky. I felt the ground slip from under me as I swung, and landed with a thud on my back. I'd slipped, and my breath forced from my lungs with a whooshing sound.

I lay there, frozen in pain as water threatened to drown me from above. Teddy was holding the shovel in one hand and the gun in the other, water pouring from his face over his wide smile. He shook his head at me like a disappointed parent before he glanced at my injured ankle. My leg exploded as he stomped on my foot.

I screamed, a primal animalistic sound of pure agony and rage. I was helpless and I knew it. He started dragging me, and I heard the shovel fall to the ground as he hefted me up the steps. My ankle hurt so badly, I thought I was going to pass out as I bumped up each step, head thudding against the stairs.

"Stop. You don't have to do this! I didn't do anything wrong," I pleaded through gritted teeth. *Clunk.* My head hit the top step, and he ignored me, pulling me toward the doorway.

"Inside now." His words were shallow, quiet drops of rain in a big lake. "Jessica Carver, prepare for your judgment."

July 13th – 2001

Finally, after another ten minutes, I saw lights from the cabin beyond Mr. Martin's. The owners were rarely there, but they must have come to town for the Kick-Off. Seeing something other than trees, shrubs, and dirt helped lift the cloud of angst drowning my teenage mind.

My mom's old necklace clung in my tight grip, and I wished she were there to talk to me about what happened. What kind of mother was she? Would she have brushed my hair, popped some corn, done my nails, and watched a bad rom-com with me?

I was never going to talk to Zoe again. She didn't deserve to be my sister any longer; that much was clear. She knew I liked Clark. Didn't she? I hadn't openly discussed it, mostly because I was worried that if I drew a target on him, she would act on it. Apparently, the fates already had her doing that, regardless of me telling her I had a crush on the boy.

Mr. Martin's cabin was dark, and I assumed they were still at the public beach. I could cross by without worry. Grandma's porch light was on, and I emerged from the trees, staring in the distance when I tripped, falling hard to the ground between Mr. Martin's and his neighbors'. Even in the dark, I could now see the pronounced tree root jutting from the ground like a gnarled orc's arm, reaching for my ankle.

I stood, brushing dirt from my knees, when I noticed the necklace was gone, dropped in the fall. I scoured the ground, cursing myself for being so clumsy. This was Zoe's fault too. If I lost the necklace… I kept looking, desperate to see the shine of the metal in the moonlight.

I stayed there for five minutes; it might have been longer. I'd return first thing in the morning. I mentally marked the tree and remembered the way the root snaked sideways and out from the trunk. When I was confident I'd be able to find the right spot again, I started to leave.

Lights emerged from above me, and I thought Mr.

Martin must have installed a new porch light, an intense motion detector. It was so bright, my eyes hurt, and I squinted against the radiance. It softened, and I now saw it wasn't coming from Mr. Martin's. It was in the sky. Thoughts of a helicopter searching for me crossed my mind, but I'd only been gone for a short while. No one would have been alerted I was missing.

I stepped from the treeline, slowly walking into the middle of the yard. The lights dimmed, and I could see at least eight individual beams forming a circle. My heart sped up as it clicked. The rumors, the chatter of UFOs, Grandma's story about seeing the lights… they were true. I was bearing witness to the lights, just like she had so long ago, and a new kind of kinship coursed through me, spreading with each accented beat of my heart.

My arms rose to the sky, suddenly so sure they wanted me to see them, to bask in their glow, to know that things like my sister kissing a boy I barely knew didn't mean anything. Nothing at all. There was life other than humans, or on Earth. I knew this now.

I was laughing, giggling like a girl, when the lights brightened again. The first time it pulsed, I thought they'd left me, and for a second, I was all alone again. The feeling threatened to overwhelm me; then the lights pulsed again, growing in speed, rising in brightness until I couldn't look in its direction any longer.

The flashing was a strobe now, and I felt the wrongness creep through my tightly closed eyelids. It was insidious, menacing. Their intentions became clear, even if I didn't know how. Anger, mistrust, resentment pulsed with the light, and finally, it all came to an end. It was dark once again, and when I looked up, I thought it might have left, until I noticed there were no stars in the sky. The ship covered it, hovering fifty feet above me.

I ran. My sore, tired legs pumped, and I shouted one word, before the light enveloped me and became all I'd ever know again.

"Dad!"

July 16ᵗʰ – 2020

I knew where he was taking me before he dragged into the cabin. The underground room was well documented during the case. I could envision the images as they flashed across the television screens of every local and major news network for over a month, at least until something newer and fresher overtook the headlines. Reporters talked about the hidden trap door in Peter Martin's cabin, and what it was used for. How many girls had he kept there? Where were the bodies? Rumors spread that Martin had abducted every girl this state had ever reported missing. Without evidence, there was no conviction on any of those cases.

"Kind of ironic, isn't it?" Teddy asked. I could no longer think of him as John. John was dead, and the man before me wore his skin, but not his face. This man was pure evil, vengeance dripping from him as obviously as the rainwater.

"What is?" I asked as he shut the door, flipping no less than three deadbolts. He wasn't messing around.

"That the first time you're actually going to be inside the supposed torture room is now," Teddy said.

I looked around, trying to find a weapon, but knew I couldn't so much as step on my wounded ankle. I tried to think logically about my situation, but there was no way out. Forcing me down there wasn't an option either. Once I was beneath this cabin, there was no helping myself.

"Go ahead. Try to scream," he taunted.

The room was sparsely furnished, and it appeared that what was in here was original to the cabin. I clawed my way onto my butt, my legs out in front of me, and I pressed my back to the wall beside the door. Teddy stood a few yards away, beside the wood-burning fireplace. I saw the utensils there, wishing I could grab one of the cast iron tools and bash his smug face in with it.

He was brandishing my gun, smiling as he waved it in front of his body. "Are you going to do this the easy way?" he asked, and I spat at him, fury rising in my exhausted body. "I take that as a no." He pulled something from atop the fireplace mantel, and I only had a second to register the dart in the tranquilizer gun before I peered down, seeing one sticking from my chest.

I struggled to escape, but he was on me, holding me still for a full minute or two, pressing my shoulders into the wooden floors until my head slumped to the side, and all went blank.

———————

"You see, if anyone was going to use this room for nefarious activities, it was me, not my dad," Teddy said, but my eyes were closed. I gasped softly, inhaling, and kept still, hoping he didn't know I was coherent. My head was spinning, and it took a moment to recall where I was.

It smelled different: stale, musty. We were in the basement. I was in a seated position, my ankle throbbing fiercely as the blood pooled to my feet. My hands were restrained behind me, the rope already chafing my wrists. I wondered how he'd managed to drug me just the right amount, and assumed he had practice on dosage over the years. He was dangerous.

"I was the one who found this room before he even knew it was here. He told me to stay away from it, saying there was a mold problem, but I didn't care. I wanted a place to sit and hide from his incessant neediness. The man was a fool, but he was my dad, and after what happened to us, I had to protect him. To keep him company, you know?" Teddy was rambling, and I couldn't believe this was the same smooth-talking man I'd met at church only four days earlier. This man sounded fully delusional.

He paused, and I heard his footsteps coming closer. "They should be wearing off now. I don't have time for this," he said, and my leg flashed with pain again. He kicked my ankle twice, and I screamed, fresh tears falling onto my face. He hadn't gagged me, at least.

"What do you want?" I begged.

"Good, you're awake. How do you feel?" he asked.

I was miserable, the drugs still lingering in my bloodstream. I was groggy, and the agony in my leg was threatening to make me throw up.

He grabbed my jaw, holding it forward as he leaned down, his face inches from mine. "How do you feel?"

"Fine. I'm fine," I lied, hoping it would calm him. I tried to get the lay of the land, but knew from the old reports that there were no windows here. The floors were packed dirt, and the walls were unfinished soil as well; wooden support beams ran horizontally along the ceiling, accented by thick posts in each corner and two in the center of the space. A crude staircase rose to the trap door above. He was blocking my exit, and I needed to escape past him. But then what?

"Now that we're past the formalities, do you know why you're here?" he asked, sitting on his own chair facing me. It was almost close enough for our knees to touch, and I wanted to reel backwards, away from him. Chester Brown's 9MM sat in his lap as he talked.

"Because you blame me for your father going to prison," I said.

"He's dead, you know." Teddy's eyes were wild but focused solely on me.

I shook my head. "I didn't know." It was the truth. I honestly had no idea.

"Two months ago. Cancer. Can you believe it? After everything he'd been through, he dies of goddamn cancer." Teddy laughed, a twisted sound.

"I'm sorry," I said, unsure what else to offer him.

"That's a good one. You're sorry. Great. Be sure to tell him when you pass by on the way to hell," Teddy said softly. "Did you ever wonder how it was that there was no evidence of you being kept here?"

My dad had talked about this with the lawyers a lot. "Your father cleaned it really well."

"So well that there was no blood, hair, skin, nothing. No evidence of you being on the property, no proof you were taken by him at all, isn't that right?" Teddy was up and moving now, a pantomime of a cross-examining trial prosecutor.

"I know. I don't remember," I said, and I caught him staring at my chest. I had the urge to cover up, until I realized he was looking at my necklace.

His hand snapped out, pulling it free. A drop of blood rolled down my neck from the clasp digging in. "Except this."

I grimaced. "Yes."

"This was inside our house. My dad claims he found it in the grass. Can you explain that?"

"I lost it."

"Where were you? What happened?" he asked.

When I didn't answer, he kept talking. "You don't remember. You were with him for a full seven days, isn't that what they said?" he asked, crossing his arms. The gun was set on the chair across from me, and I forced myself not to look at it.

I nodded in answer.

"Then wouldn't you recall this place? He was questioned during those days, early on, and that fat sheriff even searched the cabin, finding nothing. Squeaky clean. Then there were rumors of my dad leering. That was the word they kept using. *Leering* at teenage girls. Did you know what happened to my sister?" Teddy asked, and my stomach sank.

"I didn't know you had a sister," I admitted.

"That's because she died. Eight years before you were allegedly abducted by my dad. She was fourteen, my big sister. Hit by a truck on her bike ride home. Dad was obsessed with his little princess. When she was taken from us, he was so devastated. My parents couldn't handle it, and I was shipped off to live with my boring waspy mom, who couldn't even stand by her husband through a crisis. That summer was the first one I got to spend with my old man." Teddy was still pacing, and the truth of what he was telling me was evident.

"He wasn't looking at us because he was a creep." My jaw went slack, and I felt how wrong the whole trial and accusations were.

Teddy nodded, deep dips of his head. "He was watching you because you reminded him of his dead daughter."

"I'm sorry. I don't remember anything. I couldn't say one way or another. I don't remember," I cried, wishing I could take it all back. I knew now, being here, seeing Cloud Lake again; I knew what happened to me, but there was no way this lunatic would believe me if I told him.

"I don't care. All I know is, you have to pay," he said.

"How... how did you set this all up?" I asked, and then it became clear. "The lake. You were going to take me for a boat ride yesterday. A nice quiet trip around the picturesque Cloud Lake."

He laughed. "It was going to be much easier to kill you out there, sink you to the bottom of the lake."

"Like you did to Mark Fisher," I told him.

Teddy grunted. "Very good. You have a reporter's mind."

"That's why you only booked me until Wednesday. Didn't you think they'd search the receipts after I went missing?" I asked, and saw him blink in surprise. I didn't think he'd considered that aspect.

"We're dealing with McCrae here. He's not the brightest bulb. I've been tiptoeing around him for years," Teddy admitted.

"The drugs were yours too." I kept going, calling him out. "The drugs they found stashed here in 2001 were your drugs. You sold them to kids, didn't you? Unsuspecting teenagers, visiting Cloud Lake with their boring families. You'd hang out at Local Beach and sell pills, weed… what else did they find?" I pressed, seeing him so angry with me. It wasn't going to end well for me, but I had to deflect some of the blame for his father's incarceration onto him. "He admitted the drugs were his, and because there wasn't enough evidence that I was held by him, they stuck him on that charge."

Teddy's jaw clenched. A vein pulsed across his forehead as he stalked over and slapped me hard across the face. Blood pooled in my mouth, and I spat it at him, wincing in pain at the sudden attack.

"He didn't have to take the fall for me, but I was nineteen. I wasn't going to juvie any longer." He ran a hand through his disheveled hair.

"But he did go down for the stash of drugs. There were enough drugs there for them to throw the book at him. Did he ever forgive you?" I asked, knowing I was taking a risk diverting the blame from myself to the highly unstable man in front of me.

"You shut your mouth. It's all your fault. Where were you?" Teddy asked.

"I don't know."

He grabbed the arms of the chair, pulling himself directly before me. His nose touched mine. "Where. Were. You?" he shouted, spittle landing on my face.

I craned my neck to the side, not answering him.

"It doesn't matter. Maybe you were hiding out, playing a game. Show up unharmed a week later, on my dad's doorstep. Because why not incriminate a man who was only trying to be nice to you and your sister? A man who missed his daughter so much that he didn't have the time of day for his son. Maybe you were doing me a favor." He stumbled and sat down in the other chair, the wind bursting from his sails.

I had to change the subject. "What did you do? Why did the cops vacate the Kick-Off so quickly today?"

He smiled now, a proud grin. "That was perfect, wasn't it?"

I nodded, not sure what I was agreeing with.

"I saw you arrive and turn around to go find a parking spot. I called it in."

"Called what in?"

"I guess it doesn't hurt to tell you now." Those words were like the last nails in my coffin. I sensed my end was near. I worked the restraints behind my back, just like Dad had made me practice for a year after I was taken. It was part of his crazy regimen to make sure I never got captured by someone again.

"Tell me what?" I asked, trying to keep him talking.

"Your friends Clare and Dan. It seems she had an overdose, but not before she killed her husband, of course."

Teddy leaned forward, and I saw the face of a hardened killer. He wasn't just a drug dealer with revenge for his jailed father on his mind. He loved this. He wanted to kill, he wanted to play games with me, luring me here, thinking he was so damned smart for pulling it off.

"You killed them."

He nodded. "She's a mess. You saw it."

"Who were they, really?" I asked, knowing there was more to it.

"They're old customers from the area. He used to work for some resort company, but it's all bullshit now. They canned him a year ago. Caught him doing a line in his office. What an idiot. They were only too happy to get a week in the country. Come to Cloud Lake, I told them. Play a role, and they were both only too happy to be part of it."

Clare's words flashed into my mind. *Do you ever wonder what it's like to drown?*

She was clearly an addict, and Teddy was feeding her alcohol and drugs while she was here, setting her up for a downward spiral that would end in two deaths and the local department's full attention. The other tourists at Cloud Lake Cabins would have seen her stumbling about, heard the two of them yelling late at night. It would all add up, and Teddy would go scot-free while he killed me down here.

"What's killing me going to do for you?" I asked softly.

He shrugged. "Close a chapter. Once I burn this place to the ground, I'm out of here. Skipping town."

I noticed the jerry cans of gasoline for the first time, two sitting side-by-side near the stairs. Fear of being burned alive filled my entire body. Sitting here, not knowing if he was going to shoot me, stab me, or leave me to die, hadn't been as bad as knowing my future. Tears fell down my face as I imagined the flames coming closer, licking my skin as I screamed.

"It doesn't have to be like this," I told him. "Let me go. I'll never tell a soul what happened. I didn't do anything to your father. I'm sorry I misread his stares. I never once told the sheriff it was him. I never admitted it! I don't remember what happened." That was a lie now. I closed my eyes and saw the lights above Cloud Lake, moving toward me, stopping directly over my body.

I had no choice. My chin sank to my chest as I spoke. "You've heard about the sightings."

"Sightings?" he asked, a curious tinge to his voice.

"UFOs, flying saucers, the Grays."

He laughed again, this time with a little trepidation. "What are you talking about?"

"You wanted to know where I was. I remember now. I'll admit it. I was outside; I'd tripped and lost the necklace." I jutted my jaw toward his pocket, where he'd shoved the chain with a cross on the end. "They came overhead and took me."

"They took you?" His voice was nervous.

"You've seen them, haven't you?" I asked, hoping against all odds that he had.

"I've seen a lot of things while stoned," Teddy said, nearly admitting it.

"I arrived again a week later. Just like the little girl in town did. I found her, you know," I told him, and he shook his head. I had him. If I could only keep talking, he was delusional enough to believe my story, where most wouldn't. Even I was having a hard time believing it.

"Carly." He said her name, and I wished I hadn't brought her up.

"You didn't have anything to do with that?"

He looked appalled. "Why would I?"

"That's what I thought. She was taken too, I'm sure of

it." I told him my truth, because there was nothing else left.

"You can't seriously believe you were abducted by aliens?" Teddy asked. The gun was in his hand, and his finger twitched near the trigger.

"I couldn't remember then. I was outside here one moment, upset at my sister for kissing the boy I liked, and the next I was crawling toward my grandma's house, my dad running to me. There were dreams, and the drawings, and the hypnosis, but my dad and the therapist told me I was tricking my own mind. Creating something fantastical to cover what your father had done to me. I never believed them." I was crying again, unable to hold back. "My whole life has been about that week. My whole damned life!"

Teddy sat there, not speaking, but staring at me like I was a feral animal.

"I came back here to put my fears to rest. It looks like I finally know what happened to me, at least. If I'm going to die, then I'll die knowing."

Teddy was up now, standing over me. "You lie. You can die knowing what a poor liar you are."

I fiddled with the rope around my wrists, feeling it loosen enough that I might be able to slip out. It was going to be difficult without him noticing.

The doorbell rang.

Teddy's gaze darted to the stairs, and I took my chance to slide my left hand out. It almost worked, but there wasn't enough slack. I needed another minute.

The bell rang again, and again. Someone was shouting, a man's muffled voice. Teddy looked pissed and scared at the same time. He was pacing, his gaze firmly on the closed trap door. He scanned himself, as if seeing how disheveled he was.

The visitor was banging on the door relentlessly, heavy, hard sounds.

"Damn it! Stay put and quiet." He gripped my gun, running for the stairs. He was going to kill whoever was at the door, and I didn't have much time.

I fought with the rope against my wrists, not having to keep it secret any longer. Teddy's footsteps clunked across the floor above, and I broke free, yanking my arms forward. In all the excitement, I'd forgotten about my throbbing ankle, and when I stood up, I fell to my knees, groaning in pain.

I moved quickly, pushing through the agony, and grabbed a gas can. I spilled the liquid around the dirt ground, the gas soaking in quickly. I threw some on the walls, the stairs, and grabbed the matchbook Teddy had sitting beside the cans. I dragged myself up the first three steps, putting the matches between my teeth.

I heard the door open, and shouting. There wasn't much time. Thunder boomed, and even from here I could feel the breeze roll into the house and down the hole in the floor, the smell of ozone and rain entering my swollen nostrils.

I scooted up one stair at a time, using my good leg to push myself upwards. Just before the open trap door, I pulled the matches from my mouth and struck one, throwing it toward the basement. It blew out before it landed. My hands shook fiercely as I repeated the process. This time, I crouched before throwing the burning stick, and it worked. The gasoline caught, and if anything, someone would see the burning cabin. Even if I was dead, they might catch Teddy. I needed to know he wasn't going to get away.

The shouting was still going on, and I heard the struggle.

"Where is she?" a voice asked, and I knew it was Clark. My sweet Clark, the fun-loving man I'd grown to know this week; the cool kid who'd stolen my heart as a young girl was here.

"You'll find out right away." Venom poured from Teddy's voice as they rolled around the front porch. I couldn't see them, but someone was winning the battle, and I didn't think it was Clark. I was finally upstairs, the flames stretching high. It wouldn't be long before this wooden tinderbox was encompassed in fire.

I needed to help Clark, and I remembered the fireplace tools. I crawled over to them on all fours, grabbing the poker. The iron utensil was heavy in my hand, and I knew it would do just fine. I had to push myself if I was going to help, and I used a chair to pull my body onto my feet. I could put a little weight on the ankle, but not much.

I hopped across the room and saw the two men in a struggle to secure the gun, which had fallen down the front steps and into the mud. I had to get there first.

Clark was on the bottom, and rain blew in sideways, drenching the two men as they fought. Teddy's fist flew back and struck Clark the moment he saw me standing there. My appearance fueled Clark, and he threw Teddy off him, elbowing the slightly older man in the throat.

"Grab the gun!" Clark shouted to me, but I was already moving. I neared the steps, and my ankle gave out, sending me sprawling to the bottom, face-first in the mud. I frantically searched for the weapon.

Rain washed the mud from my eyes, and I glanced up to see Clark get kicked in the face. Teddy lumbered over to the steps and picked up the gun a second later. "Looking for this?" he asked, his voice loud. Lightning flashed in the sky, followed closely by its shadow thunder, and the bright strobes lit up Teddy's front side.

He peered up to the sky as Clark dove from the porch, taking Teddy to the ground. The gun flew free again, this time a yard from my position. I grabbed it, pointing it toward the two struggling men.

"Shoot him!" Clark was yelling, but I couldn't fire without risking hitting Clark too.

"I can't get a clean shot!" I called as Teddy shifted behind Clark, using him as a shield.

The lightning flashed brighter, faster, and the memory flooded back to me. I looked to the stormy sky, seeing most of it blotted out by the ship. Eight lights dimmed around the vessel, before increasing in brightness.

Clark wasn't aware, but Teddy had noticed. He stopped struggling, and Clark had him in a headlock.

Teddy's gaze met mine, and he finally understood I was telling the truth. I hadn't blamed his father; the evidence all pointed at Peter Martin, but he was innocent, and now he was dead. Teddy was the killer. Clark saw me aiming the gun at them, and he let go of the other man, ducking and rolling away.

The lights were strobing fast, making it almost impossible to see Teddy's shadow. I fired. One, two, three shots, as the vessel's lights glowed intensely. I felt the heat of the burning cabin behind me. The gun was hot and heavy in my hand, and the rain poured relentlessly as I searched for Teddy's body.

July 20th – 2001

Lights. Bright white light was all I saw, and I felt grass beneath my palms. I gripped at it, somehow feeling like it was my lifeline, my way into the world once again.

"Dad," I croaked out, trying to remember what happened. I was running home... the Kick-Off. Zoe and Clark. But somehow none of that mattered any longer. Dread spilled through me, and I rolled onto my front, ready to defend myself. My body hurt, my limbs like lead.

263

I glanced to the side, and there was Mr. Martin's cabin. I heard voices, distant ones, words I couldn't comprehend, and then they were gone, leaving me empty and drained of all purpose.

Eventually, I pushed myself to my knees. I tried to stand but fell. Grandma's cabin loomed a short distance away, but the journey looked lengthy and treacherous to my addled brain. Dad's Bronco was in the driveway, and I called for him, this time with real volume.

"Dad!" My voice cracked, my throat burning as the word escaped.

I said his name again and again, and crawled now, ever toward the cabin, scanning the area to make sure no one was watching me. I couldn't shake the feeling of being stared at. It was as if a dozen eyes were blinking in my direction, studying me from beyond the treeline.

Then I saw him. Dad emerged from the cabin, his hair wild. Even from this far away, I knew he was exhausted, red-eyed and sad.

"Dad!" I called one last time, and fell to the ground, knowing everything would be all right, yet fully aware nothing would be all right ever again.

"Jess!" His voice was an anchor I grasped hold of.

I lifted my head, watching him with lead in my body as he ran, crying and shouting for my sister.

A door opened behind me, from Mr. Martin's house, and I heard footsteps on his porch. I didn't have the energy to turn, but I knew it was him.

My dad's face twisted in anger at the man behind me as he approached, protectively wrapping his arms around my frame. He picked me up like I weighed nothing, burying his stubble-covered cheeks into my face.

"Jess," he whispered. "The police are on the way, Martin."

I could see our neighbor now, standing there with a bewildered look on his face. "I didn't do anything! She just showed up here!"

Dad didn't engage. Zoe was running toward us now, and Dad carried me to our house. Already I heard sirens in the distance. Zoe must have called them as soon as Dad came for me. I didn't know what day it was. I must have fallen asleep out here after falling to the ground. Images of the night before, the lights strobing, flashed through my memory.

"Where have you been?" Dad brought me inside the cabin, straight to my bed. Zoe came in seconds later with a glass full of water, shoving it into Dad's hand. "Drink," he said, and I obeyed, finding the cool water soothed my sore throat.

"I must have dozed off last night. I was coming back from the Kick-Off…" My pillow was so soft behind my head.

"Last night!? Jess, you've been gone for a week!" Dad said as the tears fell. Zoe was crying too, standing behind our father as if she were scared of my presence.

A week! It couldn't be. He was wrong. Another thought raced into my mind. "Where's Grandma?"

The two of them shared a look, and I instantly knew the worst had happened. I cried freely then. For the loss of my grandma, the one adult female to truly ever love me completely, and for my strange situation, one I couldn't understand.

"She didn't make it through the week. The stress… She wanted to tell you she loved you." Dad was hardly able to choke out the words.

I'd been gone for a week? But where? It didn't make sense. And my grandma had died thinking I was gone. It was too much to bear.

There was a knock on the door, and Zoe went to answer it. Muffled voices carried to the bedroom, then booted feet followed my sister into our room.

"Good God. Jessica Carver." The uniformed man came to the bedside, kneeling close to me. "We've been looking for you everywhere. What happened?"

"I don't know," I said.

His gaze narrowed. "You don't know?"

"Sheriff McCrae, we found her in Martin's yard. It was him. We told you it was him," Dad was shouting, and McCrae stood up.

"We're going to bring him in. Search the house again. We also need to get your girl to the hospital, run some tests, okay?" The sheriff was calm, and I liked him.

"It was him. She knew it all along. The way he watched her."

"He was there at the Kick-Off. I remember. He tried to talk to me. Called me Zoe," I said the words, aware after the fact that I was incriminating the man, even though I didn't think he'd actually done anything to me. But maybe I was drugged. I'd heard stories of roofies in drinks, that kind of thing. Plus Dad was so sure, I felt the need to go along with him.

Zoe stood in the corner of the room, wearing an oversized sweater, and crossed her arms, staring blankly at me. I remembered her kissing Clark but didn't care anymore. They'd all been so worried about me, but in my head, I'd blinked and it was a week later.

"Jessica. You stay put here for an hour or so, and when we have Mr. Martin squared away, we'll take you to the hospital. An ambulance is on the way. The hospital's only a town over. You'll be home before you know it, back in bed, okay, honey?" McCrae asked, talking to me like I was a little girl. I didn't mind at that moment. I almost needed the coddling.

The two adults left the room, leaving my sister and me alone.

"You scared me so much," Zoe said.

"I'm sorry. I don't know what happened. I'm serious," I told her.

She nodded, accepting my words. "Clark saw you run away. He went after you."

"He did?" I asked, recalling hearing my voice being called as I bailed from the Kick-Off.

"He grabbed his bike and took the road. I guess he didn't make it there in time." Zoe was looking at her bare feet, standing by the doorway. "He was there for every search party, and was here every day, asking how he could help."

My heart melted, but I didn't say anything.

"They're taking him," Zoe said, and I got up out of bed. I had to see this.

I glanced at Grandma's closed bedroom door, and sadness washed over me. I'd lost a lot in the past week.

The police car drove by, and Zoe and I watched it from behind the screen door. Dad and the sheriff were outside, and Mr. Martin's head turned toward our cabin, his gaze locking with mine.

The window was open, and I could hear McCrae's loud voice from here. "We found the room, Brian."

"What do you mean?" Dad asked him.

"There was a trap door under the carpet in the living room. Leads to a cellar. We're bringing in a forensic team from Portland to scour it. This is Cloud Lake. We're not equipped for a case like this," McCrae said.

A room? They were acting like Mr. Martin had taken me and locked me up for a week. Could that be?

"She had no signs of injections on her arms. No

wounds on her wrists," Dad said.

"The doctors will run tests. Find out what we're working with. There's something else. We found a stash of drugs. A little of everything. It was like a pharmacy down there," McCrae said. "We also found this." He held his hand out to my dad, and I saw my necklace in a plastic bag.

"That's my wife's. Or was. How did…" Dad's eyes met mine, and I nodded to him, confirming I'd been wearing it.

An ambulance arrived, lights flashing, the siren turned off, and I flinched as Zoe reached out to touch my arm. "We'd better go. Do you need anything else? Water? Bathroom?"

I nodded, accepting her help as we went to the bathroom. "I'll be right here." Zoe shut the door behind me, and I stared in the mirror. I felt two years older; my skin was pale and tight on my emaciated face. I was all eyes and cheekbones, my hair a mess of tangles.

The vanity strip flickered with a common power surge, and I screamed, thinking they were back. Zoe was inside a moment later, cradling me as I lay on the cool tile floor in the fetal position.

"It'll be okay." She stroked my head in her lap, repeating the phrase over and over, acting like the mother I never knew.

She was wrong, though. I wouldn't ever be okay again.

July 16th – 2020

I was on all fours, and I saw the figure approaching, the lights no longer flickering. "Dad!" I shouted, instantly knowing I was in the wrong time. Clark's face appeared, and he bent down, carrying me from the burning building beside us. It was engulfed in flames, and he set me on Grandma's grass, the same area I'd cut only a day before. It felt like forever ago.

"Where is he?" I asked Clark, his face inches from mine. I was sure they'd taken him. The Grays had returned for me but had taken Teddy instead.

A light turned on abruptly, and I recoiled in fear. Wind blew hard, scattering rain against us, and I now understood the whooshing sound. A helicopter was lowering to the ground, its searchlight scanning as it arrived. It hadn't been a UFO after all.

Clark's face was grim. "Teddy's right over there."

I couldn't believe it. It had been them. The flashing lights, the same place as I'd been taken.

I scrambled away from Clark, trudging through the

269

mud to get to Teddy's side. The gun was still in my hand, and I flinched when I noticed it, tossing it away. It landed with a sickening squelch ten yards from us. My hands found Teddy's face, and I pulled his head up. His eyes stared lifelessly, his knowing grin wiped from his demeanor.

Clark was there, grabbing my shoulders. He dragged me from the body. "Jess." He kissed me on the forehead, pulling me into a protective embrace. "Jessica Carver. How can it be you?"

"How did you find out?" I shouted over the sound of the helicopter.

"I can't believe I didn't clue in earlier. Now that I know, I can't unsee the teenage version of you trapped in this beautiful woman," he said, and I loved him for it.

"Isabelle?" I asked, assuming he had to have talked to the waitress.

He nodded. "She called me. Told me about your story. About Teddy Martin. I haven't seen him in years but assumed he still lived out here. And I still remember where your cabin was," he told me.

"I must have blocked it, along with so much else, but you came for me that night. The night I saw you kissing Zoe."

"That wasn't me. I found her, asking where you were. She kissed me. I didn't initiate it…"

I put a finger to his lips. "Thanks for coming."

"I was too slow. I rode my bike that night but got lost. I'd only come out with you once, and I took the wrong turn. Maybe I could have stopped him."

"You stopped Teddy now."

I hardly noticed the helicopter landing, or the men pouring from inside, until one of them was pulling us apart. Clark was shouting at them, but I didn't hear his words.

They held him back, separating us.

They dragged me past the dead body, and seconds later, I was inside the helicopter, the very same object I'd mistaken for one of *their* vessels. My ankle throbbed as I sat there, my head pounding alongside it.

"Stop!" I yelled, finally letting my voice out. I'd been in shock, and the picture around me was becoming clearer. These were military men, and one of them was outside, detaining Clark. "He comes with us."

A uniformed woman glanced at a man beside the pilot. He wasn't wearing a uniform like the others; he was in a black suit, and the man didn't even hesitate as he made one small nod.

"Bring him!" the woman called to the man restraining Clark, and soon the two of us were together inside the military helicopter. His fingers stretched over, enveloping my hand. As we lifted from the ground, Teddy's corpse came into view. Dead. I'd killed him.

We were in the air for less than ten minutes, so I knew the base was close to Cloud Lake. I found the fact intriguing. Now that my head was screwed on straight, I took in my surroundings. It was ominously dark out, rain pounding the exterior, and the two soldiers held guns firmly, though they weren't pointing them at us, which I took as a good sign.

Clark peered around nervously, and part of me wished I hadn't mixed him up in any of this. On the other hand, I knew I'd be dead without his intervention, and I was eternally grateful he was at my side. His arm was draped around me, and he was helping me walk across the wet grass, taking the brunt of my weight.

"Where are we?" he whispered into my ear as we were led across the grassy patch toward a barn on the outskirts of a cornfield.

"I'm not sure." I was sensing a strange energy from this whole place. I considered demanding they call McCrae so we could tell him what happened. Talk to him about how Teddy had killed Clare and Dan, how he'd set up this entire thing to seek vengeance on a young girl who was now a woman. But I didn't think this group was interested in dealing with local law enforcement.

"How did we not know there was a government agency sniffing around?" Clark asked.

I shrugged, careful not to say anything specific within earshot of the soldiers.

They directed us into the barn, which had several rooms erected along the old walls. From the looks of this place, they'd been here a while. The woman patted us each down, finding nothing of use. She pulled the folded drawing from my pants and passed it to the man in the suit. He shoved it into his breast pocket.

Clark and I stood beside each other, dripping pools of water onto the wooden floor. All signs of hay had been swept away, and the soldiers moved out, leaving the two of us with the suit.

He was tall, maybe forty-five, with short black hair flattened from the rain. "Normally I'd separate you two and see what I could learn. But I have the feeling that's not going to work this time." He looked at the way Clark was holding me up, and almost smiled.

I shook my head, unsure of what to say.

The man pointed to the nearest room. "Come. Let's get settled inside."

The female soldier returned right before we entered the doorway and passed a towel to both Clark and me, as well as to the suit, who waved it away. We dried off as best we could, and a chill coursed through me as my brain realized the implications of tonight. I'd almost died. I'd killed a man.

"It's okay," Clark whispered, helping me into the room.

The walls were stark white, the table black and cheap, just like the matching folding chairs. It all looked sterile and quickly thrown together. Nothing adorned the walls, but I saw blinking lights on cameras mounted on either side of the space.

The unnamed man motioned for us to sit at the far side of the table, and Clark nearly had to carry me there. My ankle was aching so badly. I sat, relieved to be off my feet, and rubbed my raw wrists where the rope had dug in.

In the light, I finally saw the damage Teddy had inflicted on Clark. His eye was already puffing out, and his lip was split. Dried blood caked under his nose. My heart melted for the man who'd come to my rescue. I didn't care if this suit was inside the room or not. I lifted an arm, carefully touched Clark on the face, and kissed him softly.

"Thank you," I told him.

"For what?"

"For saving me."

"You seem to have done a fairly good job yourself," he said, forcing a smile.

"Just… thank you."

The suit cleared his throat. "What happened tonight?"

"Who are you?" I asked him.

"That's not important," he retorted.

"It is to me," I said.

"You killed a man. We witnessed this."

"What are you going to tell McCrae?" I asked. "You took me from the crime scene. I need to speak to the sheriff and tell him what happened."

"Better yet, you tell me, and I'll relay the details." He opened the door, and a young man in uniform walked in with three cups of steaming coffee on a tray and a carton of cream. He pulled a few sugar packets from his pockets and set it all down in front of us, passing a black coffee to his comrade.

"He's bribing us with coffee. You better tell him everything," Clark said, jokingly but with a hint of malice.

"Seriously. What are you? FBI? CIA? Why is the military in Cloud Lake?" I asked, trying to gauge his reaction. He didn't flinch.

"As I stated, that's not important. Tell me what happened." He finally sat, getting on a level playing field with us.

I grabbed a coffee, feeling the need for the heat, poured a dab of cream in, and sipped it. Instantly, my brain was less fried. Clarity in caffeine. It was something Harry at the office used to say. I resigned myself to opening up, figuring there was no harm in telling him a version of my story.

I told him about going missing for a week as a teenager, about the trial of Peter Martin, and how his son posed as John Oliver, luring me to Cloud Lake by bribing my down-on-his-luck boss. He listened, only asking the odd question. By the end, I told him how Teddy was going to kill us both, and I shot him in self-defense.

He asked where I'd found the gun, and I told him it was Teddy's. I wasn't going to rat out Chester, and if they somehow traced it back to the old farmer, we could always suggest Teddy had stolen it from him. I doubted it was registered to Chester anyway.

At no point did I mention UFOs or flashing lights, or my memories, which were seeping back with vivid lucidity. The man must have sensed this, because he opened his jacket, unfolded the paper, and slammed it down on the table. Our coffees shook, Clark's spilling.

"What is this?" His voice was low, but I could see the intensity in his eyes.

It was the drawing of me in what appeared to be a hospital bed. A figure watched me from across the room: a long, slender one, with eyes as black as coal.

I closed my eyes and remembered. I felt the tubes entering my arms, my legs. The liquid coursing through me, the blurry drugs they fed me. I knew they were watching me, taking notes on tablet-like devices I didn't understand. I heard their voices, clicks and grumbles I couldn't comprehend. Beads of sweat dripped down my sides.

I couldn't tell this man about it. I might never make it out of here alive. "It's only a drawing from a kid with too much imagination."

He nodded. "And Carly Miller?"

I straightened in my chair. "What about her?"

"You found her, am I correct?" he asked.

"I did."

"And what do you think happened to her?" The man leaned toward me, as if his life's work hung in the balance of my answer.

"She got lost in the forest and fields. I found her," I lied. I knew what had happened to her. It was the same thing that happened to me when I was her age.

"Right. Lost in two acres of trees. Are you telling me you don't believe you were abducted as a girl, and that the same Grays didn't take Carly?" he asked, unable to hide his interest any longer.

"I think you've been drinking the Kool-Aid of Cloud Lake. You know it's all a publicity scam, right? UFO sightings and missing townsfolk. This town is dying, and without something to wet the tourists' whistle, there is no Cloud Lake," I told him.

"I know you don't believe that," the man said.

275

Clark stood. "Listen here, guy with no name. Do you know what we've been through tonight? What Jessica has been through for her entire life? She's answered your questions; now we'd appreciate you letting us visit a hospital."

The man smiled, almost as if he was impressed with someone standing up to him. "Very well." His gaze slid to meet mine, and he shook his head slowly. "I know you, Jessica Carver. Maybe one day you'll share the truth." He pulled a business card from his pocket and passed it over to me. It was white with black lettering, spelling out an unremarkable email address. "When that time comes, contact me."

He left the room, and moments later, the female soldier was in the doorway. "I'll drive you to the hospital."

August 18th – 2020

"Are you ready to come out?" I asked Zoe. Our connection kept cutting out, and her face froze in place on the laptop screen before she smiled.

"I can't believe you're keeping the cabin, Jess." My sister used my real name, and I didn't correct her. Eva Heart had died alongside Teddy Martin. She'd washed away with the rain that night.

I looked at the cabin from the picnic table. The construction crew was packing up for the evening. Already, only a month later, the place had been fixed up from top to bottom. It helped having a boyfriend who could do the plumbing for free. He also had a lot of skilled friends who'd made quick work of the repairs.

"Wait until you see it. Grandma would love the upgrades," I said, smiling at the thought of Grandma walking around the newly renovated space. I'd kept a lot of the same décor she'd held on to for decades, while mixing in my own personal tastes.

"I'm sure she would. And yes, we're all ready to come out this weekend. Are you surprised Dad's coming?" Zoe asked.

"No. After he found out about Teddy, he seems in a better place," I told her. Clark and I had visited my dad a week after everything had gone down, and I'd told him about Peter Martin. How he was innocent. I knew it would wreck my dad, but there was no hiding the truth from him. He needed to know.

"How's the ankle?" Zoe asked.

I was still wearing a brace, but it was much better. "Good. I'm hobbling around just fine." I laughed, feeling a freedom I hadn't felt in my entire adult life. The cloud over me was gone, and I was finally able to let the sun shine on my face.

"And Clark?" She waggled her eyebrows.

I closed my eyes, recalling the first night we'd spent at his place. It was unlike anything I'd ever experienced. "He's wonderful. Things are really great."

"Good. You know… I'm sorry about that night. I didn't know," Zoe said, for the hundredth time in the last month.

I waved it away. "Enough already."

"What about Chris Barns? Any word?" she asked.

Harry and I had been in touch. He'd moved out of the city and was working for a small publisher in Buffalo.

"They couldn't stick anything on him, since the trail was mostly dead. He disappeared, as far as Harry can tell." As angry as I was with Barns, I wasn't going to let it consume me.

I heard a car door shut, and I smiled. "Okay, I have to go. See you this weekend. I can't wait for you to get here. And you kids are going to love the lake!"

"I can't believe they're going to see Cloud Lake. See

you soon, missy." Zoe grinned, and the call ended.

Carly walked down the gravel driveway, and I waved at her father, who was staying inside the car.

I rose to meet her. "Hi, Carly."

She was such a beautiful young girl, but I could see the effect this whole traumatic experience had had on her. She was thinner, her eyes sunken, and dark bags hung under them. Still, they glimmered as she met my stare and wrapped her arms around me.

"Eva… I mean, Jessica," she said. I'd explained my story to her in detail, two days after Teddy was shot. She'd accepted it with a grim strength.

"I Googled you," she admitted.

"And?"

She shrugged. "Was it hard?"

I knew what she meant. "Growing up with this looming over me? Yes."

"It is hard," she said.

I led us to the dock, and we walked it, her in sandals, me in bare feet. The sun was lowering, but still hot and intense in the August evening. The air was potent with campfires, and music crawled across the water, reaching us as we sat at the end of the dock.

"What do your friends think?" I asked. I remembered my own thinking I was a stranger, someone they could no longer have fun with or joke around. That summer had changed everything.

"They ask me things. I just tell them I don't recall. Amnesia, my dad says." She glanced back to her dad in the waiting car.

"And your parents?" I asked. "What do they think?"

"The sheriff tells them he's still working on it, but they know the truth. They're in denial, though, Jess. They don't want to believe that someone took me. Someone from…"

I nodded. "I think I know what might help you."

"What?" she asked, her eyes going a little wider.

"What if you and I had a night every week where we hung out? Talked about girl things, watched movies…" I lowered my voice. "Discussed boys."

She laughed, and a single tear rolled over her cheek. "I'd like that, Jess."

"Then it's settled." I patted her on the knee, and we sat in silence for a few minutes. "You're going to be fine."

"What if they come again?" she asked, and it was a question I'd been asking myself almost daily.

I put on a brave face, one that I didn't always feel, especially during the nights I was out here alone. "Would I move back here if I was concerned about that?"

She shook her head. "No."

"Good. Now, about that girls' night. We can't start this weekend, but I'd love you to come over for dinner Saturday night. My sister and her family will be here, and my dad too," I told her.

Sitting with Carly reminded me of the hours Zoe and I had spent out here, chatting away the summers, and it felt right.

"As long as my parents say I can, I'd love to." Her mood already seemed better, and I was going to make it my mission to see Carly Miller through this hard time. I wasn't going to let her end up like I had for the last twenty years.

The car honked once, a solitary unobtrusive sound. "Sorry. We have dinner in town. See you Saturday?"

"You bet." We hugged quickly, and I watched Carly run down the dock and into the car. I waved at her dad before they took off, backing out the driveway.

My phone buzzed, and I pulled it from my pocket to see Clark's name across the screen. "Hello," I answered.

"I'm going to be late. Got held up at a job. Can I bring supper when I'm off?" he asked.

"Only if it's Buddy's," I told him with a scolding tone.

"Deal. You going to be okay alone?" he asked softly.

I looked around and told him the truth. "I haven't felt better in years. Come over when you can."

"Okay. Jess… I… I love you," he said, not for the first time.

"I love you too." And with that, the call was ended.

I limped across the dock, then the stone pathway that led to the cabin. Grandma's cabin. I felt her around me as I entered through the replaced door, the hinges no longer squeaking in protest.

The kitchen was new, the floors still not completed. I looked at the pile of bagged aprons in the corner of the room and knew I'd put them to use. My laptop was inside my room, and I went to get it, taking it from the desk where I'd found the drawings of a scared little girl.

Minutes later, I had a hot cup of tea, and I sat at the kitchen island, a white quartz countertop under my laptop, and I opened the computer.

I clicked a blank document to life and smiled to myself. The card the man in the suit had given me was inside my bedroom, safely tucked away, but it gave me comfort to know it was there. To know that I wasn't crazy, that the military and government were interested in the same story. I wasn't sure if what I was about to write would ever see the light of day, but I needed to pen it, to let my tale out, for my own sanity.

The cursor blinked at me, staring from the screen, and I began to type. I started with a title: four simple words.

Lights Over Cloud Lake

The End

ABOUT THE AUTHOR

Nathan Hystad is an author from Sherwood Park, Alberta, Canada. He writes about aliens, and heroes, and everything in between.

Keep up to date with his new releases by signing up for his newsletter at www.nathanhystad.com

Printed in Poland
by Amazon Fulfillment
Poland Sp. z o.o., Wrocław

52015311R00171